THE GIRL WHO FOUND JOY

Shee McQueen Mystery-Thrillers
Book Six

Amy Vansant

Vansant Creations, LLC / Amy Vansant
Jupiter, FL
http://www.AmyVansant.com

Editing/Proofreading by Effrosyni Moschoudi & Meg Barnhart

CONTENTS

CHAPTER ONE

One month ago

Something about her *throat*.

The length, the curve, the striking *whiteness* of it. There was something familiar about the dark-haired woman standing at the Palm Beach Art Fest jewelry booth.

Joy Zabić stopped to stare, but not for long.

Someone clipped her shoulder and sent her stumbling forward to keep from falling.

Someone not looking where they were going. Someone *sweaty*.

She spun to glare at the man, who was laughing with his buddy as they walked away in their khaki shorts and high-end polo shirts.

Jackasses.

Money can't buy class.

She whirled and almost walked into a large man in a soaked black tee shirt holding his palm aloft—the universal symbol for *my bad*. She showed him a tight smile and allowed her flash of anger to dissipate.

Deep breath.

Okay. Moving on.

Joy stood in the sun as the mob split around her—an island

in a stream of people. She held her flat palm above her sunglasses, cursed herself for forgetting her visor, and watched the dark-haired woman in the jewelry tent hold a turquoise pendant against her chest.

The woman was attractive, tan, and slim with mid-length dark hair and enough muscle tone that Joy could tell she *worked* at keeping fit.

She had good taste in jewelry, too.

Joy waited for a gap in the traffic and stepped toward the merchant tent, narrowly avoiding a stout terrier lapping ice cream at the feet of a wailing, smeary-faced toddler.

Tourist-season art fests were like the seventh circle of hell. Jostling in the searing Florida sun left her irritable. She should have made her boyfriend, Liam, come with her so he could experience all the *fun.*

The woman in the tent was Liam's type—slight, exotic without feeling *foreign*, showy with a small-town undertone. Joy could tell she hadn't been born with money but appreciated it and liked to be near it. She was a fine reproduction sitting amongst the originals, undetected.

"That's pretty," Joy said as she slipped into the shade of the jeweler's tent. She motioned to the necklace.

The dark-haired woman looked at her.

"Isn't it? I think I might have to pull the trigger." The corner of her mouth curled in a conspiratorial smirk, making Joy feel like she was in on a secret.

You understand me, it said.

The good looks, the smile—Joy felt the whole package drawing her in.

"It's got an old-fashioned thing to it without being fuddy-duddy," Joy said. She winced at the sound of her own words.

Who says fuddy-duddy? What am I—a hundred years old?

But the woman's eyes widened, and she pointed at her. "*Exactly.* That's what I was thinking." She held it up to admire it again. "I like old things."

She chuckled, and Joy aped her laughter with a titter of her own.

"Me, too. I was just thinking I should learn how to play mahjong like the old ladies around here."

The woman sucked in a breath and touched her arm.

"That's so *weird* you should say that. I want to learn how to play mahjong, too."

Joy's face twitched.

Whoops.

She hadn't *seriously* considered learning mahjong. She'd only been making conversation.

Serves me right.

She looked away. "Um—"

"Do you live here? Year-round?" the woman continued, the necklace swinging from her fingers, bouncing to punctuate each question.

Joy nodded. "Yes. Now. Made the move."

The woman rolled her eyes. "You and everyone else on the planet. I'm Rowan, by the way. Nice to meet you."

"Joy."

"I hate that everyone is moving here—" Rowan put her flatted palm to the side of her mouth and leaned in to whisper, "—*but you seem like one of the good ones.*"

The merchant behind the counter finished conversing with another shopper and focused on Rowan. She'd watched the necklace swing as the women talked and probably felt tense, worried the item might disappear into Rowan's oversized bag.

"Did you want that?" she asked, motioning to the necklace.

Rowan smiled with the light of a thousand suns.

"I don't think I've ever had a necklace look more beautiful on me," she said.

The vendor's forced smile softened into something more genuine. "I spent a lot of time picking out the perfect larimar—"

"Here you go." Rowan whipped a credit card from her purse. "You don't have to box it. I'll wear it."

The woman took the card, and Joy glanced over her shoulder, thinking it was time to leave. She watched Rowan struggle to get the necklace's clasp latched around her neck.

"Let me help," she said.

Rowan let her take the ends of the necklace.

"Maybe we could learn together," said Joy as the clasp locked.

"Hm?"

"*Mahjong*. Maybe we could learn together. Do you live close?"

Rowan leaned into the mirror to inspect the necklace and straightened to motion somewhere inland without any real precision. "Not far."

"I'm in Shoreline Ocean," said Joy, naming a large and popular community nearby.

Rowan's eternal smile became more wistful. "I lived there for a while. Bayside, though."

Joy didn't ask her why she'd moved.

"Maybe we could go to lunch?" she asked instead.

Waiting for an answer with Rowan's wide eyes on her, Joy felt locked in her gaze, like a frog in a flashlight beam about to be gigged.

Rowan grinned. "I would *love* that."

The vendor returned the credit card and turned to help someone else. Joy noticed a man's name on the card.

"Are you married?" she asked.

Rowan laughed. "No." She scanned the counter and then turned to Joy.

"Do you have a pen?"

Joy nodded and searched her purse. When she found one, Rowan took it from her, signed her slip, and then dropped the pen into her own purse. Like a sleight-of-hand magic trick, the pen disappeared, and she produced her cell phone.

"Give me your phone—I'll add my number to it," she said.

Joy handed her phone to her new buddy.

Rowan tapped away until her phone rang. She glanced at the screen and nodded with satisfaction.

"Okay, I've got your number. I'll give you a call and give

you a date?"

Joy paused, finding it odd *she'd* suggested lunch, but *Rowan* was exclusively picking the date.

"Okay," she said, accepting her phone and fate.

Seemed easiest.

That's me. Ol' go-with-the-flow Joy.

Without an additional word, Rowan waltzed out of the tent, waving goodbye before disappearing into the crowd of meandering, sweaty art lovers.

Joy noticed the cherub-faced jeweler behind the counter staring at her.

"Can I help *you* with anything?" she asked.

Joy shook her head and peered around the edge of the tent. Rowan was gone from sight.

She smiled.

I have a new friend.

It wasn't a small thing. People underestimated how hard forging new relationships could be.

Making friends as a child was uncomplicated—*I'm me. You're you. Let's hang out.*

As adults, people knew themselves.

They knew why people shouldn't like them.

CHAPTER TWO

Shee awoke to find Mason hovering over her, which seemed *sexy* until she realized his hands were on her throat.

Not good.

She grabbed his wrists, and the pressure on her airpipe eased. The snarl on his lips dissipated, and confusion replaced the anger in his otherwise vacant eyes.

"*No*," he said.

He threw himself away from her and off the bed with such force he almost toppled. In his hurry, he'd forgotten he only had one leg remaining from the original set. He caught himself on the mattress with one arm as he found balance on his good leg.

"Whoa, easy there, sailor," said Shee, sitting up. "Find your sea *leg*."

He glowered at her. "Very funny."

Mason's tall dog, Archie, had scrambled to his feet at the sound of the commotion to peer over the edge of the bed. Shee rubbed the poodle-mutt's curly head to reassure him the world wasn't ending.

"It's okay. Daddy just tried to kill Mommy in her sleep."

Mason sat on the edge of the bed and hung his head. "It's not funny, Shee. I could really hurt you."

"You didn't. Whoever you're wrestling in your sleep, you must have lost because you weren't trying very hard."

He ran his hand through his hair, and she watched his jaw

flex.

"Do you *remember* what you were dreaming about?" she asked.

"I dreamt you made a joke about my leg."

She pointed at him. "Ah, see? It *is* funny."

He shook his head. "No. I'm sorry. It's not. And *no*, I don't remember what I was dreaming about. Not specifically."

"Are you sure? Is it one of those *if I told you, I'd have to kill you* things? Oh wait, you already tried—"

He stood. "Okay, *enough*. We can't share a bed like this."

She shrugged. "I don't know. It's *exciting* going to sleep at night, not knowing if there'll be an attempt on my life."

His frown deepened, and she rose to her knees on the bed to wrap her arms around his broad shoulders.

"I'm sorry. Come here, handsome."

She pulled him down and adjusted to lay beside him. With a sigh, he placed his head on her chest, and she kissed his hair.

"Next time Doc Ginny comes by, maybe you should talk to her. Maybe make an appointment," she suggested.

"I don't need a shrink."

"Of course you don't, *big tough guy*, but maybe she can help, and I won't have to sleep with the Boston Strangler anymore."

"Hm. Maybe."

"Somehow, I doubt you'll be the first Navy SEAL—retired or otherwise—to go to a psychiatrist. Heck, they should have sent you to one just for *wanting to be* a SEAL."

Mason chuckled. "You're not wrong there."

"Maybe you need to retire *more*," she suggested.

He shifted his head to peer into her eyes.

"What does that mean?"

She shrugged. "You know. You still play soldier with us. With Loggerhead. Maybe you need to *fully* retire. No more gunplay. Take it easy."

He scoffed. "And what? Take up golf?" Sitting up, he looked at his watch. "At least I waited until a half-decent hour to murder you. We might as well get up."

Shee sighed. The topic change didn't go unnoticed. He didn't want to talk about *real* retirement anymore. He'd already be halfway down the elevator and far away from her suggestions if he didn't need to strap on his prosthetic leg first.

"Time to get up," she agreed, standing to throw on comfy clothes.

Mason mounted his leg, and the three of them—Shee, Mason, and Archie—took the Loggerhead Inn's elevator from the third floor to the lobby, an awkward silence hovering between them. As the doors opened, Archie burst out to look for Angelina, the hotel manager, and her miniature Yorkie, Harley.

Harley looked like a chunk of adorable dirt that fell off Archie—so great was the size difference between the dogs—but they'd become best friends.

Mason whistled for his dog and wandered outside, with Archie pushing to lead the way. Shee headed to the kitchen to start the coffee, assuming she'd be the first to arrive.

She was wrong.

She smelled coffee brewing and found Snookie, Angelina's sister, waiting for the pot to fill. Freshly retired from the FBI, Snookie'd found a place at the Loggerhead, helping her sister streamline their agency.

She wore a thin robe splattered with so many colors and shapes it made Shee's eyes cross.

"Wow. That robe is a *lot* for this early in the morning," she said, holding up a hand to ward it off.

Snookie glanced down. "This is my favorite. You don't like it?"

"It looks like a circus threw up on it."

Snookie grunted and poured herself a cup even though the pot hadn't finished dripping.

"Good morning to you, too," she said, replacing the pot on the sizzling burner.

They were an hour too early to steal coffee and donuts from the breakroom, where the hotel's receptionist, Croix, set them out every morning for the hotel guests.

Left to fend for ourselves like animals.

"I want donuts," moaned Shee. "We'll have to tell Croix to start getting up earlier."

She held out her mug so Snookie could pour, and Snookie cocked an eyebrow at it.

"Good luck with that. Get your own."

Shee chuckled and poured herself her cup.

Snookie sighed. "No one loved those donuts as much as your father. Part of me thinks he turned this place into a hotel to guarantee himself a continental breakfast."

"I'm sure that's true," said Shee. "Turning a mercenary den into a tourist hotel doesn't make any sense *at all* without the donuts."

She smiled at the memory of her father and the insane legacy he'd left her. Occupancy at The Loggerhead Inn was generally at a fifty-fifty tourist-to-mercenary ratio. He'd started the place as a haven for ex-military looking to redeem their souls by doing good.

For a profit, of course.

They didn't overthrow governments or kill anyone who didn't deserve it.

That had to count for something.

Her father must have hit a slow patch at some point because suddenly, he had the place operating as a beach hotel for tourists, too. Angelina probably got into his ear, hoping she could slowly wean him from mercenary work to hotel manager.

That never worked out.

They'd recently wrapped a case and were awaiting the next assignment. Hopefully, they'd have something soon to distract Mason before he waterboarded her in his sleep.

"Is Mason around? I wanted to talk to you two about a potential job," said Snookie.

Shee looked over her mug at the woman.

Speak of the devil.

"Were you reading my mind?"

Snookie nodded. "Always."

"I'm right here," said Mason, entering the kitchen.

She smirked.

Funny. As soon as someone whispered there might be work, the retired SEAL Commander magically appeared like an action-starved genie.

He tossed the newspaper on the table. He liked reading a *real* paper in the morning. Shee teased he was forty-something going on *ninety*-something but suspected after thirty years in the military, he enjoyed the sheer *normalcy* of a domestic morning ritual.

It's not like any of the news was ever any good.

"Get yourself some coffee and take a seat," said Snookie.

Mason did as he was told. When they were sitting, Snookie took a long sip of her coffee and began.

"You know I'm still moonlighting for the FBI, and as Feds, we're not allowed to hire private agencies for work."

"Not *officially*," said Shee.

Snookie smirked. "Not *officially*. But that being said, they've got some cases on the periphery they haven't officially *accepted*. It's been mentioned they wouldn't mind if I checked one out. And by *I*, I mean *you*, of course."

Shee nodded. "I assumed. Whatcha got?"

"Some sort of black widow character they're calling Portia."

"They're *calling*? They don't know her real name?"

Snookie shook her head. "That's the thing. They've gathered enough intel to know there's something there, but no one knows who she is or what she looks like."

"But they know her name is Portia?" asked Mason.

Snookie chuckled. "No. The story behind the name is actually kind of funny—but let me give you some background first. From what they've gathered, this woman hooks up with rich men and drains their bank accounts."

"That's original," muttered Shee.

"This one's got a twist. She doesn't marry them—she frames other women for the crime. That's why getting a clear picture of her is tough."

Shee scowled. "But the *men* must know what she looks like? And, presumably, the women she's framed?"

"Nope. They both disappear—sometimes dead, sometimes missing. Money's gone, witnesses gone—she moves on, picks a new name, a new hair color, who knows. She travels—they've got cases fitting Portia's profile scattered all over the country. That's why it took this long for someone to spot a pattern."

"How did they *ever* spot a pattern?" asked Shee.

Snookie shrugged. "You kill enough rich guys, and people start to notice."

"They think she's here now?"

Snookie nodded. "Palm Beach."

"Makes sense. Plenty of rich men. What do we have to go on?"

"I'll get you the file. They have a suspect—her name's Rowan Riley. No *confirmation* she's our gal, but a solid guess. I thought maybe you could be the friend she befriends."

Shee snorted a laugh. "You mean the one that ends up dead?"

"Right. That one."

"Great."

"Anything for me? Can I be the rich guy?" asked Mason.

Shee laughed. A little too hard, maybe. He scowled at her.

"Sorry," she added.

"I guess anything is possible. Depends on how far along her story arc she's gotten. She might already have someone lined up for both spots—in which case, you two would fall to straight surveillance."

"Stakeouts," muttered Mason. "Fantastic."

Shee patted his arm. "We'll try and find you someone to shoot. I promise."

He side-eyed her and turned his attention to Snookie.

"You said the Portia tag meant something?"

She pointed at him, head bobbing. "*Right*. The guys at the home office named her Portia. Someone said she's smarter than the average black widow and took the time to Google *smartest spider*—which happens to be the *fringed jumping spider*—also known as *Portia*."

Mason rolled his eyes. "Anyone who says the FBI isn't a bunch of nerds..."

Snookie laughed. "Can't argue with that."

CHAPTER THREE

One month ago

"There you are," said Rowan, dropping into the seat across from Joy. She looked flustered.

As promised, Rowan called the day after their meeting at the art fest. Sometime during their ten-minute conversation, Joy agreed to meet at Osteria, a high-end Italian restaurant off the beach. The spot had been Rowan's pick. Joy didn't remember saying more than a few words during their exchange, for which she was grateful. Having a new friend who did all the talking meant she didn't have to spend time thinking of things to say.

Not that she wasn't good at small talk. She was *very* good at it when she had to be, but that didn't mean she *enjoyed* it.

They'd agreed to meet at noon. It was twelve-fifteen when Rowan dropped into her seat across the table from her. Her lips pouted with all the drama of an aggravated teenager.

"Did you order a bottle of wine?" she asked as she placed her purse on a spare chair at the table.

Joy's gaze dropped to her glass of Pinot Grigio.

"No, I didn't know what you drink. Or *if* you drink—"

"*If* I drink?" Rowan snorted a laugh and raised a hand to catch the eye of a server talking to another table of diners. He bobbed his head to show he'd seen, and after wrapping up his specials speech, strode over and clasped his hands behind his back to beam down at them.

"Good afternoon, ladies. How—"

"I'll take a glass of rosé," said Rowan. She'd changed her mind about abandoning her purse, pulled it back to her, and frowned into a compact mirror.

The server glanced at Joy, who flashed him a tight, *nothing-for-me* smile.

He headed off.

Rowan looked up from her mirror. "Whew," she said, smiling as she dabbed her forehead with pressed powder. "I must look *crazy*."

"Not at all," said Joy.

She didn't need to lie. Rowan was a knockout in any state, with raven hair and cheekbones like ski slopes.

Rowan rolled her eyes. "I'm *sweating*."

Joy shrugged. "It makes you *glow*."

The comment started Rowan giggling. "I guess I do look *shiny*. That can't be all bad, right?" She looked around the small table as she slipped her compact back into her bag. "Did you bring the board?"

"The board?"

"The mahjong board?"

Joy frowned. "No. I thought this was more of a *getting the lay of the land* meeting. I didn't think to bring anything."

Rowan nodded. "Sure. You can bring it next time. Good idea."

Joy nodded.

She didn't *own* a mahjong board.

She made a mental note to order one when she got back.

The waiter brought Rowan her wine and suggested an appetizer. Rowan waved him away.

"I need a moment," she said.

Frozen smile shielding him from her rebuttal, he wandered off.

Rowan watched him leave but continued to stare in his

direction even as he rounded the corner and disappeared somewhere in the back. Joy followed her gaze to find her new friend had locked onto a gray-haired man sitting alone at another table. He wore a seersucker green suit jacket and a colorful striped shirt. Joy didn't notice anything special about him other than he seemed overdressed for lunch, and his jawline was unnaturally taut for his age.

He'd had some work done.

Vanity, thy name is...well, pretty much everyone.

Some just had enough money to pander to vanity.

"Do you know him?" she asked.

Rowan's attention swiveled to her. "Who? The old guy?" She sniffed. "No. He's a widower, though."

Joy glanced at him again. "So you *do* know him?"

"Nope."

"Then how do you know he's a widower? Because he's alone?"

Rowan shook her head. "Because he's got a R.O.C."

"A *rock*?"

"A *ROC*, R-O-C." She gave the necklace around her neck a tug to demonstrate. "*Ring on Chain.* I passed him on the way in and noticed he's got a lady-sized gold ring hanging from the chain around his neck."

Joy looked at the man again. She couldn't see his necklace from her angle.

She turned to find Rowan smirking at her.

"I specialize in widowers," said the brunette, leaning in and dropping her voice to a conspiratorial whisper. "It's my dirty little secret."

Joy sat up. "Really?"

Rowan pursed her lips and lifted her chin. She looked like a professor preparing to explain her area of academia to yokel parents at a college mixer.

"Widowers treat you like *gold*," she said. "They're desperate for love and attention. Throw them a bone, and they'll *shower* you with gifts."

Joy remained silent. She was *thinking*. For a split second, she'd found it *odd* to hear Rowan confess her predatory inclinations to a relative stranger.

She moved past her surprise.

Clearly, Rowan didn't consider what she did *predatory*. Her relationships were simple, common-sense transactions—men needed companionship, and she needed money. She wasn't ashamed of her 'dirty little secret.'

She was *bragging*.

Across the table from her, Rowan had stopped breathing. She watched Joy with wide sapphire eyes, waiting for her reaction.

Joy imagined the people with whom she shared this secret reacted one of two ways—horrified or fascinated. She guessed Rowan enjoyed either response.

"If you're going to date someone, it might as well be someone rich," said Joy, taking a sip of her wine.

Rowan sat back. Her flash of disappointment at Joy's lackluster response twisted into a smile.

"Yes. You *get* it," said Rowan, looking satisfied.

"I get it."

Rowan turned back to the old man. Her eyes darkened as if someone had flicked off her switch.

"What's wrong?" asked Joy, turning.

Ah.

A smiling champagne-blonde woman had arrived at the man's table. He stood to greet her and rested his hand on the small of her back, guiding her to her seat. The new arrival looked like a photo negative of Rowan—this one tan and blonde. There was one notable exception—her breasts were *enormous* for her frame.

Joy guessed the old guy wasn't the only one who'd had some work done. Maybe he'd gotten a two-for-one special.

"Looks like someone beat you to him," said Joy.

Rowan glanced down at her chest, where two respectable C-cups stared back at her.

"Seems like it," she agreed. "Do you think she's younger than me?"

Joy shook her head. "No."

Probably.

"Do you recognize her?" she asked.

Rowan's forehead creased. "Who? His date?"

Joy nodded. "I thought maybe you'd seen her prowling the area. Or maybe you're members of the same chapter of the Gold Digger's Guild, and you've met her at one of the meetings?"

Rowan's lips parted as a tempest rolled across her expression.

Joy waited.

Rowan's scowl released.

"*Oh.* You're *teasing* me," she said, laughing.

"I *am*." Joy scanned the restaurant. "You know, we should meet at Bahama Betty's next time. Do you know it?"

Rowan tilted her head to the side. "It's over in that new development, right?"

"Right, on the ICW."

"The ICW?"

"The Intracoastal Waterway. They've got a bunch of docks. My boyfriend loves it there, and I've joined him a few times. It's a parade of men in midlife-crisis boats grabbing drinks with their buddies—post-fishing and post-golf. I think you'd like it."

"Sounds *perfect*." Rowan nodded approvingly. "I promise not to pick up your boyfriend."

Joy lifted her glass and smiled at Rowan over the rim.

"Tell you what, if anything ever happens to me, you can *have* him."

Rowan laughed. "Awesome. Is he rich?"

"He's a dermatologist."

Rowan's eyes widened.

"Ooh. That'll work."

CHAPTER FOUR

Shee and Mason took a day to prepare—gathering what intel they could on Rowan Riley, aka *Portia*—and then hopping into Mason's truck for the drive. Palm Beach was only half an hour south of Jupiter Beach, but Snookie used FBI money to rent them a house so they wouldn't have to drive back and forth.

They needed a home base Rowan would appreciate, should Shee get as far as inviting her over. She'd be a less attractive victim shacked up in a hotel. How could Rowan frame a *tourist* for murder? Who'd believe Shee went on *vacation* to rob and kill a man?

Black widows liked to nest before they got down to business, didn't they?

Maybe fringed jumping spiders, too.

Shee felt Mason's eyes on her as they drove and glanced his way.

"Why are you looking at me?" she asked.

He sighed. "I don't know. I guess I was thinking about the whole, uh, *throat* thing."

"*Throat* thing?"

"You know—" He mimed choking someone.

"Your *nightmare*?" She scoffed. "It's fine. You didn't know what you were doing."

"That doesn't make it *fine*. I could have hurt you."

"But you didn't—and you snapped out of it right away."

He squirmed in his seat. "*This time.*"

"How could you have done what you did for as long as you did it and not come out with some scars?"

"I left my leg behind. That's not enough? That was U.S. Prime beef."

She laughed. "Gross. You know what I mean. *Mental* scars."

He sighed.

"So, *do* something about it," she said after a moment.

He scowled."Like what?"

"Go see someone. You're a modern guy. You're not one of those old-school *real men don't go to psychiatrists* guys, are you?"

"No," he said, looking away to stare out the window. "I had a friend who went to a headshrinker. He took out one of our own during a night raid—accident, the whole situation was FUBAR—but it ate him alive. Couldn't shake the guilt. He went to a doctor, got on medication—"

"See?"

"—still killed himself."

"Oh." She eyed him. "You're not thinking about killing yourself, are you?"

"*No*. That's not what I meant at all."

"Good. So, talk to someone. Maybe get a little medication to help you sleep."

He grunted. "*You're* the one who should have PTSD."

She laughed. "Me? Why?"

"*Why*?" He ticked the reasons off on his fingers. "You saw your sister killed in front of you—by people aiming for *you*—you ended up on the run for twenty years, no contact with Mick, our daughter, or *me*—"

She smirked. "In all fairness, *we* were already *not in contact*."

"That wasn't my decision." He frowned. "Whatever. You get my point."

She shrugged. "Other than the fact I had to keep a low profile, I've had a mostly normal life. I wasn't being shot at—"

She reconsidered. "Well, not as often as you, anyway."

"Sorry to be the one to tell you, but moving from town to town helping cops find killers is not a normal life. Avenging wrongs like some second-rate superhero is *not* a normal life."

She squinted at him. "Did you just call me *second-rate*?"

He shrugged. "Because you don't have real superpowers."

"Oh," she said with a sniff. "Well, maybe all that *was* my therapy."

He pointed at her. "Bingo. I get that. *Like Loggerhead is for me.*"

She sighed. "You tricked me."

He grinned and tapped the side of his head with his index finger.

"Uh-huh. You and your big brain," she said, smirking. "Well, I guess that *was* my dad's idea, right? To make Loggerhead a place for exorcising demons? Maybe offer people a chance to give back as much as they took?"

Mason nodded. "And the old man might have been on to something."

He tapped a beat on his thigh with his fingertips, and Shee waited, expecting more to come.

"This isn't the first time your dad saved me, you know," he said, finally.

"What do you mean?"

"Out in the desert. He didn't hear it."

"Hear what?"

Mason swallowed and leaned his skull against the headrest. "It was my first or second mission with your old man. I was eager to do my thing—we all were—but he stopped us, and he was *right*. It was a trap. We would have all died that night if it hadn't been for him. We hadn't heard anything, but he did."

Shee made a left. "What did he hear?"

"*Nothing*. That's just it—he heard *nothing*. We'd reconned this place for days—there was always a television on—people talking—*something*. Right before we moved in—*nothing*. No sound. They were waiting for us—trying *too* hard to be still."

"Hm." Shee nodded. Mick had rarely shared war stories with her. Whenever he did, it was only to illustrate some lesson.

Actually, the stories always fit the lesson so perfectly she doubted any of them were true.

A wave of sadness swept over her, and she fought off tears. She'd gotten good at hiding her mourning since her father's death. She couldn't always stop the sadness, but she *could* stop the tears. The key was making her mind go blank, or if that wasn't possible, to think of something happy, like Archie's eyes popping up over the edge of the bed that morning. Dogs were always good for a cheap, happy thought.

Now wasn't the time to get maudlin about Dad.

Mason patted her leg and let his hand stay there.

"Now that I think of it, when your father saved me, he probably knew you were pregnant. I'm lucky he didn't let me die for knocking up his daughter."

She laughed. "Actually, when he found out about Charlotte, killing you *was* his first instinct, so you can thank *me* for saving you, too."

Mason slowed to a stop and pulled into the neighborhood where they'd rented their house.

"This is the place?" he asked.

She nodded. "Good thing we've got government money to burn because the place was a three-month minimum rental."

"I can see why," he said, pulling into the driveway. "Nice place."

The neighborhood *was* cute—a collection of newish, single-family Key-West-style bungalows. Nicer neighborhoods always wrote minimum stays into their HOA contracts to keep out the undesirables—like mercenaries out to capture gold-digging serial killers.

Nobody wanted that kind of riff-raff bopping in and out of their neighborhood.

Mason hopped out of the truck and opened the back to gather their luggage while she punched in the door code and let them inside. The home's main living area was a large square with an open kitchen and a cool white and gray interior. As they walked in, their heads fell back to appreciate the tall ceilings.

"Not bad," said Shee as Mason took their suitcase to the primary bedroom.

She followed him in and checked out the spacious attached bath. She could swing a golf club in the glass-enclosed shower without cracking a pane.

"Sweet."

When she turned, she found Mason staring at her like a wolf.

"What is *that*?" she asked, pointing at him.

"What?"

"You look like you're starving, and I'm a hamburger."

He smirked, and she smirked back.

Naughty boy.

Mason moved toward her to put his hands on her hips, the tips of his fingers tracing the inside edge of her shorts.

"Oh, you're not hamburger, sweetheart. You're *U.S. prime*," he said, doubling down on his leer.

"Like your *leg*?" she asked, horrified.

He shook his head. "Sorry. I guess that phrase was in my head."

She giggled. "I'll let it slide."

His hands moved up her back to better pull her against him. He kissed her neck, and she felt her body flood with *want*.

"What's this for?" she whispered.

His lips moved to her ear. "I need a reason?"

"Nope."

They twirled like dancers, moving toward the bed, his breath speeding with hers. His biceps flexed as he lifted her rear onto the bed and leaned forward to press against her. Her legs wrapped around his waist, and they rolled until she found a perch on top of him. She bent forward, letting her hair frame his face, their gazes locked.

"I think I like this therapy best," he said, stroking her face with his thumb.

She grinned. "I'm warning you. My hourly rate is pretty hefty."

He rolled her again, lowering his weight on her hips. She moaned. He felt *good*.

The line beside his mouth curved around his lips like the world's sexiest parenthesis.

"If you're flexible on forms of payment, maybe we can work something out," he murmured.

She grinned.

"Oh, I'll show you *flexible*."

CHAPTER FIVE

Three weeks ago.

Joy found Liam in the bathroom, freshly showered and combing his wet hair. A white towel encircled his waist.

He did a doubletake as she entered.

"What are you doing here?" he asked.

It was a fair question. She'd told him she wouldn't stop by until the afternoon.

She'd lied.

"Changed my mind," she said. "I thought you were playing golf?"

He shrugged. "Guy bailed on me. I went all the way to the course for nothing."

In the mirror, she noticed his gaze run down her body.

She left the room.

"I'm meeting my mahjong friend for lunch," she said, entering his walk-in closet where she kept some clothes.

"Are you two still trying to learn that stupid game?"

She chose a new shirt. "Not really. Mostly, it's an excuse to drink wine. You'd like her."

"Oh yeah?"

"Yeah. She's your type. Exotic. Athletic but not hard. Younger than me."

Silence.

Joy waited.

Shit.

She didn't feel like getting into things with Liam *now*.

A shadow appeared on the floor beside her, and she felt his presence at the entry of his closet.

"How long are you going to do this?" he asked.

She turned to face him, eyes wide and guileless. "Do what?"

He flicked his wrist at her. "Whatever *this* is. This *woe-is-me* crap you've been pulling lately."

She turned away again and rolled her eyes where he couldn't see.

So boring. So *predictable*.

"I don't know what you're talking about," she said.

"You've been giving me the cold shoulder for days."

Joy slipped into a new breezy top and turned to face her boyfriend again. Liam filled the doorway. He was a large man, six-two, and muscular without trying. He'd never hit her or threatened to do so, but to confront anyone while trapped in the closet would be stupid.

She changed the subject.

"So you drove all the way to the course, and the drug rep didn't show?" she asked, sliding by him into the bedroom.

Not the most subtle segue.

She heard him sigh.

"Yeah. I mean, he *called*. Some last-minute family thing, I don't know."

"Guess he lost a sale."

"You can say that again."

Liam padded back into the bathroom.

She watched him go.

Hm.

He'd given up too easily.

Idiot.

Should I bother to check?

She didn't need to. She already knew everything she

needed to know.

Eh. Might as well.

She walked through the house to the attached garage, where she opened the door of Liam's Land Rover to check the odometer.

It had rolled six miles more than when she checked it that morning.

The golf course was half an hour away.

He didn't go to the course. He'd driven three miles one way and three miles back.

His other girlfriend lives nearby.

How convenient.

Probably the blonde at the restaurant. She'd seen the looks.

She shut the door and returned inside, her mood dark.

A few minutes later, Liam appeared wearing his usual weekend khaki shorts and polo uniform.

"What's for lunch?" he asked.

She looked at him. "I don't know what *you're* having—I have a lunch date, remember?"

"Can you make me a sandwich before you go?"

"Make it yourself." She paused to let him work up his anger and then added, "You're having an affair."

The jaw he'd been clenching dropped.

"What?"

She shrugged. "I thought you should know I know."

"Are you crazy? You're kidding, right?" He ran his hand over his head. "Wait. Is that why you've been—"

She held up a palm, shaking her head. *"Don't."*

"Don't what?"

"Don't do that thing where you deny it, and I pretend to believe you. How about we act like adults? You admit it, and we move on from there."

Liam stared at her. She took his silence as confirmation. He hadn't really *tried* to hide his infidelity. Even if she were lobotomized, she'd be able to see the signs. Somewhere along the way, his need to rub his cheating in her face had outgrown his instinct to hide it.

"You know, you're not exactly warm and fuzzy," he said.

She smirked.

Blame it on me. Classic Liam.

She cocked her head. "Is that what you need? Warm and fuzzy? *Get a teddy bear.*"

He straightened. "I *did.*"

"*Teddy* bear. I get it. Does she get dressed up for you? Does she try *so* hard to please you?"

He scoffed. "It's nice *someone* did for a change."

"Oh, poor baby."

He squinted at her. "Did you follow me?"

"Today? *No.* Why would I waste my time?"

He put his hands on his hips and chewed his lip with agitation. She imagined he was calculating if she'd *actually* caught him or was fishing.

"If you hate me so much, and if you're so sure I'm cheating on you, then why are we doing this at all?" he asked.

She grinned. "I'd rather stay here and make you miserable."

She walked toward him, and he flinched, thinking she intended to hit him. Instead, she kissed him, her hand cupping his jaw.

Stepping back, she saw his face redden.

"I don't get you," he mumbled, but the anger had drained from his expression.

He took a deep breath.

"What if *I* want to move on?" he asked.

She shrugged and pulled her sunglasses from the hook by the door.

"When you're single, put a wedding band around a chain on your neck. It'll help you pick up women."

He scowled. "*What?* What are you talking about?"

"Chicks love widowers."

She opened the door to leave.

"You're *sick*," she heard him say as the door shut behind her.

Joy put her interaction with Liam behind her and drove toward Bahama Betty's to meet Rowan. She glanced at the clock and knew she'd be twenty minutes late. That meant Rowan would be the first to arrive.

That would be a first.

She didn't bring a mahjong board. *Again.* She'd ordered one, but keeping Rowan focused on the game would be futile— what with wine, food, and widowers screaming for her attention.

Joy texted Rowan her ETA at a red light and sped past a slow-moving Lincoln when the light changed. Once she reached the restaurant, she spotted her raven-haired wine buddy sitting at their usual table by the docks.

"Sorry I'm late," she screamed over a rumbling boat engine pulling up to the waterside location.

Rowan shrugged. "No problem. Traffic?"

Joy stared at a man scrubbing the deck of a docked boat, her mind a million miles away.

I'm losing Liam.

That much was clear.

She noticed Rowan staring and realized she'd been asked a question.

"Hm?"

"I said, did you hit traffic?"

"No. Sorry. Just lost track of time," she said. "Liam and I had a fight."

"I'm sorry. What about?"

"He's having an affair."

Rowan gasped. "Oh *no*."

Joy sighed. "He got really mad when I confronted him

about it."

Rowan nodded. "Been there, done that."

And just like that, the spotlight had shifted back to Rowan. Joy could count on her for that. Rowan never stopped regaling her with tales of her dating conquests. The woman had an endless catalog of insane stories to share. Dating mishaps, fights, lovers' quirks—the drama never ended. She'd thrown plates at a man who called her a whore. Smacked another across the face for a similar offense because she knew he'd never hit her back. Miscalculated mouthing off to a guy over the phone and had to pack in a hurry—but still didn't leave his house until she'd flattened all the tires on his off-road vehicle...

Rowan was chattier when she'd been drinking, and judging by the half-empty bottle sitting on the table, she was well into her second glass.

If you can't beat 'em...

"How about a round of shots?" blurted Joy as the boat engine cut and yacht rock melodies flooded the restaurant.

Rowan perked. "Shots? *Seriously?*"

"It's my birthday," said Joy.

It wasn't.

Rowan's eyebrows bobbed upward. "It is?"

Joy nodded.

"Yep."

Nope.

She heard animated male voices and glanced toward the docks. A group of four middle-aged men had arrived, a hurricane of high-end UV-treated fishing shirts, khakis, and expensive watches.

"We can show that pack how to party," Joy added, thrusting her chin at the men.

Rowan turned to watch the skulk of silver foxes enter the restaurant. She turned back to Joy with a smirk.

"Whoo, shots!" she yipped a little too loudly, leaping to her feet.

The men's heads swiveled in her direction—which was the

point. Four smiles glowed in four tan faces.

Rowan shot them a flirty glance and wiggled her way to the bar, where she ordered two shots. Joy couldn't hear what flavor she'd chosen. When they arrived, the shots were *pink*.

Rowan held out a shot for Joy to take.

"To your birthday," she said.

"To my birthday." Joy sipped the shot. It wasn't bad. She finished it.

They looked at each other, grimacing. Silently admitting defeat, they ordered wine.

Rowan exchanged a come-hither glance with one of the silver foxes. Joy realized by encouraging Rowan to catch the attention of the men, she might have missed her chance to hear more of Rowan's dramas—the one thing she wanted to hear today.

"The one in the pink shirt has a serious money feel to him, don't you think?" Rowan mumbled into her wine glass.

Joy nodded without looking. "I'd think you'd be over men by now."

Rowan arched an eyebrow. "Hm?"

"I mean, with all the trouble you've had with them."

"Trouble?"

"Like when you said someone called the cops on you?" Joy fought not to laugh at the memory of Rowan's tale from their last lunch. It involved Rowan in her underwear in a pool—

"*Pfft*." Rowan rolled her eyes. "People are always calling the cops. So, I'm *passionate*. Excuse *me*."

"They were probably worried for your safety."

"Who?"

"Your neighbors."

Rowan tilted back her head and let her mouth gape at the ceiling for a few seconds. "*Neighbors* need to mind their own business," she said once her chin had dropped back into place.

Agitated and buzzed, she set her wine on the table with such force Joy winced, expecting the glass's stem to snap. Rowan pulled her purse to her and turned it to face Joy. Flipping away the flap, she flashed a small silver pistol.

"It's *me* they have to worry about," said Rowan.

Joy gasped. "You have a *gun*?"

"You bet I have a gun," said Rowan, her chest puffing. She opened the bag wider for Joy to get a better look. "I know how to use it, too."

"Have you ever used it before?"

"Once." She winced. "Well, *twice*, but only once that—" Her eyes dropped to her glass, and she lifted it for another swallow.

"That what?" prompted Joy.

"It was a *warning* shot," said Rowan, looking across the restaurant. "I mean—it was *supposed* to be."

"Wow," said Joy.

Rowan smiled and pulled a small pill box from her purse. "How did we end up talking about guns?" she asked, selecting a pink pill and popping it into her mouth.

She washed it down with wine.

Her attention drifted back to the men.

"What's that?" said Joy, nodding toward a small journal.

Rowan pulled the book from her purse, beaming.

"It's my Book o' Conquests."

Joy laughed. "Your *what*?"

"It's a book where I write down the name of each guy I date and what I got out of them."

Joy's brain stalled for a moment. "*Why*?" was all she managed to say.

"So I can compare year to year. Once I start to slump too hard, I know it's time to land a big fish, permanent-like, right?"

"And you carry it around with you? Aren't you afraid one of your *conquests* will find it?"

"No." Rowan leaned in and dropped her voice to a whisper. "I keep it behind my bureau. The back screws off."

Joy giggled. "You're *crazy*. How are you doing this year?"

Rowan flattened her palm and wobbled it. "Not great. Might be time."

Joy couldn't hide her amusement.

Too much.

She nodded to the men.

"Do you want to go over there?"

Rowan shook her head. "No. *No*. It's our lunch, and it's your birthday..." She allowed her sentence to drift downbeat.

"No, go ahead," said Joy. "To be honest, I'm not feeling that well."

"Are you sure?"

"I'm sure. Go ahead. I'm going to head home."

"Okay..." Rowan's gaze lingered on the nearly empty bottle of wine. "I guess we need to, uh—"

"I'll get the tab on the way out," said Joy.

Rowan gasped. "But it's *your* birthday."

"No, it's fine. I've got it."

Rowan stuffed her Book o' Conquests back into her bag and gathered it up. "Okay. That would be *great*. Thanks. I'll get you back."

Joy smiled. "No problem."

The next day, Joy awoke eager to enjoy her swim time.

Whenever she told someone she swam in the ocean every morning, they invariably told her she was out of her mind. *Aren't you afraid of sharks?* they'd ask. *Isn't it cold? What about rip currents?*

She'd only started the habit a few weeks earlier. It *was* cold sometimes. Other times, she sat on the beach and didn't swim at all.

Today was a swim day.

Joy walked onto the beach with the early morning sun's glow on her face. She dropped her towel and bag to the sand before reaching the ever-present line of seaweed at the shore's edge. The seaweed smelled. She'd read that burning vegetation in South Africa, nitrogen discharges in the Congo, and other environmental abuses thousands of miles away were responsible.

A flutter of butterfly wings.

No one deforesting another continent considered how their transgressions would inconvenience people trying to swim off the Florida coast.

No one cares.

It was that way with everything. Nothing made sense anymore. No one cared. Every man for himself.

She sighed.

The sea lay flat today. A smattering of people dotted the beach—yoga people, daily affirmation mumblers, meditators, sunrise photographers, and early risers walking dogs.

A woman in shorts and a tank top jogged toward her. She looked familiar.

"Good morning, *you*," said Rowan as she arrived, covered in sweat. "Fancy meeting you here."

Joy's eyes widened. "*Rowan.* Good morning. You look shiny again."

Rowan laughed. "You were serious. You really do swim every morning."

Joy shrugged. "I'm up early. Why not?"

"Because swimming out there is *crazy*."

Joy pulled her shirt over her head. Rowan took it from her as she looked into the breeze to pull her long dark hair into a ponytail. When she refocused, Rowan stood with her pre-swim orange juice in her hand. She'd found it in her bag—she must have seen it when she put her shirt inside for her.

Joy smiled. "You didn't have to neaten me up. My shirt can lay here in a pile until I get back."

Rowan shrugged and handed her the OJ.

Joy took it and drank a long gulp. She grimaced at the bottle.

"*Blech.*"

Rowan cocked an eyebrow. "Blech?"

"Tastes funny. I need to get a new bottle. I think this one has been reused too many times."

Rowan laughed. "How do you *reuse* bottles of orange juice?"

"I bought one of those little ones and refilled it from the larger container. It's like a perfect shot of instant energy for a swim, but I don't want to buy a thousand tiny ones."

Joy finished the bottle, and ever-helpful Rowan took it from her.

"I'll throw it out for you if you can bear to buy a new one, cheapo," she said, shaking the container.

Joy smirked. "Thanks. I'll find the strength."

"Do you want to get lunch today?"

"Sure. Bahama Betty's?"

"Naturally."

"Sounds good. I'll meet you there. How did things go yesterday with the guys?"

Rowan smirked. "It didn't work out. The boat was a rental." She cheered Joy with the empty bottle. "See you at eleven?"

Joy nodded. "See you then."

Rowan jogged up the beach to the trash, tossed the bottle in, and waved before continuing on her way.

Joy pulled her goggles from her bag and put them on before entering the water. She slogged through the seaweed barrier and stroked toward the sun. Searching for a clean lane, she swam farther than usual. No one stopped her. The lifeguard didn't arrive until later. She swam east until the people on the beach looked like ants.

She closed her eyes, her arms and legs swaying to keep her afloat.

What if I went to sleep here?

She stopped moving and began to sink—first her legs and then the rest of her until her head went under.

Peaceful, floating downward.

She thrust upward and broke the surface again. Took a breath. Scanned the beach.

No one had seen her go under.

If she stopped swimming, no one would notice.

She *was* tired. If she lay on her back, she could probably take a nap, rocked by the soothing undulations of the ocean. Floating like another clump of seaweed. Maybe she'd travel to the coast of Africa. There, she could chastise them for sending so much seaweed to her little part of the world.

Joy stroked southward.

CHAPTER SIX

Snookie's people had reported Rowan Riley headed toward a restaurant she frequented—Bahama Betty's. Shee thought it would be a nice spot to bump into her and see if they could connect.

She left Mason at their rental house and took his truck. As she left, she noticed a man berating an older woman next door. The pair stood outside the open garage door of their identical house.

The man seemed *irate*—drunk, maybe.

Shee paused to watch, concerned for the woman's safety.

Such a nice neighborhood, and we get the crappy neighbors.

The man noticed her and sneered almost cartoonishly.

"What are you looking at?" he asked.

Before she could think of a witty retort, he got into his car and peeled away.

Shee watched him go.

Dick.

She turned her attention to the gray-haired woman.

"Are you okay?" she asked.

The woman nodded. She looked flustered.

"He gets that way," she said, disappearing inside the garage. A moment later, the door lowered.

Shee checked her watch and frowned. She didn't have time

and knew she shouldn't get involved anyway. Team Loggerhead was on the job. They needed to keep a *low* profile—not wedge into the neighbors' domestic arguments. The woman said she was okay, and unless Shee saw evidence to the contrary, she'd have to believe her.

She headed for Bahama Betty's. On the way, she worked on her *persona*. She didn't need to go deep undercover. She even planned to use her real first name. Well, her nickname, anyway. No one wanted to deal with *Siofra*. The name was easy enough to say—*Shee-fra*—but it was unusual, and heaven-forbid anyone saw the spelling.

She'd had so many aliases during her years on the run that she was surprised *she* remembered her real name.

From now on, if possible, she didn't want to be anyone but herself.

Even with such an uncommon given name.

Thanks, Dad.

She couldn't be *totally* herself with Rowan, of course. She had to be the perfect patsy—someone *Portia* could set up as a thief-slash-murderer. Someone others would believe had committed a crime and then disappeared, but who, thanks to Portia, was probably *dead*.

She didn't want to be *that* perfect, of course.

If Portia didn't pick her to play a part in her plans, she had to at least stay close enough to gather evidence.

As she drove, she called Snookie for a quick refresher.

"Tell me again what Rowan's looking for in a woman friend," she said when Snookie answered.

Snookie grunted. "Well, someone who's moved around a lot. You can't be someone who's been in the area a long time. Her first priority is to be sure no one suspects her of the most recent crime, but it doesn't hurt to leave a trail of missing people who could have been Portia in other cities."

"Got it. Where do we think she was last? I'd be *perfect* if I'd just come from the location of her last murder spree."

"Hm. That *would* be a bonus, but because we know so little

about her, it's hard to be sure. We think New York City."

"Okay, New York's as good as any place."

"Try and stay fluid. Don't cement yourself in New York, just in case."

"Hm, also a good idea. What else?"

"We think she has dark hair and likes her fall-girls to be brunettes as well."

"Check."

"Ooh, mention your rich boyfriend. Maybe she'll go for him if not you—or both."

"A *twofer*. Mason's on deck, ready to be *rich guy* should the occasion call for it, though I don't know if he's terribly comfortable with the role."

"Other than that, I suppose it would help if you're gullible *and* have a history of being an awful person."

Shee chuckled. "This is complicated, this thing she does. Seems like a lot of balls to keep in the air."

"You're not wrong. Rarely do these people make avoiding jail a *major* part of their crime—all this setting up a fall-guy stuff...it's odd. Smart, but odd. She takes her time, too—*oh*, I should mention—you might have competition."

"Another agency's on this case?"

"No, another woman might already be her patsy. There were a few spotty reports Rowan went to lunch with a dark-haired woman, but nothing lately."

"Do we have an ID on her?"

Snookie huffed. "No. The Bureau's been real half-assed with this—which is why you're involved, of course. Rowan could not be Portia at all. Hell, Portia could not exist at all. We could be barking up any number of empty trees."

"Fine with me as long as they're throwing us hounds some meaty bones." She paused. "I mean *money*."

Snookie laughed. "Yeah, I got it. Anyway, my point is, if you see another woman, you might have to hone in—maybe save this poor sucker from becoming the next victim."

"Got it. Thanks, Snook."

"Thank *you*. Try not to get killed."

Shee nodded on her end of the line. "I'll move that up my to-do list. *Ciao*."

She hung up as she pulled into Bahama Betty's valet parking and let the young man take the truck.

She took a deep breath.

Here we go.

She strode into the open-air restaurant only to find herself lost in foliage. The place looked like some kind of tropical amusement park. By sheer luck, she reached the hostess stand without tripping over tiki totems or getting smacked in the face by fat-leafed greenery.

Passing the inattentive hostess, she scanned for a woman matching Rowan's description. An attractive dark-haired woman sat alone by the water at a two-top table, watching a small group of men secure a boat to a floating dock.

Hm.

She moved closer to watch the woman. She didn't worry about being spotted—the brunette couldn't take her eyes off the men. She had a predatory look—more like she was choosing a steak than watching men play with boats.

Shee decided.

That has to be her.

She walked to where the restaurant's thatched roof ended, and a back porch opened to the dock. Standing two feet from the presumptive Portia's table, she watched the men fiddle with their boats, doing her best to mimic the brunette's rapt attention. She turned and smiled when she felt the woman's attention shift to her.

"They look like they're having fun," she said.

The woman smiled. "Don't they? Handsome, too."

"Is one of them yours?"

The brunette laughed, loud and open-mouthed. One of the men heard and glanced over.

"None of them are mine," she said before leaning forward to lower her voice. "Not *yet*."

She giggled, and another man straightened and turned, drawn by the siren's song. He flashed her a cocky grin, and she fluttered her eyelashes before returning her attention to Shee.

Shee herself felt mesmerized by the display.

Girl's got game.

"You looked like you were waiting for someone," she said.

The brunette glanced at her watch. "No. I used to meet a friend here, but..."

She shrugged, and Shee nodded, seeing an opening.

"I've been stood up myself, I'm afraid." She gave the woman's table a longing stare. "I'm impressed you're eating alone. I couldn't decide if I could do it. It feels *strange*."

The brunette's eyes widened. "Why don't you join me?"

Shee put her hand to her chest. "Really?"

"Sure, I—"

She paused as the men from the boat filed into the restaurant. More than one of them eyed the ladies—their attention shifting back and forth between the two women like children deciding which donut they wanted from the box. Shee flashed one quick smile before turning back to the woman.

"Are you sure? I don't want to bother you," she said. "I'm Shee, by the way."

"*Rowan.*" She motioned to the chair across from her. "Please. Sit."

Shee grinned. She'd guessed right.

Rowan Riley, exactly as advertised.

She didn't need to double-check the last name. She couldn't have stumbled across another dark beauty named Rowan—like her, the woman had membership in the Weird Irish First Name Club.

Shee pulled out the chair opposite the woman.

"Thank you. That's really nice of you."

Rowan nodded as she pulled a compact from her purse and checked her makeup.

"Who stood you up?" she asked as she shut her mirror.

"My boyfriend. Work," said Shee.

"What's he do?"

"Do?" Shee cleared her throat to stall. In all the planning she'd done, she hadn't picked a profession for Mason. *Doctor? Surgeon?* No, too many details to screw up. *Lawyer?* No. Nothing law enforcement adjacent...

"Finance," she said, settling on a choice. "He runs several large hedge funds."

Rowan's expression lit.

"*Nice.* Sounds like you're my kind of girl."

"Oh? What kind of girl is that?"

Rowan leaned in for a conspiratorial whisper. "The kind who likes rich men."

She giggled and held Shee's gaze. Shee could tell she was judging her reaction.

"The only kind worth putting up with," said Shee, punctuating her words with a naughty smirk.

Rowan laughed and tapped her on the arm.

"Oh, I like *you*," she said. "Let's *drink*."

Shee smiled.

CHAPTER SEVEN

Mason wandered around the garage of their rental home, looking for something to keep him busy while Shee lunched with Portia.

"Would it kill them to have a dart board or some horseshoes or something?" he muttered, picking through a closet full of beach chairs.

He found a child-sized boogie board.

Not useful.

The house was about a mile from the beach. He *could* walk down there and people-watch, maybe take a swim, but he hated leaving when Shee was in the field. If she needed him, he wanted to be ready.

He inspected a length of polypropylene rope and found a handle at the end of it.

Waterski towline. No boat.

He doubted he could pull it off, even if he had a driver. He was just getting good at running with his prosthesis—he wasn't ready for one-legged waterskiing.

Pushing the rope aside, he found a baseball bat, a half-rotted glove, and a ball.

"This'll come in handy as soon as I find fifteen other guys," he muttered, taking the ball. He shut the cabinet and tossed the ball up and down as he walked into the back yard, where a small but clean swimming pool sat sparkling in the sun.

Already wearing swim trunks, he set the baseball on the patio table and pulled off his shirt before squinting at the small pool.

Hm.

The water looked inviting, but the pool wasn't large enough to do laps. Not laps challenging enough for an ex-SEAL, anyway. Even one that's one leg short.

But he had an idea.

Returning to the garage, he gathered up the tow line and hauled it out back to tie it to the railing leading into the pool. He removed his leg and slid into the water to tie the rope to his waist.

Tied to the railing, he swam, rope holding him in place.

Genius.

He stroked for half an hour before an odd yipping noise caught his attention.

He stopped and stood on his good leg, cocking his head to listen.

Voices.

Two people—a man and a woman—were arguing on the opposite side of the stucco wall separating them from the house next door.

The voices were angry. Well, the male voice was angry. The female's was faint.

He heard a slapping noise. A woman screamed and sobbed.

Mason frowned.

Arguing is one thing…

Mason hopped out of the pool and strapped on his leg. He lifted a chair from the patio set and carried it to the wall. Stepping on it, he peered over the wall, using a thick collection of needle palm fronds for cover.

From his vantage, he saw two people on a stone patio. The owner of the male voice was a big guy—not rough or rugged, but not *small*. He wore bronze shorts and a higher-end pink tee shirt. Mason didn't consider himself a fashionista, but even he grimaced at the color combination.

More upsetting than the man's color choices was the fact he stood over an older woman—maybe mid-seventies? She lay on the ground, holding the side of her face. She begged as the younger man raised his fist, threatening.

Mason spotted a vodka bottle on the table.

Ah. Drunk.

"Well, do you?" the man roared.

The woman curled into a ball as he bent toward her. He didn't hit her. He seemed to enjoy her fear.

Mason gritted his teeth.

I shouldn't get involved.

The man stooped to grab the woman by her shirt to jerk her to her feet.

"Get up. You're embarrassing yourself," he said.

The woman clambered to her feet with his help and then pulled away from him to support herself against the house wall, panting. She looked terrified. The side of her face was red, and her glasses hung at an odd angle from her nose.

A surge of anger lit Mason's nerves like a box of matches. He wasn't able to stop it.

So much for not getting involved.

Hopping off the chair, he found the baseball, snatched it off the pavement, and climbed back onto his chair.

I should not be doing this. I should not be drawing attention to us—

He chucked the ball. He made some small effort to make it seem like an accident, but it wouldn't take a genius to figure out the ball hadn't exactly *arced* over the wall. A line drive from that angle would have had to come from his rooftop.

That was okay.

He wanted the man to think about it.

The ball struck the goon on the back of the head, and as Mason dropped off the chair, he heard him yelp in pain.

Ha.

How do you like it, tough guy?

Mason hustled the chair back to the patio set. As he moved,

he heard the sound of the neighbor's slider door open and the muffled sound of a door slamming shut somewhere in the house. He guessed the woman had taken the opportunity to get away and lock herself in a room until Dickhead calmed down.

He *hoped*.

"Hey!" called a voice as Mason entered the house and shut the slider behind him. He imagined the man was calling over the wall.

"Hey!" he heard again, muffled but loud enough to be heard through the hurricane glass.

Mason toweled his hair, his lips a thin, tight line.

Your move, asshole.

He felt a *little* bad. Shee was going to kill him for starting with the neighbors. They were supposed to stay low and do a job, but—

The doorbell rang.

Shit.

He'd figured the guy for a coward. It seemed the man fancied himself a tough guy.

Mason walked to the main living area and answered the door as the bell rang a third time. He opened the door, smiling.

"Can I help you?" he asked.

The man eyed him. He hadn't expected to see a man bigger than himself. His gaze lingered on the prosthetic leg.

It seemed to give him some solace, but the dumbass shouldn't have locked on the metal leg. Instead, he should have noted the tattoo on his left bicep. The one with the eagle, anchor, trident, and flintlock pistol. That told him all he needed to know.

The man straightened to his full height and held up the baseball. "This yours?"

Mason eyed it.

"I was looking for that. Where'd you find it?"

The man tilted to look around him into the house. "You got a kid here?"

"No. Why?"

The tension in the man's shoulders had relaxed a notch during his search for children. It returned.

"Someone threw it over the wall. We're next door."

"Oh, well, thanks for bringing it back."

Mason reached for the ball. The man jerked it from his reach.

"It hit me. *On my head,*" he said, holding the ball near his temple.

Mason crossed his arms against his chest.

"*Ouch.*"

The man waggled the ball. "So, you threw it?"

"At *you*?" Mason pursed his lips. "Why would I do that?"

They stared at each other.

Finally, the man thrust the ball at him.

"Don't let it happen again," he said.

Mason rolled the ball around his flattened palm as the man stormed away.

It would be funny to chuck it at the back of his stupid head right now.

He sighed and shut the door.

He heard a car roar to life and peel away.

Prick.

Mason walked into the kitchen and spotted a face staring at him through a window of the house next door.

The old woman.

He nodded to her.

The woman disappeared from the window.

Mason washed his hands at the sink, *stewing*. Job or no job, that douchebag better watch himself.

He liked little old ladies.

CHAPTER EIGHT

Thirty-Six Years Earlier – South Carolina

A bag of rocks.

Mason's mother had died for a bag of rocks.

"There's your father's loser friend," his aunt said to him as they watched the news after his mother's death.

On the screen, the police swarmed around a man who looked vaguely familiar. Mason was pretty sure he'd seen him at the house before. At *his* house, with his parents, before his entire world exploded.

"*...arrested today in conjunction with the robbery of a downtown jewelry store...*"

"How do you know he's my dad's friend?" asked Mason.

His aunt glanced at him from her spot on the sofa. She didn't like being bothered during her morning coffee, but she'd started it.

She puffed a lock of hair from her eye.

"Because I *know*. Your father ratted him out to reduce his sentence, I bet."

Mason scowled and took a step toward the television. "Daddy's in jail for robbing a jewelry store?"

His aunt squinted at him. "Are you stupid?"

Mason shook his head. "*No.*"

"Then you know your father killed your Momma."

Mason winced. He didn't like hearing those words so plainly said.

"Yes. I *know*—but did he do something *else*?"

Aunt Tildy snorted a laugh and returned her attention to the television. "There needs to be something else?"

"*...partial recovery of nearly one hundred thousand dollars' worth of rough diamonds stolen...*"

Mason watched as an officer held out his hand for the camera. A pile of cloudy rocks sat in the center of his palm.

Mason gasped.

He'd seen those rocks before.

"What's wrong with you?" asked his aunt.

Mason pointed at the screen. "Those are *diamonds*?"

"That's what they're sayin'."

"But they're not *shiny*."

Aunt Tildy shrugged. "They haven't polished them up yet. Just like your daddy to steal ugly diamonds."

Mason left the room with a portion of the news report playing in a loop in his head.

"*...partial recovery...*"

Before her death, his mother had told him she planned to run away and start a new life with him. *Finally*. After years of abuse for both of them.

Now, he understood the timing.

She *knew* his thief father and his buddy planned to steal diamonds from a local jeweler.

She *knew* she'd be able to steal them from him once he got them back to the house.

But, like everything in his life, things didn't work out.

Momma ended up dead, his father ended up in prison, and he ended up living with his nasty aunt.

Things are going to change, though.

Now, *he* had a plan. A better plan. One that wouldn't fail.

He'd move into his parents' house on the other side of town, far from his aunt and cousins.

He had it all worked out in a list on one of his art tablets. *Step One* had already been completed. He'd co-opted a neighbor's yard sale and sold enough of his parents' stuff to buy himself a bike for traveling back and forth from his aunt's to his old house.

Without his parents to pay the bills, his house had no electricity, but he filled it with snacks that didn't require refrigeration and developed a taste for warm soda. It was nice to have a quiet place to think and draw.

A few hours later, that's what he was doing when he heard someone thump against his front door—thinking about *Step Two* in the quiet of his own home.

"I thought you said you have the key," said a woman's voice outside.

"Ah said ah had *a* key, not *the* key," answered another female.

Mason felt his blood run cold.

His aunt and cousin.

Mason gathered his books. He was half out the back door when his aunt Tildy and cousin Livvy walked around the corner.

They gaped at him.

"What're you doin' here?" asked his aunt.

Mason scowled. "*It's my house.*"

His cousin looked frightened for a reason he couldn't fathom. Aunt Tildy laughed.

"It ain't your house. No eleven-year-old kid has a house. And you think I feed you for *free*?"

Mason took a deep breath.

"I'm twelve, and it's *my* house."

She blew him off with a wave of her hand. "Whuddevah."

His aunt walked down the hall toward the bedrooms, poking her head in each room as she passed.

"This place was a *mess,* last I was here..."

Livvy threw him a smug grin and bounced after her mother.

"When you said I'd have to clean it up, I thought it would be worse than this, Momma," she said.

His aunt returned to squint at Mason, her hands on her hips. "You clean up in here?"

"I want this room," called Livvy from somewhere in the back of the house.

Maybe from *his* bedroom.

Mason's jaw clenched so hard he feared his teeth might break.

Aunt Tildy looked around as if she were seeing the place for the first time. "What happened to the furniture?"

Mason swallowed. He couldn't let them know he'd sold it, or they'd demand the money. Money that looked a lot like a *bike*, now.

"Someone stole it," he muttered.

The woman sneered. "*Animals*. Figures. I shoulda got off my duff and got here sooner."

"*It's my house*," Mason repeated as Livvy jogged back into the room and threw her arms around her mother.

His face felt hot.

Aunt Tildy peeled the girl from her. "Boy, maybe on paper it *is* your house, but we're your guardians 'til yer eighteen, and until then, I'll do what I like with this place. Right now, Livvy and her boyfriend need a place to nest."

Mason's fists clenched, nails digging into the flesh of his palms.

He needed to figure out a plan for making Livvy go, but first, he had to get his runaway insurance. He had something else hidden in the house besides candy and warm soda.

Ugly diamonds.

Tildy didn't know he had the little bag of diamonds his mother had stolen before his father caught up to her. He'd thought they were rocks at first—kept them because they were interesting, but now he knew. They were supposed to give his mother a new life—now, they were going to make a future for him.

Unfortunately, ugly diamonds wouldn't get his aunt out of his house. He wanted to throw the bag at her to cover the meager bit of kindness she'd shown him, push them out, and take back his home, but he knew that would be shortsighted.

She'd take the diamonds *and* the house.

He couldn't let her *ever* find out about his mother's last gift.

He tried one last time to scare them away, stomping his foot and screaming words so loud he thought something popped in his brain.

"This is my house!"

He felt woozy.

Aunt Tildy laughed and pulled a pack of cigarettes from her purse. "Get yer stuff and clear out, Mister."

Mason clutched his sketchbook and ran for his room, clipping Livvy hard with his shoulder as he passed her.

"Ow!" she yelped. "You little—"

He slammed his bedroom door behind him and waited a moment, worried she'd follow him.

She didn't. He had a minute. He heard his cousin and aunt discussing decorating ideas in the living room.

Mason pulled up the floorboard where he'd stashed the diamonds. Stuffing them and his pad in his backpack, he crawled through his window to avoid the she-devils. He didn't want to risk Livvy grabbing his backpack, and he didn't want them to see his new bike.

He found his bike where he'd stashed it out of sight and pedaled hard for town, fighting back tears.

He'd worked hard to clean the house—to make it *his* place.

Now, everything was *ruined*.

He couldn't go back to his aunt's house.

He couldn't bear it.

He'd seen the store his father robbed on the news.

That's where he needed to go.

He pedaled downtown and pulled up in the parking lot across the street from the jewelry store.

He sat a moment, winded and thinking.

He'd considered returning the bag of diamonds to the man—it was the *right* thing to do—but that hadn't been his mother's plan.

Diamonds are worth a lot of money.

Maybe *rough* diamonds were worth even more. Maybe that's why his father had taken them instead of the shiny ones. He could buy a car and drive somewhere. Maybe buy another house. His aunt wouldn't miss him. She wouldn't even look for him.

Mason propped his bike against a tree and walked across the street to the store. The place was so quiet he could hear his heart thumping in his chest.

An old man in the back looked up at him as he entered. He had a pudgy face and bags beneath each eye. Pushing a pair of glasses up the bridge of his nose, he watched Mason with some interest.

"Shouldn't you be in school?" he asked.

Mason shook his head. "I have a doctor's appointment."

The man nodded and returned to whatever he was doing.

Mason cleared his throat and pretended to shop. The diamonds in the cases, set in rings and necklaces, sparkled the way diamonds should—the way they did in the movies.

"I was gonna get my momma something for her birthday," he said.

The man looked up from his work again.

"Yeah?"

Mason pointed at him, pretending he'd had a moment of recollection. "Hey, aren't you the guy from the news?"

The man nodded. "Yes. They found some of my diamonds."

"Just some?"

"Just some."

"How much are you still missing? I mean, how much money did you lose?"

He shrugged. "Maybe thirty thousand. I got about sixty back."

Mason whistled. He tried to remember the amount of stones in the police officer's palm on the news. It'd looked like about the same amount he had in the baggie.

"Where are the rest?" he asked, though he could feel them *glowing* in the bag on his back. It was like they were talking to him, but he wasn't sure what they were saying. Did they want out? To go back to the old man? Or did they know how much he needed them?

The jeweler sighed. "I wish I knew. The guy on the news has a partner, and he's not saying. Jokes on him, though."

"How come?"

"'Cause he's in jail for life for killing his wife. He'll never get back to those diamonds, and I got *insurance*."

Mason winced. The mention of his mother's murder felt like a slap.

"The insurance will pay you for the diamonds you lost?"

The man nodded. "Yep."

Mason looked away, smiling.

It wasn't *stealing* if the man was getting his money back. No reward for returning them would be enough. He couldn't try and sell them back—the man would only have him arrested and take the diamonds anyway.

Time to leave.

He glanced into the case beside him. "I guess these are all too expensive for me."

The man stood and stretched his back. "How much do you have? Maybe I could find a nice little pair of silver earrings?"

"Five dollars."

The man laughed and lowered himself back to his stool. "Yeah, you might want to get your momma some flowers."

"Okay. That's a good idea. Bye."

"Bye."

Mason left the store and hustled across the street. He threw his back against a tree.

The man had *insurance*.

He didn't have to return the diamonds.

Especially after he laughed about Momma.

Feeling better, Mason walked around the tree and stopped, a smile dying on his lips.

Three boys stood where he'd left his bike.

All three were taller than him by a head. One of them had

his bike by the handlebars. One said something to another, and they all turned to stare at him.

Mason gripped the strap of his backpack, unsure of what to do. He couldn't fight the boys. They were too big. They'd beat him and take his backpack.

He'd lose his diamonds.

He'd lose his escape plan.

The boys moved toward him, fanning out to better their odds of catching him when he tried to run. Like a pack of hunting lions, they didn't need to say a word to each other.

He'd hesitated too long. There wasn't time to run—

Someone touched his arm.

Mason jumped. He spun with his fist up to find a tall, old black woman at his side.

"Easy there," she said.

Her hand rested on his shoulder, pushing him forward. Mason allowed her to move him toward the boys. He wasn't sure why.

"That your bike?" she asked.

Without waiting to hear his answer, she addressed the boys.

"I know you. That ain't your bike."

The one holding the handlebars bared his teeth.

"It ain't yours either, ya old bitch."

The woman straightened and puffed her chest. "You sure about that?"

Mason looked up at her.

She was *tall*. The hand resting on his arm seemed as large as his father's.

The boys drew together again. One whispered to the other, and they all looked at the old woman with new eyes.

The largest of the three boys shoved the bike to the ground and stormed off. His friends fell in line behind him.

Mason gaped, stunned.

The old woman took her hand off Mason's arm when they'd gone.

"You best not leave that bike around here again," she said.

"I won't. Thank you," he said.

She shrugged. "Ain't nothin'. Bike didn't belong to them. There's right, and there's wrong."

He picked his bike up and inspected it for damage.

"They were scared of you," he said.

She chuckled, a low, pleasant sound.

"Yeah. I got a reputation for bein' crazy around here." She massaged above her left breast, her expression pinching. "You do me a favor back?"

He nodded, and the woman pointed to a set of metal stairs on the side of a brick apartment building at the end of the block.

"I live up those stairs. Could you help me up there? You can leave your bike around the back inside the fence. No one will mess with it."

Mason looked up the stairs, wondering what lay at the top. She *had* helped him.

Her brow beaded with sweat. She seemed suddenly distressed.

"Okay."

They walked to the building in silence. Twice, she touched his shoulder as if she needed to steady herself. Mason ran his bike to the back yard at the apartment before helping the woman up the stairs. Her door was unlocked and opened into an apartment that smelled like tuna fish.

Inside, the woman collapsed into a chair and fumbled to open a bottle of pills on the table. She took one and closed her eyes, breathing deeply.

"I'll be better in a second. Thank you. That was a good thing you did."

Mason nodded.

"You better get back. Your momma's gonna be missin' you."

Mason shook his head. "My momma's dead."

"Oh yeah? I'm sorry to hear that. Mine too. What about your pa?"

Mason didn't want to tell her the story of his father. "Him, too."

"Where you stayin'?"

"With my aunt."

"Oh yeah? She a nice lady?"

"No. She doesn't want me there. I've got three cousins. None of them want me there."

The woman grunted.

"She stole my house," he added. It felt good to have someone to complain to.

"Stole it?" she asked.

He nodded. "I cleaned it up, and she gave it to my cousin."

"That don't seem fair. Ain't it yo' house?"

"Not official 'til I'm eighteen, I guess."

"How old are you?"

"Twelve."

"Hm. You know, you're kinda young, but if you wanted to come here and help me out from time to time, I could maybe pay you a little. I gotta pension."

Mason considered this.

She continued as if she didn't want him to make the wrong decision without considering all the facts.

"I always got things need doin'. Look at this place. I'd like to paint it. And gettin' up and down those stairs for groceries..."

She huffed a sigh to show the effort it took.

Mason chewed his lip. "I can maybe come by after school tomorrow?"

"That be nice. What's your name?"

"Mason."

"Good, Mason. You can call me Miss Elly. Go now. Be careful bikin' home. Those kids might be waitin' for you."

"I'll be careful."

Mason opened the door, and she called after him.

"I can't be there every time."

He biked back to Aunt Tildy's. He could leave with the diamonds in a few days. It wouldn't hurt to help the old lady for a spell.

She seemed *nice*.

CHAPTER NINE

Rowan flipped the pages of the local lifestyle magazine she'd grabbed from the pile at the front of Bahama Betty's. She'd found reading in restaurants made it clear she was alone and approachable. She used to bring a book, but sometimes people asked her about the books she wasn't *actually* reading.

Awkward.

After that, she stuck to props she could grab at the restaurant and not cart around with her.

Local tourist magazines were handy. Nobody ever quizzed her about the plastic surgery advertisement on page two.

Forget books. Older rich men didn't like women to be *too* smart, anyway.

Rowan flipped another page as the roar of a boat engine caught her attention. She turned to spot a tall, middle-aged man backing his boat into one of the restaurant's many docks.

She straightened.

What do we have here?

She didn't know much about boats, but she knew his was expensive.

She scanned the restaurant for the woman she'd met earlier that day. *Shee.* Shee was attractive and older than her. That made her a good wingwoman. They'd clicked.

She didn't see her anywhere. They'd exchanged numbers—

she should have called her before coming back to the restaurant for the evening's hunt.

Dammit.

The man cut his engine and handed the young dock attendant a line. He hopped off the vessel, slipped the kid some cash, and headed into the restaurant.

He was handsome. Not too old. The teeth looked too white to be original but weren't too *big*—he didn't have the horse-faced look some old guys developed after replacing their choppers. This strapping fellow had *movie-star teeth.* The kind you got—not because the old ones were falling out—but because the old ones weren't *perfect.*

Expensive teeth.

He'd been in the restaurant for less than a minute, and he'd already checked several of Rowan's dream-boyfriend boxes.

Handsome, tall, rich...

He walked toward her, and their gazes met.

Hold it, hold it...

He flashed a smile with those perfect teeth. She smiled back.

Look away demurely.

He passed and went to the tiki bar, but not before she saw it.

The ring.

He wore a R.O.C. around his neck.

Rowan sucked in a breath.

No.

How could she be this lucky? A man closer to her age than her usual, rich, a widower—she'd won the lottery.

She had work to do.

Rowan's attention returned to the man at the tiki bar as the bartender handed him his drink. She stood, adjusted her skirt, and sauntered toward him, pretending to be on her way to the bathroom.

"What is that?" she asked as she neared.

He turned, the glass an inch from his lips.

"Are you talking to me?" he asked.

She smiled. "Yes, sorry. I was wondering, what are you drinking?"

He held his glass aloft and eyed it as if he'd just noticed he was holding it. "This? A Dark and Stormy—dark rum and ginger beer."

"Ginger beer?" Rowan leaned in, looking as awkward as possible, hoping he'd invite her closer. "I didn't know they made beer out of *ginger*."

He shrugged. "I guess they do. Do you want one?"

She placed a hand on her chest. "Me? A Dark and Stormy?"

He grinned. "Sure. I'll buy you one—or are you waiting for someone?"

She pouted. "No. I'm afraid my friend stood me up."

"Then join me," he said.

Score.

One of the bartenders glanced at Rowan as she sat but looked away when she glared back at him. He'd seen her at the restaurant before and knew she was hunting.

You ever want to make another tip? said the glare.

The bartender smiled, content to keep their secret.

"Did you want to try the Dark and Stormy?" he asked.

She nodded. "Sure."

She watched as he made the drink. She didn't love that he'd noticed her. *Remembered* her.

Might be time to pick a new bar.

She turned to the handsome man and smiled. She'd been told she had a dazzling grin of her own. She had expensive veneers, too. Thanks to—well, she'd have to search her book to find the name of the man who'd paid for them.

"I'm Liam."

The object of her desire offered his hand, and she took it.

"Rowan."

"That's a pretty name."

"Thank you."

And so the dance begins...

The Dark and Stormy appeared, and Liam motioned to it. "Go ahead. Do you want a drumroll?"

She giggled. Lifting the glass, she let it hover near her lips to draw his attention to her mouth. She wanted him to think about kissing it.

"Okay, here I go," she said. She took a sip and cute-winced by wrinkling her nose.

"Not bad..." she said, covering her mouth with her hand.

He chuckled. "You hate it, I can tell."

"No, no, it's good. It's an *acquired* taste..."

Clearly amused, he waited until she put the glass down and then slid it in front of himself. "Don't worry about it. I'll drink it. What's your poison?" He glanced at the table where she'd been sitting alone. "White wine?"

"Rosé."

"Bartender, a glass of your finest rosé," he said.

The bartender nodded and brought her a glass.

"Thank you," she said.

Liam nodded. "My pleasure. So, what brings you here today? You said you were expecting someone?"

She shrugged. "Oh, you know, end of the week. I thought I'd get a cocktail, and my friend had to bail. How about you?"

He shrugged. "Bored. Thought I'd take the boat out for a spin."

As he spoke, his hand slid up his chest. He pinched the ring around his chain, twirling it between his thumb and forefinger.

He wanted her to see it.

"Is that a wedding ring?" asked Rowan, careful to be sure her tone sounded sympathetic and not accusatory.

"Hm? Oh, kind of." He nodded sadly and dropped his chin to look at the ring. "I lost my girlfriend—not my wife, this was more of a promise ring, but...

"Oh no, I'm so sorry to hear that. Recently?"

He nodded and looked away. An awkward silence fell.

"Was she sick?" asked Rowan, running through her mental database of pre-planned stories. If he said she'd had cancer, she'd tell him she'd lost her mother that way. If the illness was heart-related, she'd tell him about her father's heart attack.

Neither story was true.

Her mother was alive. Her father was who-knows-where—but she liked to use the same lies. It made it easier to keep them straight. At this point, her lies felt as real as the truth anyway.

Maybe they weren't even lies anymore. Maybe that's how lying worked.

Death worked. She knew that. Bonding with people over loss was sometimes more powerful than sex.

Not that sex didn't help seal the deal.

Liam shook his head. "She drowned."

Rowan gasped and covered her mouth with her hand. "Oh, I'm so sorry."

She didn't have a drowning story of her own to share. She made a mental note to find one or two. She imagined if she kept her tragedy stories vague enough, she could use them for almost anything—drowning, car crash, slip and fall...

"I'm sorry," said Liam with a soft smile. "I didn't mean to bring things down."

Rowan put a hand on his thigh. "No, not at *all*. My God, I can't imagine. You're so young to lose someone."

He chuckled. "Been a little while since someone told me I was *so young*." He took a deep breath and clapped his hands together. "Okay, so, moving on—what do you do, Miss Rowan?"

She gave his leg a little squeeze and released him. "Oh, I'm a consultant."

She always said she was a consultant. *Consultant* could mean anything, and most of the time, the men were so busy thinking about *themselves* or getting her naked that they didn't bother to ask specifics.

She waited for a beat and turned the question on him when he didn't ask for clarification—as expected.

"How about you?"

"Dermatologist," he said.

...aaaand there was the reason he'd asked what *she* did. So

he could tell her what *he* did.

Men.

So predictable.

Rowan took a sip of her wine to compose herself. She wanted to proceed with caution. The man was semi-widowed, a doctor, rich, seemingly interested—Liam was a *trophy fish.* She needed to reel him in, drag him into her boat, and club him over the head.

"What's funny?"

Rowan looked up. "Hm?"

"You were smiling to yourself."

"Was I? I—" She turned and looked at the words painted on the back of his boat. The name stood out in flesh-colored lettering.

"*Peel Out*," she said, reading aloud.

He glanced at his boat and laughed. "Ah, yep. I do a lot of cosmetic work—face peels and whatnot." He grimaced. "Is it too douchy?"

She smiled.

Ew. Oh God, yes, but I'm going to let it go.

"No, not at all," she said aloud. "Doesn't everyone name their boat after something that means something to them?"

"Yeah, I guess. It was my girlfriend's idea."

"Oh." She sniffed. She didn't want to talk about his dead girlfriend. She wanted him to think about *her.*

Time for a subject change.

She looked at his boat. "So, do you fish?"

He nodded his head from side to side. "A little. The head of my department drags me out sometimes." He pulled his phone from his pocket. "We went out a couple of months ago and caught this."

He flipped through his photos and held up a shot of him and another silver fox holding a giant fish.

"Wow, that—" Rowan's focus shifted to a pair of women sitting together in the photo's background. The older smiled at the camera. The other dark-haired woman seemed unimpressed by the catch. She'd turned away from the lens to stare somewhere off the stern.

"Who is that?" she asked, pointing to the obscured woman.

"Hm?" he looked to see where she was pointing. "Oh, this is Joy and that's Rob's wife," he said pointing to two different women.

"Joy?"

He nodded as his forehead creased. "My girlfriend. Why?"

She placed an open palm on her chest. *His name was Liam.* Liam, the dermatologist.

Didn't Joy say her boyfriend was a dermatologist? Some kind of doctor—sometimes she wished she listened more.

"I think that's *my* Joy," she said.

"*Your* Joy?"

"My friend. She drowned? When?"

Liam blinked at her. "A month ago. You didn't know? Are you sure?"

"I used to meet her here, but then she just dropped off the face of the earth. I thought maybe we didn't get along as well as I thought we did." Rowan pulled out her phone and held her call log up for Liam. "Is that her number?"

He squinted at the screen. "*Yes.* Oh my God...when was the last time you saw her?"

"About a month ago. She was about to go swimming on the beach—" She gasped. "That's where—?"

He nodded. "We found her stuff on the beach, but no sign of her." He ran his hand through his still-thick hair. "Probably got caught in a rip current or something. I held out hope—technically, she's still *missing*—but it's pretty clear she's gone."

Rowan nodded. "I'm *so sorry.*"

"Thank you. Me, too, I guess. You were friends." He took a long sip of his drink. "This is *crazy.*"

Rowan nodded. "I'm here because of her—I mean, in this restaurant."

"How so?"

"The first time we met at another place, and then she said

we should start meeting here."

"That makes sense. We came here all the time," said Liam. "Though, to be honest, I'm here today because I got a flyer on my door."

Rowan chuckled. "Me too."

She almost told him she'd been there earlier and then returned because of the Ladies' Night flyer but decided it sounded a little *sad* that she'd returned to the same bar twice in one day. She couldn't *not* come, though. Ladies' Night always brought the men in—and she knew to come early for the older, richer ones.

The kids and starving artists could *have* late night.

He cocked his head. "Where did you and Joy meet?"

"At an art fest. We were going to learn how to play mahjong together—"

He pointed at her. "You're the *mahjong* friend."

"I guess so. She mentioned me to you?"

"Not specifically. She called you her *mahjong friend*."

Rowan smiled. "That's funny because we never actually ever learned—never even *played*. Not once. We decided it was more fun to drink."

His forehead creased. "Really? She wasn't much of a drinker."

Rowan shrugged. "She seemed pretty good at it to me."

"Yeah..." Liam ran his finger along the edge of his glass. "Did she talk about me with you?"

Rowan shook her head. "No. I mean, sometimes in passing, but not really."

He nodded. "She wasn't that chatty as a rule."

"No. Now that you mention it, I think I did most of the talking. She seemed to like it that way."

"Sounds like her."

Liam smiled and held her gaze. Rowan could tell he was attracted to her.

"It's, uh, it's nice to meet someone who knew her," said Liam.

She nodded and hoped he wouldn't ask for any more stories. She wasn't sure how well she knew Joy. Her conversation with Liam only underscored how little she knew about her friend.

"How long were you together?" she asked.

He shrugged. "Two months. Hardly any time at all. When the police asked me for a photo of her for identification, this was the only one I had, and you can't even see her face. Embarrassing, really."

Rowan turned her head so he wouldn't see her smile.

Two months.

She bet she could erase the memory of a short-term dead girlfriend *in a week.*

Sorry, Joy.

She looked at her watch.

"Oh gosh, is that the time?" she said.

This was her least favorite part of the game. She needed to leave him wanting more. Every bit of her wanted to hang around, stay until he asked her back to his place, but she knew that wasn't the right move.

Not for the long game.

Not for the *win.*

"You have to go?" he asked.

She nodded. "I do. I have a thing."

She finished the last sip of her rosé and slid off her bar seat to reach for her purse.

He put his hand on hers. "I've got it."

She gaped at him. "What? No. I had a glass before you even got here."

"No. Seriously, let me get it. It's the least I can do. I'm afraid I wasn't much fun."

"No, it wasn't like that at all."

He pulled his wallet from his pocket and pulled a fifty from it. He placed it on the bar and stood.

"I'll walk you to your car."

"Thank you."

She headed for the exit with him beside her.

She gave her ticket to the valet, and he jogged off to retrieve her car.

"Would it be wrong to tell you I'd like to see you again?" he asked.

"No," she said, tilting her chin down as she looked up into his eyes.

"Can I get your phone number?"

She rattled off her numbers, and he plugged them into his phone as her car arrived. She walked around to the driver's side, and he followed, tipping the valet for her before she could do it.

Not that she'd moved very fast.

"Thanks. It was great meeting you, Rowan," he said as she sat in the driver's seat.

"You too, Liam."

He bit his lip. "You know, at the risk of being too forward— I'll actually be back *here* tomorrow around eleven. I'm going fishing in the morning with some buddies, and we always stop here after. Maybe you'd like to join us?"

She shrugged and gave him her sauciest smile. "I'll see what I can do."

He shut the door, and, with a final flirty wave, she pulled out into the street.

She screamed with happiness.

Thank. You. Joy.

What were the chances? Joy's boyfriend. The dermatologist.

Fan-freaking-tastic.

He had to be *filthy* rich.

Had to be.

She'd won the lottery.

Joy really was a great friend.

Did she feel bad she wanted to spend every waking moment with her dead friend's boyfriend?

No.

Not really.

She giggled, remembering the ring around the chain on Liam's necklace.

What are the chances?

She was the one who'd told Joy about the R.O.C., and now Liam was wearing one of *hers*—the bait that drew her to him.

She shimmied with excitement.

Crazy.

CHAPTER TEN

"Joy's officially dead, and Rowan's moving in," said the voice on the other side of the line.

Shee sat up and glanced to where Mason lay beside her, naked, only the sheet covering his naughty bits.

It was a good look for him.

She couldn't lie.

He was awake and staring at the ceiling, or maybe he awoke when the phone rang. Either way, he was awake and looking...*pensive*? His gaze shifted to her as he waited to hear who'd called so early.

"It's Snookie," she mouthed to him.

He nodded and rolled away from her to his side.

"Who's Joy?" she said into the phone.

Snookie sighed. "She was a woman getting chummy with Rowan—Joy Zabić. I told you about her. Only we didn't know who she was then. We know now, and she's gone missing."

"Dead or missing?"

"She swam into the ocean and didn't swim back, so there's not much difference unless she can tread water indefinitely."

"You're thinking Rowan did it? Could it have been an accident? Coincidence?"

"Sure. Might have been bad luck. Except it looks like now Rowan is canoodling with Joy's rich boyfriend. Liam Bruce. Dermatologist."

"Whoa."

"Yeah, seems like less of an accident now, doesn't it?"

Shee grunted. "I met with her."

"Joy?"

"No, Rowan."

"Oh. Right. And?"

"And I set myself up as the perfect friend." She paused and then added, "I didn't get Joy killed, did I?"

"Did Rowan ditch Joy in favor of you? Maybe you were *too* good at your job?" Snookie chuckled. "Don't flatter yourself. Joy took her last fateful swim weeks ago."

"Oh. Whew. That *would* be a long time to tread water."

"Yes."

"It's less creepy of a timeline for Rowan to be dating the boyfriend, though."

"Little less creepy. No less suspicious."

Shee scowled. "Wait. If this Joy person is pertinent to the case, why am I just finding out about her?"

"Like I said, the Bureau surveillance guys weren't in it to win it. I'm lucky I got you to her yesterday. They threw us a final bone, catching her with Liam Bruce last night before being reassigned."

Shee sighed.

"What does that mean for us? We need surveillance now. I guess I could put Mason on her—though I was saving him to play my rich boyfriend—"

"I've got you covered. Croix and Ethan should be there any second. That's what I was calling to tell you."

Shee sat up. *"What—?"*

Someone knocked on the door, and Mason rolled to face Shee.

"Could everyone make a little more noise?" he grumbled, punching his pillow to fluff it.

Shee put her hand over the phone. "Croix's here. Snookie sent her for surveillance."

"Super," mumbled Mason.

She returned to her call. "Croix's here," she repeated to

Snookie. "I gotta go."

She hung up.

"Close the door on your way out," said Mason as she threw on clothes and left.

The doorbell rang again.

"I'm *coming*," yelled Shee.

She strode to the front door and answered to find Croix and Ethan, their newest recruit, grinning at her. Well, Croix was grinning. Ethan looked like he'd just woken up.

"Rise and shine," said Croix, walking past Shee.

Ethan followed as if she had him on a leash.

Shee shut the door behind them.

"Coffee?" she asked, heading for the pot.

"Yes," said Croix.

"Me too," said Ethan.

"I'll be making it to-go. I need you two following Rowan ASAP."

Croix nodded. "Yep. Snookie gave us her address. Just touching base and getting coffee."

Mason entered the main living area in shorts and a United States Navy tee.

Ethan watched him cross to the kitchen.

"I will never get used to how big that dude is," Shee heard him murmur to Croix.

"That's just because you're so *small*," said Croix.

Ethan rolled his eyes, and Croix giggled. It made Shee laugh to see this all-too-human side of Croix. The *young-person-in-love* side. Or lust. Or whatever tossed around in the heads of young people like them.

I'm sure I don't remember.

Mason arrived at her side in the kitchen, and she eyed the pecs straining his tee shirt.

Oh right. I remember now.

Lust.

"Did you say something?" he asked.

She shook her head. "No."

"We're going to put our bags in the spare room," said Croix.

The pair wandered off.

"Why are they here again?" asked Mason.

"The FBI is officially unwilling to spend manpower on this unofficial case. We lost our surveillance. Snookie sent *them* to keep an eye on Rowan."

He rubbed his eyes. "Got it. Better them than me. What's your plan for today?"

"Well, we got some new news from Snookie. It turns out Rowan might have had a patsy already, but that woman, Joy, has gone missing, presumed dead."

"Missing? Where?"

"In the ocean."

"Ah. That'll do it. She killed her?"

"We don't know. It doesn't make sense for Rowan to kill her if she hoped to frame her, but she was spotted yesterday with Joy's ex, who happens to fit the rich guy profile."

"Already? How long has this Joy person been missing?"

"Weeks."

Mason scoffed. "He moves fast."

"So does she. He might have been manipulated, but yeah. Still doesn't seem like it was hard to talk him into it."

"I take it this Rowan is hot?"

She glowered at him.

"I mean, *objectively*," he added, smirking.

She chuckled. "Yes. She's *objectively* hot."

"And this Liam guy is rich?"

"Dermatologist."

"So, maybe she needed Joy out of the way to get to this guy."

"I hope so. Otherwise, Rowan's already at the endgame. I need to get myself to her immediately, whether she decided Joy would be more useful dead or the poor woman really *did* paddle into the wrong rip current. I have to make sure I'm handy, and no one else dies—least of all *me*."

"And me? Do I play rich boyfriend today?"

"Not yet. If she killed Joy to get her man, I doubt she'll throw him over for you."

He puffed his chest. "She hasn't seen me yet."

She rolled her eyes. "Fair enough. But let's assume she's put *planning* into this. Let's see where things go." Shee poked him. "You could hang out with Croix and Ethan? Go on the stakeout?"

The kids returned from the spare room, thumb-wrestling with each other as they walked.

Mason cocked an eyebrow at Shee.

"I'll pass."

She giggled. "Well, then, I don't know. You'll have to kill another day here. Maybe you could research—"

She stopped as inspiration struck.

"Hey, Croix, Ethan, I need you two to split up."

The pair stopped wrestling and turned to look at her. Realizing they still held hands, they jerked away from each other.

"We're not *dating*," said Croix.

"*No*," agreed Ethan.

Shee frowned. "I said *split up,* not *break up*. I mean split duties for the day. Croix, you'll be on Rowan. Ethan, you stay here and get me all the information you can find on Rowan Riley, a woman named Joy Zabić, and Liam Bruce. I know he's a dermatologist—I don't have anything on Joy yet. I'll forward whatever Snookie sends me."

Croix pouted.

"I have to stakeout alone? That *sucks*."

Shee shrugged as she heard her phone ring where she'd plugged it in overnight.

"Sorry, kiddo, them's the breaks," she said, carrying her coffee to the bedroom. She figured it was Snookie calling with some bit of info she'd forgotten, or maybe Angelina calling to make sure Croix had made it safe—

The name glowing on her phone was her new buddy's.

Rowan.

She picked up.

"Hello?"

"Hi, it's Rowan. We met yesterday? At Bahama Bettie's?"

"Sure, hi, what's up?"

"I was wondering if you'd be interested in grabbing brunch with me? I was about to go alone and thought maybe you'd like to join me again?"

Shee grinned.

I knew it. I killed it undercover.

"Brunch? Sure? Name the place."

"Well, a gentleman may or may not have mentioned he might be at Bahama Bettie's around eleven this morning..."

"And you need me to be your wingman?"

Rowan barked a laugh. "*Yes.* You *get* me. I think this is a good one—and I have the craziest story."

"Really? Sounds good."

"Maybe he has some friends you'd be interested in? But— you said you have a boyfriend—?"

Shee glanced at Mason. She decided against it. Better to stay fast and light at this point.

"Eh, I like to keep my options open," she said.

She could always crack Mason out later.

Rowan laughed wickedly, and Shee smiled. She was scoring points with Rowan left and right. The woman loved her.

Hopefully, enough to frame me and kill me.

Shee spotted Rowan at the bar at Bahama Betty's and took the stool beside her.

"Hey, girlfriend," she said.

Inside, she groaned. Did real people say things like *Hey, girlfriend!* or had she seen it on television?

Ugh.

Rowan seemed unfazed.

"I'm going to have to get a frequent diner club card if this keeps up," she said.

She already had an almost empty glass of wine in front of her. Shee checked her watch. She wasn't late. She guessed Rowan had come early so as not to miss Joy's boyfriend.

Rowan put a hand on her hand. "Liam should be here soon. I'm so excited."

"I bet. He's a good one?"

Rowan tilted back her head. "A great one. Tall, handsome, rich—" She refocused on Shee. "He's not even that old. Older than me but not *old*. In his fifties still."

Shee chuckled at the woman's unabashed gold-digging. It was almost funny how *shameless* she was if you pushed aside all the dead people she left in her wake.

Rowan motioned for another glass of wine and pointed to Shee to request one for her as well. She didn't bother to ask what Shee *wanted* to drink.

Rowan tapped the bar top like she was about to explode with giddiness. "He's a doctor too. Can you believe it?"

Shee shook her head, feigning amazement like a good friend.

"No, I—"

Rowan barrelled on. "It's like he comes pre-vetted because he was with Joy. You know?"

Shee wasn't sure what to say to that. "Uh-huh."

"He should be here in a bit." Her gaze swept over the docks. "He was going fishing with his buddies and coming here after."

The bartender delivered their wine, and Shee took a sip.

Blarg.

Cheap and sweet.

"I might be able to burn the book after this one," said Rowan.

"The book?" asked Shee, attempting to palate a second sip. Sometimes, with bad booze, it was best just to power through the first few sips until you really didn't care how bad it was anymore.

"My Book of Conquests," said Rowan with a wicked smile. "I keep track of them, like accounting. What they looked like, what they gave me—"

"Like accounting?"

She pointed at Shee. "*Yes.* I didn't really think of it like that, but that's *perfect*. It helps me choose new boyfriends based on past performance, etc."

Shee's glass paused at her lips.

This woman...

She sure would like to see that book, though.

"Do you have it with you?" she asked.

"No. I keep it hidden behind my bureau—can you imagine if one of them found it?" Rowan rolled her eyes at the horror of it. She gasped. "Oh, that reminds me, I forgot to tell you the crazy story about Liam."

Rowan was in the middle of taking a sip and almost choked in her rush to talk.

"It's the craziest story." She looked both ways like a conspirator before leaning in. "He's the boyfriend of my *dead friend*."

Shee could tell it would be easier to wrestle a bear than to jerk Rowan back to the Book of Conquests topic. She made a note to circle back later.

"Your *dead* friend?" she echoed, trying to show as much excitement as the human leech sitting beside her.

Rowan nodded. "My friend I used to meet here. She stopped showing up, and now I know why. She's dead."

Shee held up a hand. "Hold on. You're dating her boyfriend, but you *just* found out she's dead?"

Shee winced, worried her comment sounded judgemental. It *was*—she just didn't want it to sound that way to Rowan.

If the woman was offended, she didn't show it.

"He's the one who told me," she said.

"He told you she was dead?"

Rowan nodded.

"So you knew him before?"

She shook her head. "*No*, that's the crazy part. I just met him, he happened to show me a picture of his *dead girlfriend*, and I recognized her."

Rowan made air quotes around the phrase *dead girlfriend* with her fingers, which Shee found odd. From the dip in her tone, Shee guessed she thought air quotes were for mocking dead romantic rivals.

"Wow," she said. "So you meet him, totally randomly, and he happens to show you a photo of his dead girlfriend, and you realize she's your missing friend?"

Rowan's eyes popped wide over her wine glass. Crazy, right?"

"*Crazy*. How did she die? Car accident?"

Rowan shook her head. "Drowned."

Shee winced. "Yikes."

"I know—it doesn't end there, either." She put down her glass and tapped Shee's knee. "Get this. I think I talked to her on the beach right before she went out and never came back."

Shee leaned in. This *was* interesting. Could Rowan be so full of herself that she'd half-confess to murder just to get a thrill? She bragged about her gold-digging—why not brag about murder? Why not give your new friend a taste of the truth, knowing she'll never assemble the pieces?

"Really? You saw her? How do you think it happened?" asked Shee.

Rowan shrugged. "Rip current, I guess. Or, whaddya call it, stitches? She might have gotten a *stitch*."

She took another sip and added, "I know she drank some bad orange juice."

Shee froze, hanging on Rowan's last words.

This is it.

It had to be. This was Rowan's equivalent to the Zodiac Killer sending cryptic notes to the police to taunt them.

"How do you know she had bad orange juice?" she asked.

Rowan shrugged. "She drank it while I was there. Said it

tasted funny."

Shee gaped. Was Rowan confessing to spiking Joy's orange juice?

Shee glanced at her wine and set it back on the bar.

"Do you think it could have been poisoned?" she asked.

Rowan's brow knitted. "Her OJ?"

Shee nodded.

"I figured it was just old." Rowan's attention drifted and then returned, her expression darkening. "Why would someone poison her? Who?"

"Her boyfriend?"

Rowan scoffed. "Liam? *No.*"

She took another sip of her wine.

"No," she repeated again.

Rowan looked as if she'd wandered off mentally, and Shee studied her expression. She didn't look like she was faking her confusion.

She's good.

The problem was she'd been a little too insightful, bringing up the possibility of Joy's poisoning. *Portia* probably didn't want friends—or potential marks—who asked too many questions.

She'd basically accused Rowan of poisoning Joy.

"Maybe someone else had a crush on Liam," she said.

This snapped Rowan from her thoughts.

"What?"

"Maybe someone wanted Joy gone so they could go after him. Or, maybe someone from her work. What did she do?"

Rowan's mouth opened a crack and remained that way for a beat.

"You know, I have no idea what she did."

She took a long sip of her wine and cocked her head at Shee.

"You think there's someone else after him?"

The question caught Shee off-guard. Instead of appreciating the idea she wasn't the murderer, she seemed panicked someone else wanted Liam.

Shee shook her head, laughing. "*No*, I listen to too many

crime podcasts. I'm sure she drowned. Lots of people drown."

Rowan nodded. "I see it on the news a lot."

Shee waved a hand as if she were erasing all suspicions. "Anyway, I'm sure the police would have checked that OJ. If it had been poisoned, they would have known."

Rowan shook her head. "I threw it out."

Shee'd been scanning the bar for potential Liams. Her attention snapped back to Rowan.

"The OJ?"

Rowan nodded. "I jogged the empty bottle to the trash for her so she wouldn't reuse it again."

"Oh..." Shee nodded.

Shit.

"Well, I'm sure it was nothing—"

"He was cheating on her," chirped Rowan, sitting up in her seat.

"What?"

"Joy said Liam was cheating on her."

Shee found herself at a loss again. She couldn't ask Rowan why she was so damn excited about some douchebag who cheated on his last girlfriend. For crying out loud—if Rowan didn't kill Joy, Liam might have—*and* he was cheating on her?

What a catch.

But she couldn't say that.

Rowan could see she was confused, even if she didn't know why.

"Don't you get it?" she asked instead.

Shee shook her head.

"That's who killed Joy. That woman."

"Because she wanted Liam to herself?"

Shee expected Rowan to grow concerned, or pensive, or—be anything other than *ecstatic*—but that's what happened. The woman scrootched around as if it were hard to keep from leaping from her seat and starting a conga line.

"She's got to be angry to kill Joy, right?" she asked, without stopping to wait for an answer. "*Obviously,* it didn't work out with whoever that bitch was because he was here talking *me up*—"

Shee nodded supportively.

Right, because it's not like he has a history of dating two women at once...

Nope. She couldn't point that out. She needed to match Rowan's growing excitement.

"*Totally.*" Shee held up her glass. "Her bad luck is your win."

Rowan grinned and cheered her.

"It's a shame, but *yes.* I think—" She paused to rap her knuckles on the bar top. "*Knock on wood*, but I think this proves Liam and I are meant to be."

"Too many coincidences," agreed Shee.

"Exactly. It *has* to be fate."

Shee held up her glass again since Rowan seemed to like it the first time.

"To fate."

Rowan grinned. "To fate."

Shee took a sip of her hopefully unpoisoned wine.

To fate. And to uncovering who this third woman is...

It could be Rowan was as transparent a gold digger as she seemed. Maybe this other woman was Portia, and *Rowan* was the fall guy.

Oh no.

The more she thought about it, the more it seemed possible.

Portia targets Liam, gets Joy out of the way, draws in silly Rowan to take the hit.

She needed to get back. She and Ethan needed to explore this *other woman* theory.

They might be chasing the wrong spider—

"Hey, pretty lady," said a man's voice.

Shee turned to see a generically handsome man making his way toward Rowan.

Rowan's expression lit, and Shee smiled.

You must be Liam.

Shee noticed a young blonde waitress glowering at them from the other side of the room. She tilted to the left to see around Liam and get a better look at her.

What the heck is that about?

The waitress saw her looking and spun on her heel to disappear into the kitchen.

Shee looked at Rowan to see if she'd noticed, but she only had eyes for Liam, who only had eyes for the bartender. He ordered a Dark and Stormy and stood between them.

"This is my friend Shee," said Rowan.

Liam nodded. "Nice to meet you."

Shee smiled and motioned to his group of boat buddies setting up camp down the bar.

"You, too. Catch anything?" she asked.

He shrugged. "We didn't end up fishing. John over there is visiting from Texas for a seminar, so we took him out for a spin."

"My mother lives in Texas," blurted Rowan.

Liam turned to her. "Yeah? He's from Houston."

"She's in Lubbock." Rowan took a sip from her wine and looked away. She seemed to regret bringing it up.

The bartender brought over Liam's beer concoction, and he took it.

"Well, I'd better get back to the guys, but maybe you two could come join us?"

He eyed Shee hungrily as if he were looking forward to feeding her to one of his friends.

Oh, hell no.

"You go ahead. I have to go," she said to Rowan.

"Really? Are you sure? You're going to throw me to the lions all by myself?" asked Rowan, giggling. She didn't seem to mind.

"We'll buy you a drink?" offered Liam.

Shee shook her head and finished her last sip of wine.

You could buy me a house.

She wouldn't get anything useful out of Rowan if she were busy flirting with Liam and his friends. She'd end up making small talk with one of the drunken buddies—a circle of hell easily avoided by leaving.

"No, I do have to go. I'll catch up with you tomorrow?" she said to Rowan.

Rowan nodded. "Definitely."

The woman was already half off her stool, one arm locked in Liam's, preparing to move to the other end of the bar.

CHAPTER ELEVEN

Mason sat outside, overlooking the pool, *listening*. Things were quiet. Shee had gone to meet Rowan for lunch, Croix was keeping an eye on Rowan should she get away from Shee, and Ethan was inside the house, nerding out.

Mason finished half a ham sandwich before he heard voices next door. He didn't have to be a genius to hear the tension in them.

The neighbor was at it again.

Mason shook his head.

Some people can't take a hint.

He heard the patio sliders behind him open and turned to see Ethan poking his head outside.

"Hey, there you are," said the kid.

"Here I am," said Mason.

Ethan's head bobbed. "Do you know, does Shee have, like, a phone number or a license or something for this Joy Zabić person?"

Mason shook his head. "I don't know. I'm more in the *thumping heads* division. You'd have to ask her."

Ethan nodded. "I'll give her a call."

Mason expected him to pop back into the house, but he remained, hanging half in and half out.

"I've got a bunch of info on the Liam guy," he said after a beat. "He works out of the hospital down the road. Pretty respected dermatologist. One previous marriage. Divorced three years ago—"

Mason side-eyed him. "I'm a little busy here."

Ethan glanced at his remaining half sandwich before the voices next door swelled. He snapped his attention toward the neighbor's property.

"Is that the neighbors fighting?" he asked.

Mason nodded. "Yup."

"What's wrong?"

He shrugged. "They're pissed the Girl Scouts ran out of Thin Mints."

Ethan scowled. "Seriously?"

Mason threw him a withering glance.

"Oh. Ha. Got it. I'm leaving."

"Sounds good."

Ethan's head retracted, and the door slid shut.

Mason chuckled to himself. He liked Ethan. He seemed like a nice kid—but the boy was *new*, and it felt like something was going on between him and Croix. He sat firmly on *Team Croix*, so he needed to keep his distance until things settled.

He didn't want to get attached to Ethan in case he needed to toss him out of a window at some point.

Mason returned to eavesdropping. He only heard the man's voice, but it didn't sound like he was on the phone. He assumed he and the woman were at it again. Bickering this time, but *loud*. They were inside the house—*a cement brick house*—and Mason could *still* hear the fight. He couldn't make out the words, though.

The voices stopped. A minute later, Mason heard a door and then a *car* door slam.

He stood to peer over the gate and saw the man's car leave.

Mason growled.

I shouldn't get involved.

He repeated that same thought the whole way through the back gate and through the yard to the neighbor's front door.

He placed his ear against the door.

Silence.

He didn't like it. The woman wasn't big. A couple more knocks like that jerk gave her the day before, and she'd end up dead.

Mason stared at the door.

Maybe just a quick chat.

He knocked and was about to rap again when the door opened. The woman peered up at him, her head cocked at an odd angle. She was doing a terrible job of hiding the left side of her face from him.

He saw the black eye.

He's a righty. Good to know.

He felt his blood boil.

"Yes?" she asked.

He considered using a ruse to explain why he'd stopped by—ask to borrow a cup of sugar or something—but decided not to bother.

"Are you okay?" he asked.

Their gazes locked. The woman stood there for what felt like a minute before her eyes welled with tears, and some invisible string holding her upright seemed to snap.

"I'm sorry," she said, slumping. "This isn't your problem. I guess you can hear—"

"Don't be sorry," said Mason, making his voice as soft as possible. He bent forward to make himself seem smaller and less threatening.

"I'm here to help," he said.

Her lip quivered so violently that she raised a hand to stop it.

"Are you a police officer?" she asked, her voice shaky.

"No. I'm not, but—"

He didn't have to convince her he was harmless. Her knees buckled, and he stepped inside to catch her as she fell.

"*Oh,*" she said as he wrapped his arms around her.

"It's okay," he assured her. "I'm going to walk you to your sofa, okay, honey?"

"I don't know."

"I can't leave you in the doorway."

She steadied herself against him and nodded.

"Okay."

He led her to her tufted sofa and sat her on a worn cushion. She tucked herself into the corner against the arm to stay upright and stared at him wide-eyed.

"Do you want some water?" he asked.

Like a dam breaking, water poured from her eyes. She dropped her face into her hands.

"I'm *sorry*," she said. "I don't even know who you are—"

"I'm your neighbor. Next door," he said, nodding in that direction. "Name's Mason."

"The rental? You and your wife?"

He nodded.

Close enough.

Obviously, she'd seen Shee.

He took a deep breath. "Ma'am, I'm sorry—"

"Janet," she corrected him.

"Janet, nice to meet you. I have to ask—what's going on here? Who is that man?"

Her crying slowed as she waved him away. "I'm sorry. I'm just having a bad day."

He spotted a box of tissue and brought it to her.

"You're *not* having a bad day. I see what he's done to your face."

She touched the bruise beneath her eye with her fingertips.

"Is he your son?" he asked. "Is that why you're protecting him?"

She shook her head. "He's my husband's boy from a previous marriage."

"Where's your husband?"

She closed her eyes as if the last of her strength had packed up and left.

"He died. Nolan came to help me take care of him in the end. He never left." She scoffed. "Not that he was any help. I just had two people to take care of instead of one."

"Nolan. That's the man who hits you?"

She nodded.

"This is your house?"

She shook her head. "I rent. I've rented for years."

"And you'd like him out?"

She closed her eyes. "*I* want to leave. I want to go live with my friend in New Mexico."

"He's stopping you?"

She nodded. "He needs me here to pay the rent. Doesn't want to lose his free ride."

"But you don't want to pay for his life, right? I want to make sure I understand. If I help you and you protect him—"

She looked up at him. "Protect him? Why would I protect him?" Her expression pinched, and he saw the anger roiling beneath her sadness for the first time.

"I *hate* him," she whispered.

"Why don't you go, dear?"

She sighed. "I need to pack. He never leaves me alone long enough. He knows I want to run. He says he'll kill my cat."

Mason sniffed.

Cat. That explained why *his* eyes felt puffy.

"You could call the police. Have him arrested?"

She shook her head. "He'd get out. He'd get bail. Restraining orders don't work—I've seen that on TV."

Mason nodded. She wasn't wrong.

"What if a time for you to pack and leave could be arranged? Say, two weeks? Would that be long enough?"

She laughed bitterly. "He'd never leave me alone that long."

"But what if he did?"

She wiped her eyes. "You're asking if I could move out in two weeks?"

"Right. Would that be long enough to get to your friend's?"

She nodded, and he could see her mind working as she considered the possibilities.

"Does he know your friend? Would he know where to find you?" he asked.

She shook her head and lifted her chin. "No. He doesn't know anything about her. I've been careful about that."

Her gaze wandered around the room as if she were packing up the place with her mind. She refocused on Mason, and her shoulders slumped.

"He won't ever leave me that long."

Mason sucked his tooth with his tongue.

"I'm sure it will work out. Can I do anything else for you while I'm here?"

She sighed. "No. Listen to me complaining to you. I'm so sorry. I'm not your problem."

"It's okay. If you need anything, you come on over, okay?"

She nodded and blew her nose. "You're sweet. I'm fine. You don't worry about me. You enjoy your vacation."

She moved to stand, and Mason stopped her.

"You stay there. I'll let myself out."

He smiled and left, her large, haunted eyes following him as he moved.

"Your leg," she said, noticing his metal limb for the first time.

He smiled. "I left it somewhere. I'll find it."

She hooted and covered her mouth with her hand.

"You're *terrible*," she said.

Mason left. As soon as the door closed behind him, his smile dropped.

He strode back to the house.

"*Ethan*," he called, shutting the door behind him.

Ethan's head popped up on the sofa where he'd slouched over his laptop.

"Hm?"

"I need some research."

The boy's brow knitted. "I'm working on it."

"Not that. Something new."

"What?"

Mason squinted.

"What injuries would keep someone in the hospital for a

week or two?"

CHAPTER TWELVE

Thirty-Six Years Earlier – South Carolina

Mason biked to Miss Elly's every day after school for the next week.

On the sixth day, he knocked, and the door opened a crack. One large brown eye peered out at him. Once she saw who it was, he saw her shoulders release, and she opened the door wider to reveal a knife in her hand.

His eyes saucered, and she laughed before stabbing it back into a block sitting on the counter of her tiny kitchen.

"Now you can see why they all think I'm crazy," she told him. "More than one person around here with a couple holes in them from messin' with me."

Mason entered and put his backpack on a chair.

"I'm glad you're here. I have a proposal for you," said Miss Elly.

"A proposal?" Mason flopped into her cratered sofa cushions. He'd never gotten a *proposal* before.

Miss Elly sat in her favorite chair and folded her large hands in her lap.

"You know how you hate livin' at your auntie's? How you

always be complainin'?"

He nodded. He did complain a lot. Miss Elly was a good listener.

"Well, how 'bout I make you a deal? How 'bout you live here?"

Mason's eyebrows shot toward the ceiling. "Here? With you?"

His gaze floated toward the spare room.

Miss Elly nodded. "Sure. I need the help. You need a place. Things aren't going too good with your house, right?"

Mason huffed.

No.

Livvy and her stupid boyfriend had moved into *his* house. He'd had no way to stop them or get them out.

"I can teach you how to get tough, too," Miss Elly added, as if getting out of his aunt's house wasn't encouragement enough.

He giggled, and Miss Ellie smirked back at him.

"Oh, you think that's funny? My son was a professional boxer. Who you think taught him everything he knows?"

"You?"

"Damn straight, *me.*"

Mason couldn't find a downside to Miss Elly's proposal, but before he could agree, she started chewing on her cheek like she did when she was thinking.

"Unless they won't let you move out. You bein' too young," she muttered.

Mason scoffed. "My aunt won't even know I'm gone, and my cousins'll have a party."

"So what do you think?"

He stood. "I *accept* your proposal."

"Okay then. Shake on it." She thrust out one of her enormous paws, and Mason stood to shake it and make it official. He stared at the way her long fingers curled around his.

Those hands.

Maybe she *had* taught her son to box.

Six Years Later

By the time Mason turned eighteen, a lot had changed. His body had grown strong and square-shouldered. He was already as big as his father. Maybe bigger.

It had been a *long* time since his cousin last messed with him.

He and Miss Elly made good roommates. She liked to cook, and he liked to eat. He ran errands, and she spilled wisdom.

Miss Elly liked a chocolate donut on Saturday mornings. She liked them on Sundays, too, but Mason took her to church first on Sundays. The Sunday donut had sprinkles because Miss Elly said *He Himself* demanded sprinkles on Sundays.

He let himself into the house and put the donut box on the counter.

"Elly? I have your donut," he called at her bedroom door. "I'm gonna eat it if you don't get up."

The coffee machine coughed its death rattle, a job well done, so she'd been up.

He knocked on her door.

"Miss Elly?"

He opened the door a crack but kept his head turned away. More than once, he'd accidentally caught a glimpse of her bony, naked frame, and moments like those kept them from making eye contact the rest of the day.

"Elly?"

He gave in and peeked inside.

The morning sun filtered through the sheer curtain stretched across Elly's only bedroom window, illuminating her face where she lay in her bed as if she were an angel. Her bony joints, shoulders, elbows, and hips poked at the thin blanket pulled almost to her neck.

Mason felt his heart sink. He didn't need a second peek.

Even from a distance, he could tell she was dead.

Elly had always been a light sleeper. No way he could have come into the room calling her name without her scolding him for sneaking up on her.

Instead, she lay there.

Still.

Mason's knees buckled with a weight he didn't want to carry. He'd known her day was coming, but he hadn't seen it being *today*. He didn't know how old Elly was. She'd refused to tell him, but he'd found enough paperwork around the house over the years to know she had to be into her eighties.

He entered the room and rested the back of his fingers against her cheek.

Cold.

Picking up the phone receiver by her nightstand, he fell short of dialing nine-one-one.

He dropped it back into its cradle.

He needed to think first. He needed things. He needed *money*. Miss Elly needed a burial. He was her only family.

Mason squeezed Elly's hand and walked to his room. He reached high to a hidden ledge in his closet until his fingers brushed his bag of diamonds. The plastic bag his mother had left them in had long ago been replaced by a soft, purple Crown Royal whisky bag with gold tassels. He'd found the bag when he was fourteen, and immediately, it was the bag for his diamonds.

He couldn't sell the diamonds in Charleston. It had been a long time since his father robbed the jewelry store—which had since gone out of business—but he didn't know if diamonds had markings like dollar bills had serial numbers. People might ask questions if a seventeen-year-old son of a thief showed up with a bag of rough diamonds.

With a final glance at Miss Elly, Mason left the house to drive to Savannah in her old Chevy. He sold one diamond at the first jewelry store that didn't look too rich or too shady. At a second spot, the man studying the diamond Mason offered sucked in his breath and offered him more money than he'd gotten for the first, even though the rock was the same size.

Either the first man had ripped him off, or there was something special about this second rock.

Mason asked for the return of his diamond.

"Sorry, I didn't mean to offer that one," he said.

The man nodded. "So you know?"

Mason nodded, though only to keep from looking stupid.

"You know why that one is special?" probed the man.

"More or less," said Mason.

Still, the man wouldn't let it go.

"It's the clarity," he continued. "It would make a nearly perfect three-carat."

Mason nodded. "Yeah, I didn't mean to sell that one."

The man smiled. "If you're going to keep one for someone special, *that's* the one."

Mason eyed the man and then poured the rest of his treasure from the Crown Royal bag. He didn't want to keep testing jewelry stores. He might never meet a man as honest as this one again.

Time to cash in.

"Would you be interested in these?" he asked.

The man gawped at the collection.

"Where'd you say you got these?" he asked.

"My father brought them back."

The man didn't ask from where. He lifted his loupe again and inspected a few before looking at Mason.

"I hadn't planned on making a purchase like this today. Can you give me an hour to gather the money? I'll need to go to the bank for cash. Unless you'd take a check?"

Mason shook his head, and the man laughed. "I didn't think so. Smart boy."

In the end, Mason headed home with nineteen thousand dollars and one very special rock.

His mouth went dry as he drove home.

He needed to decide what to do with the rest of his life.

He'd been considering joining the Marines. He'd brought home a pamphlet, and Miss Elly thought the men on it looked sharp. She told him they could help him with college and he could become an officer like the men in those fine uniforms.

But first, he'd go home and take care of Miss Elly. He'd find her a nice final resting place.

Nothing bad happened to Miss Elly—not even now.

Not on his watch.

CHAPTER THIRTEEN

Rowan dropped to the bed beside Liam, breathing heavily but not *unattractively.*

It was an art.

"Holy hell," said Liam.

He grinned. He wasn't sweaty like she was. She'd done the bulk of the work.

But it was worth it.

Liam was a *dream.*

Rowan was in heaven.

Not the way Joy was, of course.

"Hm?" she asked Liam, anxious to have him repeat his exclamation of awe.

"That was *amazing,*" he said.

She agreed. "It was."

It had been her pleasure. Well, not *literally.* She'd faked the bit at the end when it was clear Liam wouldn't be able to hold on any longer, but that didn't matter. It was a *delight* to touch taut flesh. Taut-*ish.* It'd been a while since she last spent time with someone in their fifties. And *handsome.* With his broad shoulders and square jaw, Liam looked like an aging professional baseball player. His hair was still thick and the color of sand—the speckles of gray only provided depth and texture. She'd asked him how tall he was, and when he told her he was six-two, she felt a flush of pride, as if his height was her victory.

He *was* her victory. Her prize. She deserved him.

The night before, they'd spent some time at the bar with her new friend, Shee, and then Shee had to leave, and Liam stayed. In the end, she went home with him. She probably should have waited, but she couldn't do it.

She just *couldn't.*

She turned her head to face him as his eyes closed. His breathing slowed.

She checked her watch. It was still early.

She slipped from the bed, plucked her clothes from the floor, and tiptoed to the bathroom. By the time she dressed, his heavy breathing had shifted to a soft snore.

She paused in front of the closets.

Hm.

She slid open the one to her right to find it shallow and filled with Liam's clothes—collared shirts, polos, slacks. She closed the door and opened the closet on the opposite side of the hall. The larger walk-in closet contained Liam's suits and a smattering of women's clothes.

Joy had carved a spot for her things at Liam's.

Rowan stepped inside and ran her hand over a dangling blouse sleeve she recognized—one Joy had worn to one of their lunches. She'd admired it.

We were about the same size, weren't we?

She opened a drawer built into the well-organized custom closet and found jewelry. A pair of diamond stud earrings.

Wow.

She'd never seen Joy wear the things she saw in that drawer.

What a waste.

Was she wearing jewelry when she drowned? If she was, now it was probably in some fish's stomach. Didn't fish like shiny things? She remembered some old bastard boring her to death with fishing tips.

She closed the drawer and pulled a small teal-green purse from a shelf. *Bulgari*. Slipping it back into place, she let her gaze drift from one pair of shoes to another. Joy hadn't kept many clothes at Liam's, but what she had was beautiful and expensive.

Rowan fought the urge to *shop*. What would Liam do with it all? Maybe she'd offer to clean it all away for him. It would only make him sad seeing these things in his closet, wouldn't it? Or, maybe not. She could probably even wear these garments around him—men didn't remember clothes.

She turned to leave and then turned back.

One thing.

She'd take *one thing.*

Tiny.

She opened the jewelry drawer.

Men remembered jewelry even less than clothes.

She plucked a pair of gold earrings from the back of Joy's collection. They looked forgotten, there at the back. Daisies with diamond centers. She slipped them into her pocket and shut the drawer.

Rowan returned to the bedroom to find Liam staring at her.

She forced a smile.

"I'm sorry. Did I wake you? You were asleep a second ago."

He sat up, his smooth pecs falling into place on either side of the sexy divot in the center of his chest—a valley flanked by rolling hills of muscle. She wasn't sure how he kept his physique. He hadn't mentioned belonging to a gym, but clearly, he did. He didn't sculpt a body like that with skin peels and golf.

"Would you like to go to an event with me tonight?" he asked.

"An event?"

"My boss is having some people over. Just twenty or so of his best earners."

She took a beat to hide her excitement.

"I—sure. What time? What should I wear?"

"Nothing fancy. Just normal stuff. We'd have to leave here a little after five."

She nodded.

Totally unhelpful. Case in point—men didn't know anything about clothes.

"I'd have to run home—" she said.

"Sure. I'm sorry. I should have given you more of a heads-up. I just remembered it was tonight. I understand if you don't want to—"

"No, it's fine. I'd love to meet your co-workers. Did you want to pick me up? Or I could come back here?"

He grinned and walked to her to slip his hands around her waist. "You could spend the night again..."

She kissed him. "Sounds like a plan."

"Mm. See you at five."

"See you."

She stepped out the door and pulled out her phone.

She called Liam, waited until he answered, and then walked back into the house to find him hovering near the bedroom door with the phone to his ear.

"Did you just call me?" he asked.

"Sorry. Butt dial," she said. "I just realized I'm missing an earring. I'm just going to check the bed. Go get your shower, sexy. Don't let me hold you up."

He nodded and put his phone down on the corner table before disappearing into the bedroom.

Rowan ran across the room and grabbed his phone.

Still unlocked.

Yes!

She took the phone into the bedroom, touching the screen, keeping it alive.

She heard the water turn on. The shower door's rubber scraped across Liam's tile floors. The uneven sound of someone standing beneath the stream interrupted the steady hiss of an empty shower.

Safe.

She gave his phone her full attention.

She scrolled through his recent calls and texts, looking for other women, gritting her teeth as she tried to recall *exactly* what day Joy had mentioned Liam's cheating. If he was in contact with that woman, it would show up on his phone around then—maybe that day.

She found it.

A person listed only as K.

Be there at ten, wrote Liam.

Can't wait, answered the tramp.

Rowan rolled her eyes. Did the little hooker think Joy couldn't see that exchange for what it was? That she'd think it was Liam's accountant sitting around wearing only *bells*?

Idiot.

Their last exchange had been a week ago.

See you soon, wrote K.

He hadn't answered.

That has to be a good sign, right?

She plugged K's phone number into her own to look into her later. Maybe she could reverse-lookup her number online to better understand what she was up against.

The shower was still running. She took one last longing look at Joy's closet.

No.

Best not to push it. She'd see if she could relieve Liam of her stuff later.

She put his phone back where he'd left it and walked out to her car. Driving away from Liam's house, she ran over the evening. K didn't matter.

One night together, and he's already asking me to public events.

That was much more than just a good sign. He'd probably been keeping K around as a spare until he found himself a new, *real* girlfriend.

She got the invite, not K. He wasn't worried about people seeing a new woman on his arm.

She frowned.

Or, K wasn't someone from work. He didn't have to worry about bumping into her there.

Shit.

There was that.

Hm.

She shrugged. The one he showed off was the important one. K was probably history. Some trash he'd never take to a work event.

No, she wouldn't let some phantom woman bring her down. She couldn't believe her luck. She'd worried their relationship wouldn't move to the *public* phase for longer than usual—thanks to Joy's untimely demise, appearances, etcetera—but Liam was full of surprises.

She stopped at a light and glanced at herself in the rearview mirror. Knowing how long lights stayed red in Florida, she removed her earrings and dropped them into her cup holder before retrieving the pair she'd liberated from Joy's drawer. She poked the daisy diamonds through her lobes and admired them in the mirror.

So cute.

She'd have to remember to remove them tonight. She'd bet a lot of money Liam wouldn't recognize them as Joy's, but it wasn't worth taking the risk. Not when things were going so well.

"You really blew it, Joy," she said as she hit the gas.

A little before five, Rowan returned to Liam's. He answered the door smelling of expensive aftershave that made her dizzy. The tension in her shoulders relaxed when she saw him dressed in linen pants and a polo shirt. Nothing too fancy. Her outfit fell on the same *fancy* level, and her blue, blousy top complimented the teal of his shirt.

"We match like we planned it," she said, rising to her toes to kiss him. "What a cute pair we are."

"Great minds," he said, stepping forward. "We can head right to the car."

Her brow knitted. "Am I late?"

"No. I just want to get going. I don't care if we're a little early."

He passed her, and she followed him to the driveway, waiting as he pulled his Land Rover from the garage. She recognized it as the car she'd seen Joy driving once. She'd coveted it then.

Now, it's mine.

For all intents and purposes, anyway.

Once the car appeared from the garage, Liam remained in the driver's seat, so she let herself in the other side.

She smiled at him.

He smiled back.

They drove the twenty minutes to the event, chit-chatting about nonsense. His boss's house was amazing. Everything was perfect until he introduced her to one of his colleagues.

"You must be Joy," said the man.

Her smile faltered, and she glanced at Liam.

"No, Joy is no longer with us," said Liam stiffly.

"No longer—?" The man's wife sucked in a breath. "*Liam.* I remember hearing it now. Oh, I am *so* sorry."

Liam smiled. "No problem. This is Rowan."

The couple nodded to her, and she nodded back.

The two men started talking, and Rowan caught eyes watching her.

Whispering.

She'd expected it. Nothing to be done.

The night went relatively smoothly, considering. When Liam asked, *Did you have fun?* as they pulled into his neighborhood, she could honestly say *yes*.

"Everyone was nice," she said.

"They get worse," he said, chuckling.

Rowan laughed and then froze, something twisting in the pit of her stomach like a ball of snakes.

She saw the words first.

When Liam's headlight beams hit the driveway, he was looking at *her*, still in mid-thought.

"What?" he asked, seeing her expression change.

His attention snapped forward, and he hit the brakes, stopping the car halfway into the driveway.

Together, they read the red, ragged letters scrawled across the front of his white garage door.

I know you killed her.

CHAPTER FOURTEEN

Liam slammed the car into park and swore.

"Who would do something like this?" he raged, snatching his phone from the center console.

Rowan read the words on Liam's garage door again—painted in red with so many sloppy drips it looked like blood. She thought the effect had to be intentional.

I know you killed her.

Her could only mean one person.

Someone thinks Liam killed Joy?

Rowan looked at Liam.

Shee had said as much.

Her attention floated to the camera mounted at the corner of Liam's roof line.

"You have a camera," she said, pointing. It was a dumb thing to say—Liam knew he had a camera. The words came out of her mouth before she could stop them.

"That's what I'm looking for," he snapped.

He poked and swiped his phone for five minutes before roaring and slamming his hand against his thigh.

"*Nothing.* The cameras didn't catch them."

He got out of the car and slammed the door.

Rowan winced, her ears ringing, and then joined him.

"But you know there are two of them?" she asked.

He scowled. "*What*?"

"You said *them*."

He huffed. "Him, her, them, *whatever*. I don't know. I told you, the camera didn't pick them up."

Rowan turned back to the cameras. "How is that possible?"

He ran his hand over his head. "I don't know how—they must have hugged the house, kept where the cameras couldn't see them. It's *physics*, jeezus, don't worry about it."

Rowan squinted at him.

Angles would be geometry, wouldn't it?

She turned away to keep from saying it aloud.

With her back to him, she noticed the writing wasn't centered. The right side of the door bore the burden. That put the message directly below the camera where someone could have moved without being seen if they'd come in from the side.

Yep. *Geometry.*

He must have heard the demeaning tone of his voice and touched her arm to get her attention.

"I'm sorry. This isn't your fault. I shouldn't take it out on you," he said.

She turned back to him and nodded. "It's okay. This is *terrible*. You should call the police."

He let his head hang back. "I don't know. They can be such a circus..."

He glanced up the street. She guessed he was imagining the flashing lights of a police cruiser, calling the attention of his neighbors...

"It's geometry," she mumbled, motioning to the cameras.

He looked at her. "What?"

"Not physics. The angle of the cameras. *Geometry.*"

She swallowed. She knew better.

Why can't I ever keep my mouth shut?

He looked at her.

"You should go."

"*Go*?" Her eyes widened.

Dammit. I knew I shouldn't have corrected him. Damn doctors are never wrong—

"Go home. There's no point in you hanging around here while I deal with this."

She bobbed one shoulder. "It's no problem. I can keep you company—"

He shook his head. "No. It's going to be nothing but a pain in the neck."

Rowan stopped herself from arguing further. She knew he was right. She *should* go. When men got annoyed, it was best to disappear. Otherwise, *she* might become the focus of their agitation. Her mother taught her that's where most wives made the worst mistakes—trying to help when they should disappear. End up the focus of a man's anger often enough, and then *everything's* your fault—*forever*. That's when the husband finds another woman who isn't up his ass twenty-four-seven. He finds himself a new woman who giggles and lusts and accepts gifts...

A woman like her.

"Okay." She squeezed his arm. "If you need anything, let me know."

He took her hand and pulled her in for a kiss. "Thank you. I appreciate it. I'm so sorry, but I won't be any fun tonight."

Rowan nodded and, with a final wave, headed to her car, muttering.

As she pulled away from the curb, something caught her eye in the foliage across the street from Liam's—something too *round* to be a plant, about five feet off the ground.

A *head*?

Was someone in the bushes?

She hit her brakes and did a double-take. The round object, whatever it was, was gone. She glanced back at Liam's driveway, where he stood with his hands on his hips, staring at the bright red letters glowing under the yellow light of his house lights.

She drove on.

CHAPTER FIFTEEN

Croix pulled down a side street, made a U-turn, and returned to park diagonally from Liam's house. From here, she'd be able to keep an eye—

I know you killed her.

Croix gasped.

What the—

She read the words spray-painted on Liam's white garage door several times before she thought to shut her gaping jaw.

Whoa.

She found her phone and called Shee to tell her what had happened.

"On his garage door?" Shee echoed.

"Yep. I'm watching him rage around right now. Not happy."

"Did you see anything? Who did it?"

Croix clucked her tongue. "I don't know. I was following *them*—not watching his house."

"Right. Okay. Stay on it."

"Yup."

Croix hung up.

She tapped her phone against her steering wheel. Liam and Rowan had gotten out of the car. He was looking at his phone, tapping at it like he was trying to smoosh ants on the screen.

Croix chewed at her lip. She wanted to hear what they were *saying*.

She slipped out of her Jeep and jogged across the street to

where the overgrown landscaping stood tallest. Moving from tree to tree, she worked her way as close as she dared to get and peeked through the bushes at the couple.

"What?" she heard Liam snap. He was annoyed—for obvious reasons.

She couldn't hear the two when they began talking in a relatively normal tone.

Dammit.

Liam put down his phone and pulled Rowan to him.

Croix murmured a running commentary as the two kissed.

"Someone thinks I killed my last girlfriend—so much so they spray-painted it on my garage—but you're safe, don't worry, honey. I wouldn't kill you."

She looked away as they kissed because—*ew*—and suddenly Rowan was striding toward her car.

Shit.

Croix started to stand and then dropped back to a crouch. Rowan would see her if she ran for her Jeep now.

She stayed in the bushes as her target pulled away from the curb. A mosquito buzzed in her ear, and she slapped at the little monster just as Rowan passed.

Rowan's car slowed.

Shit, shit, shit.

Croix crouched lower.

There was a tense pause, but Rowan drove on.

Croix released the breath she'd been holding. She retraced her steps to her car. Liam had opened his garage and disappeared inside.

She had to give it to him—that was one way to hide the graffiti—open the door.

She wanted to stay, wanted to see how Liam dealt with his issue, but she needed to keep on Rowan.

She pulled from her spot and caught up to her quarry before the woman could leave the winding neighborhood.

Whew.

She tailed the old Mercedes. Rowan drove straight to her

apartment, and Croix set herself up across the street to settle in for what promised to be an incredibly boring night.

She had the windows open to avoid running the air conditioning. Unfortunately, the open window turned her SUV into an all-night buffet for every mosquito in the area. She slapped at her arm and cursed the existence of the bloodthirsty little—

"Hey," said a voice.

Croix jumped and had her hand on her center console—the current location of her gun—before she recognized Ethan's face at her passenger window.

Her shoulders relaxed.

"You scared the crap out of me," she grumbled.

He nodded. "Let me in."

She unlocked the door. Ethan hopped inside.

"What are you doing here?" she asked. "You can't sneak up on me like that— I almost shot you."

"I thought you'd like some company and some food," he said, holding up a brown bag.

She nodded. "Okay. All is forgiven."

His nose wrinkled. "It's kind of stuffy in here."

"No kidding. Surveillance in Florida *sucks*. Nothing but heat, humidity, and mosquitos."

He slapped his neck.

"See what I mean?" she said. "I'll hit the AC for now."

They closed the windows, and she started the car to get relief. The only thing worse than sitting and sweating was sitting, *eating,* and sweating.

He nodded. "I'll get you some screens."

"For the car?"

He nodded. "It's a thing. You can get them online, but I'll DIY yours. The hardware megastore is open all night."

"Really? Awesome. Thanks."

"I brought you another present."

She smirked. "You're like Santa Claus."

He pulled something from his pocket and held it up for her

to see. It was small, square, and black.

She scowled at it. "A thumb drive? I don't have a computer with me."

"Not a thumb drive. A *tracker*. I'll put it on her car, and you can download the app and *bam!* you'll never lose her."

She sniffed. "I was never going to lose her anyway."

"Right, but now you can go grab a sandwich and know she didn't go anywhere."

Croix side-eyed him. "Unless she walked. Or were you going to stick one on her butt?"

He giggled, and it started her laughing.

"I'm just trying to be helpful," he said.

He looked away, and she watched him for a moment. She could tell he was still smiling.

"You like it with us, don't you?" she said.

He turned and held her gaze before rattling his head like his skull was a cocktail shaker.

"Yes, I like it. It's fun. You guys are great."

He kept looking at her, so she motioned to the tracker to get him to stop. It made her nervous. Or *something*. She wasn't sure.

"Where did you get that? Did you DIY it?"

He scoffed. "*No*. I brought it with us, just in case. I always keep some in my backpack."

She shook her head. "You're so weird."

"If by *weird*, you mean resourceful, dashing, and brilliant, then *yes*."

He grinned at her.

She rolled her eyes.

"I thought maybe I could be, like, your Q," he added.

"My Q?"

"Not *your* Q, the *Loggerhead's* Q. You know, my role in the crew."

She scowled. "What the hell is a Q?"

"Like Q from James Bond." He gaped at her. "You never saw a James Bond movie?"

She shook her head. "I mostly only watched movies with

Mick. He thought James Bond was full of himself."

Ethan shrugged. "Fair enough. Anyway, Q is Bond's inventions guy. He'd make him crazy cool stuff for his missions like pens that shot poisoned darts and watches with poison gas—that sort of thing."

Croix snorted a laugh. "James Bond sure likes *poison*—that's what I'm getting from this. What are you going to invent? iPhones that shoot poison?"

He shrugged. "I don't know. I'm working on it. Maybe a machine gun leg for Mason like Cherry had in *Planet Terror*."

She frowned. "I assume that's another Bond movie?"

He shook his head.

"Not Bond, but if you don't know Bond, you definitely didn't watch *Grindhouse*."

She shook her head as an awkward silence fell between them.

"So, what's going on back at the home office?" she asked when she couldn't take it anymore.

"Not much. Shee's sifting through the info I pulled today. Mason's got something going on with the neighbor."

Croix looked at him. "Something going on? What do you mean?"

"He asked me how to put someone in the hospital for a couple of weeks."

Croix straightened. "You didn't find that odd?"

"I found it mad odd, but who am I to question what he's up to?"

"How could you not? I mean, whatever it is, it isn't going to end well."

Ethan shook his head. "Not for whoever he's thinking of using the information on, *no*."

Croix found her curiosity piqued.

"What was the answer?" she asked. "What can keep a person in the hospital for weeks?"

Ethan ticked the options off on his fingers.

"Hip fractures, femur breaks, traumatic head injuries, and

spines."

"Yikes. I'm glad I'm not the neighbor." Croix winced. "And you have *no* idea why he wanted this info?"

"No idea."

She grunted. "I guess he can't just kill him."

"Nope. Not now that he's a civilian back here in America."

He handed her a sandwich and unwrapped his own food.

"Where *is* it okay to break someone's spine?" she asked.

Ethan took a bite of his sandwich.

"Good point."

CHAPTER SIXTEEN

Shee woke up to find herself alone in bed. She padded into the main living area to find Mason on the sofa. He turned to watch her enter the room.

"What are you doing out here?" she asked.

He shrugged. "Had a bad dream and thought it might be safer out here."

"You mean for *me*?"

He nodded and sat up. She sat beside him.

"Now, you're not going to sleep with me anymore?" she asked.

"I wouldn't phrase it like that," he said, chuckling.

Croix entered from the other side of the house.

"What are you doing here?" asked Shee.

"Ethan's watching Rowan so I could get some quality sleep."

Shee nodded and patted Mason on the leg.

"I'm going to get a shower."

"I'll get the coffee going," he said.

Shee got showered and dressed and had just sat down to have her coffee when her phone rang. It was Rowan.

Shee checked the time and scowled at the phone.

Early for Rowan to be calling.

"I think you're right about that other woman," said Rowan when she answered.

"Good morning to you, too," said Shee. "I'm right about what now?"

Rowan launched into a long, detailed story about how Liam had asked her to an office event, how dreamy that was, and how it meant he was falling for her. Shee nearly fell face-first into her coffee before Rowan reached the interesting part.

"Spray-painted on his garage?" she echoed when Rowan finally told her about the troubling end to their fairytale evening.

She glanced at Croix, who rolled her eyes with her tongue hanging out, mocking her acting job as she pretended she didn't know about the spray paint incident.

She stuck her tongue out at her and looked away so she wouldn't laugh.

"In red paint. Very scary. That's why I think you're right. There has to be some other woman doing this, and she might have killed *Joy*," said Rowan, continuing, oblivious to all the faces being made.

Shee couldn't believe Rowan was more worried about some mystery woman harassing Liam than the idea *her new boyfriend* might have killed his last girlfriend.

Of course, if *Rowan* killed Joy, she *knew* Liam didn't do it, didn't she?

"It has to be this K person," continued Rowan.

Shee sat up. "Kay? You know her name?"

"No. That's how she shows up in his phone. Just the letter K."

"How do you know it's her?"

Rowan sighed. "I tricked him into opening his phone before he got in the shower and found a text chain between them. *Flirty*. It *has* to be her. I got the phone number. I'm going to look into it today."

"Give it to me," spat Shee before thinking of a less aggressive way to word her request.

"What?"

"I'm, uh, I'm *really* good at Internet stuff," she said. "Give me her number, and I'll find her for you. No problem."

"Really?"

"Sure."

There was a pause while Rowan found the number. Shee jotted it down on the back of a tourist magazine.

Shee heard a thumping on the line.

"Someone's knocking on my door," said Rowan.

"Okay, I'll let you go and call you back when I have the info," said Shee.

Rowan laughed. "Thanks. This is exciting. I feel like a spy."

She hung up, and Shee shook her head as Mason went into the kitchen.

"I'm starving," he said.

She followed him, her mind still processing.

"What the heck is going on with these people?" asked Shee, watching him root through the refrigerator.

"Which people?" he asked, unwrapping the pound of ham he'd picked up to keep them from starving.

"This—I don't know—incestuous group of psycho lovers. I couldn't decide if Rowan killed Joy, and now I'm wondering if Liam or maybe Liam's mistress did."

Mason looked at her without comment.

"Why are you staring at me?" she asked.

"Because I'm going to say something that is operationally solid but not *nice*."

"What's that?"

"*Who cares?*"

She squinted at him. "Who *cares*?"

"Yes—who cares who killed Joy? Or if someone killed her at all?"

Shee gaped. "The woman is *dead*."

"Yes, and that's a shame, but we're here to catch *Portia*. You're letting yourself be distracted by an accidental drowning or, at worst, a domestic."

Shee frowned. "Okay. That *is* cold, but not wrong. But how can her death *not* be related?"

"By being an accident."

"But what if it isn't? And what if Rowan isn't Portia? What if Liam's lover is?" She sucked in a breath and pointed at him. "Or Liam? Maybe *Liam* is Portia. It might be like that doctor joke."

Mason peeled off a piece of ham and dropped it into his mouth. "You lost me. What doctor joke?"

"You know—a father and son are in an accident, they're both admitted to the hospital, and when the boy goes for an operation, the surgeon says *this is my son!*"

Mason blinked at her. "What the hell are you talking about?"

"The father was *in the accident*, so how can he be the surgeon?"

Mason squinted at her. "This is a trick question, isn't it?"

Shee laughed. "The surgeon's his *mother*. People assume the surgeon has to be a *man*. It shows preconceived notions about men and women."

Mason hooked his mouth to the right. "And that has *what* to do with our case?"

"We haven't considered *Liam* could be Portia."

"Because we assume black widows are female?"

"*Right*. And the spiders that kill their mates *are* all female, but that's not the important part."

"Is the important part that Liam's been moving from town to town seducing men masquerading as a woman with dark hair?"

Shee frowned. "Hm. I suppose that isn't likely."

"*No*."

"But Snookie said the Bureau has been doing a crappy job with this, so we have to keep an open mind."

"Always."

She held up a finger as her gaze drifted. "Wait..."

"Oh no, she had a thought," muttered Mason. "Everyone hold still."

Shee ignored him. "Rowan might have killed Joy. That

seems most likely... Or, what if Rowan *pushed Liam* to kill Joy?"

He squinted one eye. "I don't love that idea. From what you tell me, they've only known each other a few days, but I guess it's *possible*. I don't expect she's been one hundred percent honest with you, and if the Bureau isn't paying attention—"

"But who *knows* it?" said Shee.

"You lost me again."

"Who's leaving threatening notes? Who *knows* Liam killed his girlfriend?"

"Rowan?"

"Ooh..." Shee tapped her tooth with her finger, thinking about the possibilities. "You think Rowan killed Joy and then spray-painted his garage—to make him paranoid? Scared? Why would she do that?"

Mason nodded. "Maybe to get the neighbors talking? To make Liam look like the bad guy so no one looks into her and why all his money disappeared—assuming it will at some point?"

Shee gasped. "It would look like he and his money disappeared because he's running away from Joy's murder—when in reality, *Rowan* took his money and killed him."

Mason nodded. "That's not bad. Ties up nicely."

Shee grinned. "It's not bad at all, huh? Sounds like something Portia would dream up."

"One problem."

"What?" Shee held up a hand. "Wait. Let me guess. We need to prove all this before she kills Liam?"

"No, well, *yes*, obviously, but I was thinking something else. Didn't you say Rowan was at a party with him when the paint went up?"

Shee's shoulders slumped. "So she couldn't have painted the garage."

"Nope. Not unless she sneaked out without Croix seeing her, drove back, did the deed, and drove back."

Shee let her head fall back. "Ugh. Seems unlikely, huh? I have to find out more about Liam's affair."

"Maybe. Either way, I think we need to keep eyes on both of them now—Rowan and Liam. Lucky for us, we have two kids here at our beck and call."

"Okay. Good work. I feel like we've made progress. I need to look up this woman, K." She laughed. "You know Rowan tricked Liam into leaving his phone unlocked and found the affair's phone number?"

"She's a pro."

"No kidding. She gave it to me—said he had it under just the letter K. Hopefully, that will be enough for me to find out who she is."

"Sounds good."

Mason's gaze drifted out the kitchen window, piquing her curiosity.

"Whatcha thinking about?" she asked.

He shrugged. "The lady who raised me after I left my aunt's."

"Miss Elly? You haven't mentioned her in forever. What has her on your mind?"

He shrugged. "Old ladies."

She glowered at him. "You better not mean *me*."

He smirked and stepped forward to wrap his hands around her waist.

"Not you."

She breathed in the scent of him.

"Say something sexy to me," she whispered so Ethan wouldn't hear.

He leaned down and brushed her ear with his lips.

"Brad Pitt."

She exploded with laughter and pushed away from him, but he held her hips against his.

"Not your thing? Sorry. Let me try again," he said, leaning in. "*Porterhouse steak.*"

She giggled and thunked her head against his pec.

"You're so *stupid*."

He kissed the top of her head and released her with a shrug.

"I guess we find different things sexy."

"Uh-huh. I'm going to go back to work. You can snuggle up with your honey ham."

He glanced around the house. "Hey, quick question—how long do you think we could keep someone captive here if we had to?"

She paused.

"What?"

CHAPTER SEVENTEEN

Someone knocked on Rowan's apartment door while she was on the phone with Shee about K. Before that, she'd been awake and staring at the ceiling, thinking about Liam's garage door and working out all the possibilities until she had to vent to someone and Shee was the one person who knew most of all her recent dramas.

Shee was the new Joy.

She didn't know what to think about the knock. It was only seven-thirty. Too early for people to be knocking on her door.

She hung up with Shee, slid out of bed, slipped into her silk robe—a gift from George Patterson, 71, four years previous—and padded to her door to peer through the peephole.

Liam stood outside.

What the hell?

She raised a hand to her cheek. She was barely awake and hadn't put on her makeup. It was too early in the relationship for him to see her *in the raw*.

"Just a second," she called through the door before bolting to her bathroom. She ran through her morning routine in double time, skipping over face washing and cream applications.

After a final inspection in the mirror, she ran back to the front door, took a deep breath, and opened it, smiling.

"What are you doing here?" she asked. It took all her energy to hide her irritation. He was cute, but not *arriving at seven-thirty in the morning unannounced* cute.

Liam grinned, holding up a white bag. "Breakfast."

She opened the door wider to let him in and let her robe fall open to expose the matching silk slip she'd slept in—also from George. Hopefully, her exposed skin would keep him from focusing on her half-assed makeup job.

"I felt bad you had to deal with that last night," he said, setting a cardboard tray holding two coffees onto her countertop.

His gaze swept over her apartment. She could tell it underwhelmed him. She'd put *some* effort into decorating but couldn't do much about the low ceilings and lack of space—and she wasn't home that often.

"*You* were the one who had to deal with that nightmare," she said.

He shrugged. "I know, but still. You did me a favor going to that boring party, and your evening was ruined." He handed her one of the coffees and frowned. "I didn't know how you take it—"

She moved toward the refrigerator. "I have creamer. What did the police say?"

He shrugged. "Nothing. I didn't call them."

"You didn't?"

He wandered to the sliders to stare at her ocean view. "Nah. More trouble than it's worth."

Rowan had never considered he might not involve the police.

Is that a bad sign?

"I think it was the asshole down the street," he added.

She perked. "Oh? One of your neighbors? Why do you think that?"

He shrugged. "I called him out for putting his dog's poop bags in my trash, and he didn't take it well. He probably heard about Joy and thought he'd be a funny guy."

"I don't see what's *funny* about that," Rowan mumbled.

"What are you going to do?"

He pulled out his phone and held it up to show her a picture she recognized as his house. The words were gone.

"I painted over it last night. I had spare paint," he said.

"No, I mean, what if he comes back?"

"If he does it again, I'll catch him. I ordered another camera I can use to cover the blind spot out front."

She nodded.

That's when it hit her. Her head cocked.

"How did you know where I live?"

He chuckled. "Anyone with Internet can find anyone." He motioned to the room. "Want to give me the tour?"

She turned her palms to the ceiling. "It'll be a short tour—"

She took a step and then stopped, remembering what she'd seen on her bureau while rushing to answer the front door.

Joy's earrings.

Shit, shit, shittity shit.

She'd left them in plain sight. She never *dreamed* Liam would make an unscheduled stop.

"It's not worth a tour," she assured him.

He shrugged. "Anyway, I just wanted to let you know I appreciate you for putting up with everything last night."

She nodded.

He glanced to his left.

She followed his attention to her bedroom.

Oh.

That's why he came.

She put down her coffee.

"Um, could you give me two seconds?" she asked.

Before he could answer, she strode into her bedroom and shut the door behind her. She threw Joy's earrings into her jewelry box, straightened the bedsheets, snatched all the dirty clothes from the ground, and wiped down the bathroom sink.

After checking herself in the mirror, she opened her bedroom door and batted her lashes at him.

"Still want that tour?" she purred.

Liam set down his coffee.

"I *do*."

He entered the bedroom. She'd worried for nothing—he didn't even look around. Like a man on a mission, he moved her to the bed, put in his time—a valiant effort—and threw his legs back over the side of the bed.

"I've got to get to work," he said.

Rowan sat up. "It's Saturday."

She spotted the flash of a smile as he pulled his polo back over his head. "No rest for the wicked."

She stood, wrapped her robe around her, and walked back into the main living area as he finished dressing. He joined her a second later, gave her a peck on the cheek, and reached for the door.

"I'll give you a call later," he said.

She smiled and nodded. "Talk to you then."

He left.

Rowan remained staring at the door.

Hm.

That hadn't felt right.

This early into a relationship, she could usually feel the power dynamic *fully* in her favor.

Not this time.

He already had an aloof, entitled air about him. She couldn't shake the feeling she could drop off the planet, and he wouldn't notice.

Sort of like Joy did, come to think of it.

Not good for this early in the relationship.

Not good at *all*.

She'd have to find another way to get him focused on *her*. For all she knew, he *was* dating K—maybe even *other* women.

She liked the idea of a handsome, wealthy mate close to her age, but the young ones were a lot more difficult to control.

She needed something to bring them *close*. To *bond* them. Something that made her stand out. It wasn't going to be sex. Sex was all she needed to render the old men dumbstruck.

Liam treated it like his God-given right.

She rubbed her face with her hands. Maybe she was being too hard on him. He *lost* his girlfriend only a few months ago…maybe he was *confused.*

Don't panic.

She took a deep breath and spun on her heel to head back into her bedroom. She'd get a shower and think about what might bring them closer together.

She always thought better in the shower.

Her robe was sliding off her shoulders when someone knocked on her front door.

Liam? Again?

Had he forgotten something?

She pulled the robe back on and scanned the room for something he might have left behind. A watch? A phone?

She didn't see anything.

As she approached the door, she noticed a sheet of paper on the ground and rolled her eyes.

A sales flyer stuffed under the door?

She scooped it up with a huff to find the offender's name. She'd report them to the head of the condo association and—

It wasn't a flyer.

It bore no logo—just a simple sheet of typing paper with a message written in red marker.

Don't trust him.

CHAPTER EIGHTEEN

Mason saw Ethan walk into the main room with his backpack. The boy nodded to him.

"I've been given a mission. I'm off to follow Liam around," he said. "Shee here?"

Mason shook his head. "She had some errands to run. Hey, do you have any trackers small enough to swallow?"

Ethan scowled. "To *swallow*? You mean like some kind of *pill* tracker?"

Mason shrugged. "I guess."

"No. It wouldn't be practical. I mean, a person would pass it in a day or two."

Mason nodded.

Makes sense.

"What about one I could stab under the skin?"

"Sure. I mean, sure, they *exist*, but I don't have any. I mean, ever since I retired from the CIA..."

He chuckled.

Mason stared at him.

He cleared his throat.

"But seriously, I don't have anything like that, sorry. It, uh, doesn't come up that often."

Mason grunted.

"I have a car tracker left?" offered Ethan.

Mason turned. "Yeah?"

Ethan put his bag on the counter and rooted through it to find the device.

"Here," he said, handing it to Mason.

Mason inspected it. He'd used trackers before, but it had been a while. This one was smaller. "I just stick it on the car? What is it, magnetic?"

Ethan nodded. "You can generally find a spot under the back bumper." He frowned. "Are you working on the same case as us?"

"Hm?"

"The *sending people for lengthy hospital stays* question, the tracker—it seems like you're working on a different case than the rest of us."

Mason shrugged. "It's a need-to-know thing. How does this thing work once I have it on the car?"

"You download the app. Let me see your phone."

Mason gave the boy his phone, and Ethan set up the app. Mason checked it when he was done and saw the tracker's location in the house.

"Perfect. Thanks," he said.

"Anything else?"

"Nah. You go ahead."

Ethan zipped up his bag and moved to leave. When he opened the front door, Mason spotted movement in the driveway next door and headed that way to get a better look.

Nolan was washing his car in the driveway next door.

Hm.

Now was the time—while he had the house to himself.

Nolan. Nolan. Nolan. What should we do with you?

He'd run through a list of ideas and decided keeping Nolan captive in their house was a bad idea. Too many complications. For one, he'd have to be around to feed him, bathroom breaks— and he wasn't sure when Shee might need him for active duty in their *real* case. Plus, so many people were in and out—he couldn't keep the guy a secret for long. He didn't think anyone would call the police on him, but maybe not *all* the Loggerhead staff thought keeping a stranger chained to a wall for a couple of weeks was *cool*.

Then there was Shee. She probably wouldn't love having a bound man in the corner of the spare room. She'd put up with it better than most, but still, it would be pushing the limits of her patience.

He'd also accused *her* of being distracted from the case. She'd throw that back in his face as soon as she found out about the neighbor.

He didn't want that. She already won more of their arguments than he wanted to admit.

He wandered to the garage and gathered the bat he'd seen there. He brought it inside and propped it behind the bedroom door.

The bat would come in handy if he needed it for *Operation Broken Femur*—number three on the lengthy hospital stay hot list.

He glanced outside to be sure Nolan was still washing his car.

He was.

Operation Broken Femur was a last resort, requiring Nolan to bust into his house and Mason to *righteously* send him to the hospital. After all, then he'd be a man protecting his home.

He couldn't go next door and just break the guy's leg.

Well, he *could*, but that caused complications of its own.

Getting Nolan to come to the rental was crucial to every plan he devised.

Mason opened a few cabinets until he found a stash of liquor—old whiskey the owners had probably had in there for a decade.

That'll do.

He pulled out the bottle and was about to close the cabinet when he noticed a little silver button inside—lying on the shelf, the size of a dime.

Hm.

He moved to the front door and made a mental inventory. Bat, booze, button—he'd forgotten one B.

Beretta.

He found his gun and stuffed it under the sofa cushions.

Perfect.

Mason grabbed the bottle of whiskey and went outside to stroll across the lawn to the neighbor's. He took a swig from the bottle as he moved.

"Hey, asshole," he said.

Nolan straightened and eyed him.

"What do you want?" he asked.

"Nothing."

Nolan stood at the front of his car, watching. Mason walked around the back of the Porche like he was inspecting his car-washing handiwork.

He pretended to stumble and fell to one knee.

Oh, I'm so drunk. Look at me. I'm weak. Vulnerable.

He glanced up and flashed a sheepish grin.

Look at me, Nolan.

Nolan laughed.

"The gimp's a drunk?" he said.

Mason slapped the tracker under the Porche's bumper before straightening.

He felt it stick.

He had to admit, the kid had some pretty cool toys.

He smiled and clambered to his feet to take a fake swig from the bottle.

"You're a piece of shit," he said to Nolan. "Fancy car, and you're living with your grandmother?"

"She's not my *grandmother,* and you better get off my property," said Nolan, walking towards him.

Mason took a few steps onto his own property and pointed at Nolan.

"I'm going to beat the crap out of you," he said, slurring heavily. Probably too much. He should maybe tone it back a bit.

"You don't want to push me," said Nolan.

Mason snorted a laugh. "You can't take me."

Nolan scoffed. "You can't even stand."

They exchanged f-bombs in several creative ways until

both were screaming.

Nolan took a step toward Mason, and Mason pretended to stumble as he rushed to his front door.

Look. I'm so scared.

Nolan laughed.

"*Run*, Peg-leg."

Hovering at his door, Mason held up the bottle.

"Cheers. I'd like to stay and talk, but first, I'm going to take a nap, and then I'm going to come back out and *kick* your ass."

Mason ran the words into one almost unintelligible sentence.

"*Pass out* is more like it, you prick," said Nolan. Mason could tell the man was bristling.

Good.

"Whatever," said Mason. He threw out a few more choice insults and then stumbled into the house, leaving the door ajar.

He collapsed onto the sofa to wait.

Come on. Take the bait, Nolan.

Ten minutes went by. Fifteen. Mason started to lose faith that his fishing expedition would pay off.

Then the front door moved.

From his position on the sofa, Mason saw only the very top of the door, but he could tell no breeze had moved it. The door opened far enough to let a large man inside.

Mason smiled and lowered his lids, keeping them open enough to watch as a figure appeared at the end of the sofa.

Hello, Nolan.

Mason snored.

Smirking, Nolan moved toward him, fingers curling into a fist. In his other hand, he held a gun.

Oh, Nolan. Shame on you.

Nolan raised the weapon.

"Wake up, you—"

Mason's hand shot up and locked on the man's wrist, bending it to keep the nose of the gun pointed toward the ceiling.

The men locked eyes.

Mason smiled.

"*Surprise.*"

Nolan roared and wrestled to free himself of Mason's grip. Mason jerked him off balance and punched him hard in the temple. He twisted the weapon from his hand and tossed it like a frisbee through the bedroom doorway and onto the bed.

Even he was pretty impressed by the accuracy.

Nolan stumbled back. He shook his head like a wet dog to clear it.

By now, Mason was on his feet—

Foot, he heard Shee's voice in his head say. She never missed a shot at him. Even when she wasn't there.

He beckoned the man forward.

"Come on, Nolan. It's been a while. Give me a dance."

Nolan's eyes telegraphed his fear—but driven by rage and no doubt a history of bad decisions—he lunged forward. The men collided like battling circus bears. They grappled to gain the upper hand as Nolan's momentum and a wobbly metal shin sent Mason stumbling back against the hurricane glass sliders.

Mason slid down and hit Nolan with three rapid rabbit punches to his midsection. Nolan gasped for air. When he fell back, Mason straightened and struck him in the jaw. The man slammed against the entertainment stand. He grabbed a glass fish statue there and threw it at the SEAL. Mason blocked it with his forearm, and it snapped in two before shattering to the tile floor.

Mason frowned at the mess.

There goes the deposit. Shee's going to kill me.

Nolan pushed off the unit to throw a roundhouse. Mason sidestepped the punch and came in with a glancing body blow. Nolan went for the obvious move and attempted to sweep Mason's fake leg out from under him. Mason saw it coming. He moved out of the way.

They squared up again. Nolan threw several lumbering punches, growing more winded by the second.

"Should have kept the gun," teased Mason.

The comment made Nolan glance into the bedroom, and Mason used the distraction to move in. He struck his foe in the face and then hit him with a solid shot to the stomach. Nolan doubled over, and Mason circled to wrap him in a headlock.

Nolan slapped at the arm around his throat. Mason tightened his grip.

"Calm down, and this will all be over soon," said Mason.

Nolan twisted to break free and failed as Mason pressed on his windpipe. He dropped his hands to his side to show his submission.

"Good boy," said Mason. "You invaded *my* house, Nolan. I can kill you right here, right now, and walk away."

"I'm sorry. I effed up," Nolan croaked.

"Oh, you definitely effed up," said Mason. "The hardest part of this fight was trying *not* to accidentally kill you. But I'm going to give you three options, which is pretty generous, considering. I want you to think hard. Ready?"

Nolan nodded. Mason felt the man's weight growing in his arms and released pressure to let him get a good gulp of air. Unconscious Nolan would be of no use to him. When he felt the man regain his legs, he began.

"Option one, I kill you and tell the cops you broke into my house to kill *me*. That gun of yours will go a long way toward proving my point."

Nolan shook his head.

"You sure? That one ends your miserable life. Could be a good option?"

Nolan shook his head again.

"Okay—option two, I break your femur with a baseball bat. That's the bone in your thigh, in case you're wondering. I'd need the bat because it's a *big* bone, Nolan. The biggest. It'll put you in the hospital for about a week. Very painful."

"No," grunted Nolan.

"No? Well, once you hear number three, you can revisit it. Option three is—you go away. That's it. You go away five hours from here in any direction you like and *stay* away for at least *two* weeks."

Nolan didn't respond, and Mason eased up on his throat again.

"Did you hear me, Nolan? Do you like that option? Or should I get the bat? I'll choke you out, and when you wake up, your leg will be at a right angle—"

Nolan shook his head as best he could. "No, no, no—"

"No? So that's it? Option three?"

Nolan nodded. "Where? Why?"

"I don't care *where* as long as it's at least five hours away. Go to Vegas. Take in a show. In two weeks, I'll be gone. Probably. If you get back and my truck is still parked out front, you should probably go back under your rock because I might remember how you sneaked into my house with a gun. It was rude, Nolan, and I'm deeply offended."

Mason leaned down to whisper in his ear.

"Did I mention I have a camera?"

He pointed Nolan at the camera sitting on the entertainment shelf. Nolan made a little *gerk* noise as Mason moved him by his neck.

"The police might be interested in seeing you and your gun creeping on a sleeping man in his home. Have you spent any time in jail, Nolan?"

He shook his head.

"I'll be honest. I don't know if you'd like it. Big guys like messing with big guys like you who aren't so good at fighting. They like a *challenge*." Mason grinned. "Though, it's not really a *challenge* when there's six of them. You know what I mean, Nolan?"

Nolan nodded. "Option three."

Mason patted him on the head. "Option three. Good choice. Any thoughts on where you're going to stay?"

"I have a buddy up in Jacksonville."

"That'll work. I'll need you to do something for me, though."

Mason pulled the silver button from his pocket with his free hand and held it up in front of Nolan. "Swallow this."

"Why?"

"You heard me."

"But what is it?"

"It's a tracker, so I can make sure you stay far from here."

"A tracker?" Nolan strained to look at Mason. "Who the hell are you?"

"You don't need to know that, Nolan. Just know I've killed more people than you pass on the street on an average day."

Nolan fell silent.

"You really didn't know the lengths to which you effed up, did you?"

He shook his head.

Mason gripped his throat tighter. "Open your mouth."

When Nolan didn't immediately comply, he pressed harder, and the man's jaw dropped. Mason popped the button inside his mouth.

"Swallow it."

He eased his grip and felt Nolan's Adam's apple bob.

"Good boy." He reached behind him and pulled his gun from his waistband. He released the man and pushed him forward.

"Turn around."

Nolan did, eyes saucering at the gun in Mason's hand.

He rubbed at his throat.

"You had a gun?" he said.

"The whole time. Didn't need it for the likes of you. Let's go get your stuff."

Mason pushed the man ahead and walked next door. He had Nolan open the door to Janet's house and pushed him inside.

Janet sat on the sofa watching a talk show. She turned and gasped as they entered.

"What is this?" she asked, her eyes wide.

"Sorry to startle you. Nolan just needs to pick up a few

things," said Mason.

Mason followed Nolan to his room and watched as he packed to be sure he didn't come out of the room with a weapon. Janet remained on the sofa.

"Should I call someone?" asked Janet.

Mason waved her off. "No, dear. He's just packing. Give us a few minutes."

When Nolan finished, Mason walked him to his car and watched him drive off.

He waved as the Porche headed down the street. "See ya, Nolan."

Mason turned to the house. The door he'd left ajar slammed shut as he approached. He slipped the gun back into his waistband and knocked.

"Let me in, Janet. We need to talk."

"You have a gun. I'll call the police," she called from inside, her voice shaky.

Mason frowned. He hadn't gamed his plan past putting Nolan in his car. He hadn't imagined Janet's response.

Hm.

This is where Shee always came in handy. She thought about the civilian reactions.

"I'm not going to hurt you. I did this for you."

"What happened to him?" asked Janet. "He looked like he was hit by a truck."

Mason pulled his phone from his pocket and checked the tracker Ethan helped him set up. He saw Nolan's vehicle heading away from the neighborhood.

"Hello?" called Janet.

"Sorry," he said. "I was just checking. I arranged for Nolan to head out of town. We have an agreement. He won't be back for two weeks. At *least*. That's long enough for you to pack up and get to your friend's house, right?"

Through the frosted glass, Mason saw the outline of Janet's body move closer to the door.

"Yes, but—how do you know he won't come back?" she

asked.

"I gave him a few options, and he picked the least painful. I'll be here for a while anyway, don't worry. He's not coming back."

Janet took another step closer. "This is my chance?"

"Yep. Take it or don't, but this is your chance. Start packing." He moved to leave and then turned back. "Hey, before I go, do you know Nolan's phone number? Can you give it to me?"

Janet rattled off the number, and Mason plugged it into his phone. He heard the door open and looked up to see Janet peering outside. Her eyes were wet with tears.

"Are you okay?" he asked. "This is what you wanted, right?"

She nodded. "How can I ever thank you?"

"By getting out of here. I'll be next door if you need anything."

He nodded to her and left.

The rest would be up to Janet, but he felt pretty good she'd take her chance.

On returning to the house, he checked his phone and saw Nolan's beacon on the bridge headed for the interstate.

He dialed the number Janet gave him to ensure Nolan knew the button "tracker" he'd swallowed worked. He didn't want the man checking his car for the *actual* device.

Nolan answered.

Mason didn't wait for him to say *hello*.

"I see you're on the bridge, Nolan. Good boy," he said. "I'll be watching."

He hung up before Nolan could respond. Chuckling, he put down his phone and walked to the glass slider doors to stare at the pool.

He thought Miss Elly would be proud of him for helping Janet. She'd always taken care of her neighbors, and she'd always encouraged him to do the same.

He brushed the bumpy scar on the outside of his right

bicep and traced it with his finger. It had started to itch lately.

His last diamond lay beneath that scar. He'd carried it into his military service and asked the doc to place it under his skin after being wounded. He'd always kept it close, and sitting under his skin seemed safer than dangling in a locket on a chain around his neck.

He was young then—scared he'd lose the stone before he could put it in a ring for Shee.

So many years ago.

Finally, they'd found each other again, and the stone was working its way out of the scar tissue like it knew it was finally its time to shine.

CHAPTER NINETEEN

Shee saw Ethan calling and answered her phone.

"What's up? Any movement on Liam?"

"No. He's been shuttling back and forth between work and his house following a brief visit to Rowan's this morning."

She nodded. "Great, I'm sure I'll hear all about it."

"I think I've got your K," added Ethan. "I'm looking at her social media right now."

"You do?" Shee was impressed. Access to a hacker through Croix had always been handy, but now that Ethan had joined the team, he was even more helpful.

"How's she look for spray-painting garages?" she asked.

"Not great. She's only twenty-two."

Shee chuckled. "Right. Young people don't do stupid things, I forgot."

"It's not that it's—I dunno. I guess it's possible, but she seems *happy*. She has a lot of friends. She doesn't seem like the *spray-painting threatening messages* type."

She shrugged. "You never know. People don't usually post photos of themselves stewing over boyfriends."

"True."

"What did you find? Where does she live?"

Ethan sniffed. "I'll send you her address. She's a waitress at Bahama Betty's, too."

Shee's jaw dropped. "You're *kidding*."

"No—I'm looking at a staff photo she posted."

Shee smiled. "Let me guess. Blonde? Thin? Ponytail?"

"Yes—how did you know?"

"I saw her giving Rowan and me the stinkeye at Betty's. It's Liam's favorite hangout—makes sense he met the girl there. I'll swing over there—see if I can get anything out of her."

Ethan sighed. "I'll be sitting here, staring at Liam's house."

Shee hung up and headed for the restaurant, thinking she needed to get a frequent customer punch card if this kept up.

She approached the hostess, smiling.

"Hi, I wonder if you could help me? I had a waitress the other day I really liked—twenties, blonde, thin—I think her name started with a K?"

The girl nodded. "Kimmy? That has to be Kimmy. Do you want me to seat you in her section?"

Shee clasped her hands together. "If you would, that would be *great*. Thank you *so* much."

The hostess led her to a two-top, and she sat, waiting. Her phone rang, and she saw it was Rowan.

Again.

Good Lord. The woman was *needy* for a serial killer.

She was about to answer when Kimmy appeared, glanced at her, did a double-take, and then approached.

Shee put down her phone.

Sorry, I'll catch you later, Rowan.

Kimmy arrived tableside and grinned broadly, trying to push a friendly vibe, but Shee could tell she'd been recognized, and the girl was wary.

"Hi, my name's Kimmy. I'll be your waitress today," she said. "Can I start you with something to drink?"

"Hi," said Shee, cocking her head. "Do I know you?"

Kimmy's smile wobbled. "I don't think so."

"No, I think I do. Didn't I see you with Liam?"

The waitress's smile disappeared.

"I don't know what you're—"

"You do," said Shee. "You were looking at me yesterday. I

was there at the bar with Liam and a dark-haired woman, Rowan."

Kimmy straightened and tried to reset it. "Oh, *that's* why I recognize you. You're friends with that other one. *Rowan,* you said her name is? That's a pretty name."

"Uh huh. Seems like she and Liam have a thing now."

Kimmy scoffed. "Great. Good for her. Good for *them.*"

"You don't care?"

"Me? I couldn't care less."

"Are you sure?"

The girl scowled. "Look, what's your problem? My life isn't any of your business."

"Well, it is when I'm investigating the death of his last girlfriend, and I see you eyeing the new one."

The girl paled. "You're a cop?"

"Detective," said Shee. It wasn't a lie, and it sounded homocide-y.

Kimmy looked around. "He told me she drowned. Joy."

"That's one story," said Shee, trying to sound as vague as possible.

Kimmy leaned in. "You think *he* killed her?" Her attention swiveled to the bar where Shee and Rowan once sat. "Or *her*? Do you think *she* killed Joy?"

"What do you think?"

She shrugged. "I don't think *he* did."

"No?"

Kimmy looked around to see if her manager was watching and sat across from Shee.

"He seemed genuinely broken up about Joy."

"So you don't think it was him?"

She shook her head.

"And there's no reason to think it's *you*?"

Kimmy slapped her hand to her chest. "*Me*? Why would *I* kill her?"

"To get Liam for yourself."

She laughed. "I don't want him. He's *old.*"

"But you were dating him, weren't you? When he was with Joy?"

"Not dating him. It was like a one-time thing."

"One time?"

"Couple, few times, maybe. I've got a boyfriend."

"Does your boyfriend know about your couple-few times with Liam?"

"No. That was before."

"So, *new* boyfriend."

She nodded.

"And you wouldn't, *hypothetically*, be so bitter about how things ended with Liam that you'd spray-paint nasty messages on his garage door? For example? Hypothetically?"

The girl's brow knitted. "What are you talking about?"

Shee sat back. Kimmy didn't seem like her girl. She'd been pretty forthcoming with the details of her short romance with Liam, and she seemed genuinely clueless about the spray paint.

"Why were you glaring at us the other day?"

Kimmy huffed. "He's just such a *man whore*. He was with some redhead two days before at the same spot at the bar. I guess—I dunno. Working here, you see it all the time—I guess I just get tired of it."

Shee nodded. "I can see that—"

"He said he would hook me up with some free skin treatments, too, but that never happened." She pouted. "*Jerk*."

Now that she had the girl talking, she didn't want to stop.

"I maybe wouldn't pressure him about skin peels now."

Kimmy barked a laugh. "*Hell* no. Don't worry about that."

"Okay. Well, I appreciate you talking to me."

"No problem." Kimmy stood. "Oh, can I get you anything?"

Shee handed her a folded hundred-dollar bill she'd prepared just in case.

"If you see anything weird about him or that other dark-haired woman he was talking to, let me know."

"Weird *how*?"

"Just weird. Fights. Anything strange."

Kimmy took the money.

"Cool. And you'll tell me if, like, they're *murdering* people, right?"

"Absolutely," said Shee.

"Cool."

"Cool."

Shee headed out no wiser than she'd come in. They still didn't know who'd spray-painted Liam's door, but she felt confident it wasn't Kimmy.

That was one thing off the list, she supposed.

Cool.

CHAPTER TWENTY

When Liam called later, Rowan had mixed emotions.

On the one hand, the fact he'd called, as promised, was a good sign that her fears about losing her grip on him had been overblown. That he'd asked her over meant he wasn't tiring of her.

On the other hand, someone had slipped a note under her door that could only be about Liam. Joy died, someone accused Liam of killing her, and now someone was warning her away from him.

She didn't *love* the math on all of that.

She struggled with it on her way to Liam's house. Should she mention the note? Would it drive a wedge between them? Would he try to prove he hadn't murdered Joy? Or would he cut ties with her for doubting him?

Or...would he murder *her*?

She sighed.

Seducing rich old men seemed like a walk in the park compared to this mess. And none of what she knew explained who left the graffiti or slipped her the flyer. Was it angry, bitter K? Or someone serious, too scared to come forward?

Liam thought the spray paint was his neighbor—but would a disgruntled neighbor, embarrassed over a poop bag dispute, follow *her* home to try and break them up with an ominous note?

That didn't feel right.

She needed to talk to someone.

Someone who really knew how to handle men.

She called Shee, but her new friend didn't answer. She wasn't entirely disappointed. She preferred it when people thought her life was *amazing,* and she'd been moaning to Shee a *lot.*

Rowan made a hard and sudden right to pull into a grocery store parking lot.

She parked and called Liam.

"Hey, I'm going to be another half an hour. I have some things I need to finish up."

"No problem. I'll be here," he said.

He sounded in good spirits.

Men.

Why can't it ever be easy?

She called her mother.

"What's up, baby girl?" answered her mother.

Rowan heard the television in the background and pictured her mother on the sofa where the woman had been growing like a fungus for years.

It had been a while since she'd last gone home to Texas. When she was young, her mother had been the most beautiful woman in the world. Whenever her friends and *their* mothers gathered, Rowan swelled with pride at how much prettier her mother was than the others. Tall, curvy without being overweight, long legs—Rowan's good looks hadn't come from *nowhere.*

There were downsides to having the prettiest mother, though. Rowan had had a lot of "uncles" over the years. Back then, it felt like her mother had all the men in the neighborhood wrapped around her finger—or other parts.

At the sound of her mother's voice on the phone, Rowan stalled. Suddenly, she didn't feel like explaining the situation with Joy and the threatening notes.

It all felt *embarrassing.*

Calling had been a mistake. What advice could her mother give? All she could say was *move on*, which she didn't want to hear.

"I've got a man my age," she said instead. "More or less."

"Yeah?" Her mother laughed, a sharp rattle snapping in her throat. "That means one of two things: Either you're going to make my mistake and fall in love, or—"

"Or what?"

"Or you're just *old* now. You've caught up to your marks." She cackled again.

Rowan shook her head. "He's *rich*."

This news stopped her mother's amused rattle.

"How rich?"

"*Move you out of your shithole and into an assisted care neighborhood* rich. That kind of rich."

Her mother's voice perked. "Yeah? That's what you said about the last one."

Rowan looked away. She *had* said that.

She *had* siphoned a good amount of money from the last sucker but needed it to catch up with the bills. There wasn't enough left to share.

"No, this one really is the answer," she assured her mother. "He's a dermatologist."

"Ooooh. I'm raising my beer to you, so you know," said her mother, her voice dripping with sarcasm.

"Thanks."

"So why the call? What's the problem? I taught you everything you need to know to seal the deal."

"It's different. Like I said, he's not as old as most of the guys—"

"So? Same rules apply."

"I know, but..." Rowan winced, trying to find a way to define her feelings. "I feel like I need something *more*."

"Like some secret weapon? Magic bullet? I can't tell you about any new sex positions. It's been a while." Her mother started laughing again until it turned into a cough. "That be a good name for a sex position, though—the *magic bullet*."

Rowan rolled her eyes. "Yeah, you're hilarious. *No*, I was thinking something that would make him—I dunno. *Connect* with me."

"Connect with you? What kind of new-age hippie bullshit is that?"

"Not like that. Just—something to bring us together. To make it feel like it's him and me against the world."

Her mother grunted. "I got you. Hm. What can you give him that no one else can?"

Rowan grimaced. "Nothing. He could easily go younger than me. He's good-looking and rich."

"And it really only takes rich," muttered her mother. "Life is so easy for those bastards."

Rowan nodded but didn't answer. She didn't want her mother to spin off on a man-hating tangent, or she'd be on the phone the rest of the day.

She heard her mother take a drag from her cigarette.

"What can he give *you*?" she asked, in that breathless way people spoke when they were delaying an exhale.

Rowan scowled. "I think I've explained all that."

"No, not *money*. Could he want to take care of you? Could you work the Big Daddy?"

Rowan didn't have to consider this option for long. "I don't think that will work for him. He's not mushy like that."

"So he's a self-centered prick."

Rowan's cheeks felt hot.

"*No*," she said.

She hated she knew she was lying.

She tried again. "He's just not *soft*. I don't think appealing to his daddy instincts would work."

Her mother grunted again. "Then I got nothing except *The Island* play. You've got to isolate him."

Rowan tilted back her head. "But *what* island? He's got a busy job, friends, co-workers, a career—how can I become his whole world?"

"*Baby Island* isn't an option, I suppose?"

Rowan frowned. "No. I won't pull what you pulled with my father—even though it worked out *so well* for you."

Now, it was her turn for sarcasm.

Her mother snorted. "I wouldn't complain about that if I were you. If it weren't for *Baby Island,* you wouldn't be here."

"Yeah, yeah. But Dad left anyway, and you were stuck with me."

"Yeah, but he *married* me first. The money you brought lasted me until I was almost forty."

Rowan sighed.

But look at you now.

She wouldn't end up like her mother. She wouldn't be happy with money that lasted her until she was *forty*. She needed to score big. She'd already done much better than her mother, but Liam was the pot of gold at the end of the rainbow.

"I imagine it's too late for you to work Baby Island anyway," said her mother. "You're dried up by now—"

Rowan swore at her and held the phone away from her ear.

Why did I call? What was I thinking?

She took a few deep breaths and then again put the phone against her ear to hear her mother reining in another coughing fit.

"Why do you always have to be such an asshole?" she asked.

Her mother sniffed.

"Find your island, baby. Find it for both of us."

"I've got to go. Do you need anything?"

"Wine."

"I'll have some delivered."

"I like the boxes."

"I know. Anything else? Do you have all your pills?"

"Yeah."

"Have you and Sasha been up to anything fun?"

"I don't talk to that bitch anymore."

Rowan nodded. Her mother and her best friend Sasha had

broken up and reconciled more times than she and her mother ever had, which was saying something.

"Okay. Well, go make up with her."

Her mother scoffed.

"Screw her *and* that stupid bald parrot."

Rowan hung up without another word and ran her hand across her face.

Great conversation, as always.

She put the car in drive and headed for Liam's.

Rowan watched Liam slap at a bug on his neck. They'd gone to an early dinner and were strolling around his neighborhood. He seemed eager to show off the place.

She hoped that was a good sign. He'd started talking about Joy, though. That seemed less hopeful.

"Honestly, I'm glad she's gone," he said.

Rowan gasped and slapped his arm playfully. "You're *terrible*. She was always nice to me."

He shook his head. "She was nice to *me* in the beginning, too. Then she turned into a first-class bitch."

"Wow..."

Rowan wasn't sure what to say. He seemed bitter, but the person he described wasn't anything like the Joy she knew. She didn't stop him, though. She needed to get a list of what he hated about his ex so she could be the *opposite*.

Liam's head suddenly snapped to the left as they passed a side street.

"There he is," he said.

"Who?"

"The guy who painted the garage."

Rowan turned and saw a short, stocky bald man glaring back at Liam. She grew uneasy. She didn't want to come all the way from her mother's trailer in Texas to wind up *dead* in a Florida sub-division front yard because two men had a beef.

"You *know* it was him?" she asked.

"It had to be." He pointed at the man. "Hey, *you.*"

The man didn't say anything—just watched Liam close in.

"You wrote that shit on my garage," said Liam.

The man's brow knitted. "What?"

Liam repeated his accusation, and the man shook his head.

"I don't know what you're talking about."

Liam poked a finger at him. "Do it again, and I'll have you arrested. I've got cameras."

The man scooped up his small dog and took a step back.

"Get out of my face."

"Do it again, and I'll *destroy* you." Liam spun to storm off, tapping Rowan's arm as he moved. She assumed the tap meant she was supposed to storm away, too. He'd left her behind with the steaming short man.

She broke into a jog to catch up with Liam and glanced over her shoulder at the man, who clutched his dog to his chest, watching them leave.

Liam strode in silence. *Seething.*

"He looked confused," said Rowan.

Liam shook his head. "He knows what he did."

Rowan nodded and didn't answer. She supposed Liam knew the man better than she did.

"He doesn't know who he's messing with," muttered Liam. "Did you see his door?"

"His *door*?"

"Red."

"Was it?" she looked over her shoulder, knowing she wouldn't see anything from where they were now.

Liam nodded. "Yep. He did it. The evidence is right there. *Idiot.*"

Rowan sighed. The idea that someone would write something so awful on Liam's door over a poop bag disagreement seemed *crazy*, but maybe Liam was right.

"He's not the only one," said Liam.

"What do you mean?"

"Some people at work blame me for what happened to Joy."

"They say that?"

"Not directly, but I can feel it. I can tell. I can tell by the way they look at me."

"How could her drowning be your fault?"

He shrugged. "That's the stupid part. How *could* it be my fault? I wasn't even there. What was I supposed to do—forbid her to swim?"

"No. That's crazy."

"I know. I've done *everything* for that group of losers. If it wasn't for me, the whole practice would be nothing, and they turn on me. It's like someone is poisoning them against me."

A car approached and slowed as it passed. When she tried to peer inside, it took off.

"Did you see that?" he asked.

"What?" she asked, though she knew what he'd meant.

"That car that passed. It slowed down like they were looking at us."

"Looking at us, *how*?"

"I don't know. It just didn't feel right."

Liam turned and stared in the direction the car had left.

"Something's up," he muttered.

CHAPTER TWENTY-ONE

Liam watched Rowan smile and slipped into the bathroom to get a shower.

They'd had a nice night together.

Too bad.

In another world. At another time.

Rowan was something special—but something was *off*. He couldn't get as excited as he thought he should about his new lady friend. Didn't look forward to seeing her as much as he thought he *would* after the first night. He'd taken her to that party, and it didn't feel like people *looked* at her enough.

He wasn't feeling it. Couldn't put his finger on it. Maybe it was the fact she'd seen him at his weakest—people spray-painting his garage—it was *embarrassing*.

She'd always see him as *that guy.*

They didn't have much in common. The conversations felt forced and strangely old-fashioned, somehow. She *was* kind of old. Probably, what? Fifteen years younger than him? But...

Nah. He could do better. She wasn't it.

Still, no reason not to keep her around for a while.

He walked to his closet to pick out something for dinner and noticed the light glowing in the walk-in closet. The one he hadn't entered since Joy died.

He scowled and opened the sliding door.

He eyed the few things of Joy's still hanging there, unsure what he should do with them.

Should I give her stuff to Rowan?

Maybe she'd been looking at Joy's stuff—she'd said she felt underdressed to go to dinner in what she had on.

He ran his tongue over his teeth.

She seemed *tacky*.

Maybe that was it.

All of it—her *looking* at Joy's stuff, him even thinking about *offering* Joy's stuff—all of it felt tacky. Say what you want about Joy—she could be a first-class, prize-winning bitch when she wanted to—but she had that *thing*. He couldn't put his finger on that, either.

Would Rowan even want some dead woman's clothes? Maybe not. Maybe it was rude to even ask. He didn't want to make her feel like some charity case, but from what he'd seen so far, she could use a few wardrobe upgrades—

His gaze fell on a leather case—stuffed between some other clothes.

Joy's satchel.

He hadn't noticed it before.

How did I not see that before?

She must have left it there before she went swimming that day.

He opened it to find it empty but for a laptop. He pushed aside his rarely worn sweaters and sat it on the shelf to open it. It sang the usual song, and the desktop appeared.

No password.

He blinked at it, surprised.

Would it be wrong to poke around a little?

He flipped through the files, searching for anything interesting, and found a directory called *Rowan*.

He scowled.

Weird.

Joy and Rowan were drinking buddies. Why would Rowan

have a directory dedicated to her on Joy's laptop? Especially when it seemed that was *all* there was on the laptop. It had to be new.

He clicked on the folder icon and found a saved thread of emails between the two women. Rowan was talking— laughing—about her history of seducing rich men.

Older rich men.

Liam sneered at the thought.

Ugh.

He snorted a laugh. That explained the old-fashioned feel of her conversations. She'd accused the waitress of *lollygagging* the other night, for crying out loud.

He read a little farther.

"...you know the best part? They're so grateful. It's like I saved them from the void, you know?" she said in one.

Whoa. What the hell kind of woman was Rowan? Some kind of hooker? Was she shaking him down somehow, and he didn't even know?

Joy's answers to her predatory new friend were supportive but not overly so. Short. Perfunctory. So much so he found it shocking that Rowan went on, but she did.

On and *on.*

Liam felt his anger growing.

"...You should have seen the face on his sister when I showed up at the funeral in his car. LOL. She was always trying to get his money out of him. Sorry, honey. She was awful."

He realized Rowan knew more about him than he'd known.

"...You're so lucky to have a younger, handsome, rich guy," said Rowan in one email.

"You can have him," replied Joy. *"If I'm hit by a bus, feel free to take him. LOL."*

"...Remember, tell him to wear the R.O.C., and I'll find him!" said Rowan.

"What does that mean again?" asked Joy.

"Ring on Chain."

Liam touched the ring on his chain. Joy had told him to

wear one to attract women if something happened to her. She'd said it in anger—

He'd actually done it—thought it was genius. Not only had it elicited sympathy from his co-workers and patients, but it had attracted Rowan.

Joy learned it from Rowan?

He turned to look toward the bathroom where Rowan had showered.

The message on the garage.

Was it for Rowan or had she done it? He couldn't imagine how she could have done it—she was with him at the party—but maybe she had a partner? Was she trying to blackmail him or something? Make it look like *he* killed Joy?

He shut the computer.

Had *Rowan* killed Joy to get *him?*

He pushed the case behind a row of hanging slacks and straightened, steaming.

No love was lost between him and Joy in the end—but there'd been *something* about her. Rowan felt like a cheap knockoff of Joy.

Now, he knew why.

His head swiveled as he heard the familiar squeak of his shower valve. The hiss of the shower stopped. He pushed the case aside and shoved the laptop between the shorts in his closet so Rowan wouldn't see it.

His face felt hot.

He clenched his fist, trying to decide whether he should confront her or not.

Golddigging *bitch.*

CHAPTER TWENTY-TWO

While Rowan and Liam were at Liam's house, Ethan slipped into Croix's car to nap in the back seat. They were watching the same house at this point, so it didn't make sense not to do it together.

Croix's head started nodding when she heard something and sat up.

"Did you hear that?" she asked.

"Hm?" grunted Ethan.

She reached back and shook him. "Wake up—someone's screaming."

"Screaming?

Ethan sat up, and they both leaned toward the window, peering outside, their attentions locked on Liam's house.

That's when they saw her.

Rowan stood outside in the driveway, screaming, holding something in her hands. She wore only a towel. Something about her looked...*blotchy*.

Ethan grabbed for the door handle, and Croix reached around her seat to snag the back of his shirt as he tried to leave the vehicle.

"What are you doing?" he asked. "We have to go help her."

"*Don't*," she said.

"We *have* to."

Croix shook her head. "We're not here. Whatever this is, we

can't be involved."

She pulled a small pair of binoculars from the center console and trained them on the screaming woman.

Ethan huffed. "Are you kidding me? We have to help her. She's covered in—"

"*Blood*," finished Croix, her gaze locked on the woman in the driveway. "Let it play out."

"But what if she dies?"

She grunted. "I don't think she will."

"How can you say that?"

Croix handed him the binoculars.

"*She's* holding the knife."

Shee parked her car down the street from Liam's house and took a circuitous path to where she knew Croix and Ethan waited for her. She found them in the backseat of their car, taking turns peering through binoculars at the situation at Liam's house.

The *situation* had become just that—police cars and flashing lights surrounded the property like a swarm of patriotic lightning bugs. Neighbors with concerned expressions gathered nearby, whispering and watching an officer cordon the area with the familiar yellow tape.

Shee knocked on the window, and the two inside jumped before Croix leaned over to unlock the door for her.

"This is all looking suspiciously *murdery*," said Shee, hopping into the passenger seat. "Do we know what's going on?"

Croix handed the binoculars to Ethan and turned to face Shee. "Liam and Rowan took a walk. Liam got into a shouting match with a neighbor—"

"Bad?" asked Shee. "*This* bad?"

"I didn't think so." Croix looked to Ethan. "You saw that part. Tell her."

Ethan lowered the binoculars. "I didn't see *all* of it because I had to keep cruising by, but I'd call it *a heated exchange of words*."

"So no fists, nobody screaming *I'm going to kill you*?" confirmed Shee.

"No."

"I guess you couldn't hear what it was about?"

Ethan shook his head. "No. But, like I said, they didn't look *that* upset. They argued, then Liam and Rowan went back to the house. I parked, joined Croix here—next thing we know, Rowan's in the driveway with a knife in her hand, wearing nothing but a bloody towel and screaming bloody murder."

"In a towel? Like she'd just gotten out of the shower?"

"That's what we're thinking. Her hair was wet too—" Croix paused.

"What is it?" asked Shee.

"I mean, her hair *looked* wet. Unless it was all *blood*. It's hard to tell in this light. She *did* have that *Carrie* look."

Shee squinted at her. "What do you know about *Carrie*? That's before your time."

"It's not that old," said Croix. "It's one of the few movies Mick and I watched in color. I think it was Halloween."

"They remade it," explained Ethan.

"And, honestly, that's how I imagine all proms end anyway," added Croix with a snort of laughter.

Shee chuckled and motioned to the scene. "There's no ambulance?"

Ethan raised the binoculars again. "It already left. *Not in a hurry*."

"So, we can assume Liam's dead?"

Croix shrugged. "Didn't look good, and I don't know who else would be in there."

"Where's Rowan now?" asked Shee, motioning for the binoculars.

Ethan handed them over and pointed to one of the cruisers. "She's in that car."

Shee saw an officer standing on the opposite side of a cruiser. She assumed he was talking to Rowan. She scanned over the scene as she processed. She liked the group of chatty neighbors gathering.

That seemed like a place she should be.

She handed back the binoculars.

"Okay, you two find out what happened to Liam. Check with the coroner, the cops, whatever you need to do. I'm going to see if I can get to Rowan."

"I don't think the cops will just let her go home," said Croix.

"Probably not, but I didn't get the impression she's got a lot of friends. I want to be the one she talks to next time she can talk to anyone."

Croix offered a little salute. "Aye, aye, Captain."

She sighed. "You know I hate it when you do that."

Croix smiled. "I know. That's why I do it."

Shee hopped out of the car. A light rain started to fall.

Figures.

She sped to the scene, hoping to get there before the rain picked up and sent the gawkers hurrying home. Police and detectives walked back in and out of Liam's home. She imagined there wouldn't be much evidence left to paw through by the time they finished.

She walked close to the cruiser where Rowan sat, straining to listen.

"I think that's my friend," she called to the officer. "Rowan? It's Shee. Are you okay?"

Her raised voice brought another officer to her, but not before she saw Rowan stretching forward to see who was calling her name.

She looked *terrible*.

Rowan's hair was wet and *not* covered in blood like *Carrie*, but her haunted expression spoke volumes. Shee couldn't see the bloody towel Croix and Ethan described—someone had draped a coat around Rowan's shoulders, and she gripped it to her.

Shee waved to be sure she was seen.

"*Anything you need*," she called.

"I'm going to need you to stand back," said the approaching officer.

Shee stepped back. She wanted Rowan to see her but didn't need the officers remembering her—just in case she needed to sneak around later.

She moved to the crowd of neighbors whose attention had already shifted to her.

"Do you know that woman?" asked a woman in a purple tee spotted with raindrops. Her question sounded more like an accusation.

"That's Joy, his girlfriend," said a man.

"Joy's *dead*," said another woman.

The man looked at her. "I thought they took *him* away. Joy's right there."

"*That's not Joy*," hissed the woman. Shee could tell by her exasperated tone she was the man's wife. "I told you, Joy *drowned*. Remember?"

The man looked away with a tiny shrug.

Shee realized Purple Shirt was still waiting for her to answer.

"I don't know her well," she said.

"What's her name? Did she kill him?"

"She's a new one," said Exasperated Wife.

She was clearly in charge of neighborhood's dating gossip.

"Did you see her?" asked a tall woman. "She was covered in blood. I posted pictures on my Facebook if you want to see."

She held up her phone, and Shee watched as she flipped through a collection of blurry shots of Rowan wrapped in a bloody towel in Liam's driveway.

"You can see in this one she has a knife in her hand," said the woman.

Shee nodded as her attention pulled to a sour-faced, heavy-set woman with her arms crossed against her chest.

"I think he killed his other girlfriend," said Sour Puss when she saw Shee looking at her.

A woman at her side nodded enthusiastically.

Shee nodded to acknowledge the woman's logic. She didn't know if Liam had killed Joy, but clearly, *something* was going on.

She turned to stare at the cruiser where Rowan sat.

"You think Liam tried to kill *her*?" she suggested.

Sour Puss shrugged. "Yes, and I think she *won*. He tried to kill her, and she beat him to it."

"About time," muttered her friend.

Purple Shirt wasn't buying it.

"I saw her creeping around outside right before it happened."

"Creeping around?" echoed Shee.

The *whoop whoop* of a police car cut the conversation short. The cruiser Rowan had been sitting in rolled forward.

Shee frowned.

They're taking her.

While she thought the neighbors might provide a font of information, she couldn't tell what was real or wild speculation. She turned to where Croix was parked and saw the kids pulling away from the curb to follow the police car taking Rowan.

That was their job, after all. Follow Rowan and Liam—even if it took them to the morgue.

Shee watched the vehicles turn the corner at the end of the street, her mind a million miles away, loitering somewhere quiet where it could process information.

She snapped from her trance when Purple Shirt poked her in the arm.

"I saw her sneaking around. Next thing I know, she's out here, covered in blood, and he's *dead*," said the woman.

When Shee didn't respond, Purple Shirt scoffed with the bitterness of a thousand lifetimes.

"*You* do the math," she added.

Shee nodded grimly to avoid a confrontation and headed to where she'd left her car. She called Snookie on the way.

"Hey, Snook," she said, trying to sound upbeat. "Quick

question."

"Yes?" asked Snookie. She sounded half asleep.

Shee cleared her throat.

"Were you hoping no one else would die?"

CHAPTER TWENTY-THREE

"She's going to be in there a while," said Croix, staring at the police station where Rowan had just disappeared into.

More surveillance. Yay.

"I guess I'm off the hook," said Ethan.

Croix frowned. "You're so lucky. Yours died. You suck."

Ethan laughed and then sobered. "You know, you promised a lot of excitement working for Loggerhead, but it seems like we spend an awful lot of time *staring* at things."

Croix nodded. "Believe me, when the action happens, you'll *wish* you were on a stakeout. Less chance of ending up dead."

Ethan blinked at her, and she shrugged.

"Anyway, nice try, but I need you to stay here and watch for Rowan. I'm going to the hospital to see if I can get a peek at Liam."

He gaped. "You're going to leave me here?"

"Yep. Duty calls." She patted him on the thigh and hopped out, hoping to close the door before the daggers he was staring at her pierced her flesh.

She called the largest hospital in the area to see if Liam had been taken there.

He had.

By the time she hung up, her rideshare had shown up.

"*Come back with food!*" she heard Ethan scream at her as she stepped into the car's back seat.

She had the driver drop her off at the hospital, where she roamed the tile hallways, following signs to the morgue. She took an elevator to the lowermost level to find the corridor lights dim and flickering, making the echoey hall feel like a horror movie scene. The buzz of them sounded like angry flies.

She eyed the lights with disgust.

"Really? Kind of cliché, don't you think?" she muttered to them.

They didn't care.

Several gurneys sat parked against the walls. No bodies. That was a bonus. All she needed was a zombie to rise from beneath some sheets, and the effect would be complete.

She heard nothing but the low rumble of distant air handlers until she rounded a corner. Open double doors allowed light to splash across the hallway and against the opposite wall, brightening her mood by the *tiniest* increment. She heard a voice and paused to listen.

"How many miles did you go this morning, dude?" said a man.

There was a pause.

"*Dude.* We took A1A up to Juno, but I think one of my pedals is bent, and it was slowing my roll, *bad*, man."

Croix scowled.

Pedals?

Croix peeked into the room and spotted a middle-aged man in a white jacket sitting on a stool with a phone to his ear.

From what she could see, he was the morgue's only living resident. She remained in the hall another few minutes, listening to him wax poetic about his bike, shoes, and sports drinks—the guy could bore the peel off a banana.

She heard him end his largely one-sided conversation and had an idea worth a shot. If it didn't work, she'd wait until he had to go out for something and sneak inside then.

This looked like a job for *Georgio Sanfreddi*.

She took a deep breath and walked inside.

The man's eyes were on his phone—no doubt, he was

wondering who he could call next, like some pre-teen who got his first ten-speed for Christmas.

Croix squinted. Walking into the morgue after standing in the dim hall was like stepping on stage. The lighting felt capable of stripping the skin from her bones, and the air changed.

Chillier.

Croix wrapped her arms around her body. The smell of antiseptic cleaning products made her nose twitch.

"Hey," she said, pointing a finger gun at him. "You're the bike guy, right?"

He sat up. "Me?"

"You *bike*, right?"

He offered a crooked smile. "Yes, how'd you know?"

His chest puffed. She could tell he thought she'd guessed it from his body mass index score or something. He *was* in good shape—she had to give him that. His skin had that tight, stretchy look people with no body fat had. His eyes had that wide, eager bulge gym rats always had.

He radiated health and douchebaggery.

She glanced at the biking magazines and catalogs he had open all over the autopsy table beside him, and he offered her a sheepish grin.

"Dead giveaway, right?" he said.

She hit him with the finger gun again, figuring it was a jackass-sign language he'd understand.

"*Dead* giveaway. I get it," she said, trying to look amused.

He chuckled and nodded as if he'd meant the pun.

He hadn't. She could tell.

She clapped her hands together. "Anyway, I thought you should know they've got Georgio Sanfreddi upstairs, and he's giving out swag. *Tons of it.* You'll lose your mind, dude. His sponsors must have sent him a *crate*. I thought you'd like to know."

The man's jaw dropped a little, and he cocked his head. "Georgio...?"

She tucked in her chin to demonstrate how shocked she

was that he didn't know the name. "You know—*Georgio Sanfreddi*. The famous Italian racer. *The* Georgio Sanfreddi?"

He nodded. "Right, *right*—I know who you mean—I didn't hear you. What's he doing here?"

She smiled. Georgio Sanfreddi was a fake name she liked to use sometimes to amuse herself. It was working.

The guy was such a *tool*.

She shrugged. "I don't know, dude, but how awesome, huh? I guess he was in town for something—but as soon as I saw all the signed, uh—" She wracked her brain for what bike guys called those stupid shirts with all the logos. "—*jerseys* and stuff, I knew you'd kill yourself if you didn't know about it until it was too late."

He slid off his stool. "I appreciate it." He looked around the room and then back at her. "Do I know you?"

"I'm pretty new," she said. "I brought down a couple of the bodies?"

"You're an EMT?"

"Mm-hm." She nodded. That works. The title that had popped to mind was *orderly*, but she wasn't sure that was even a thing or if orderlies even moved bodies around. He'd given her a raise, no doubt, dubbing her EMT.

He looked around again as if trapped, and she realized why.

"You want to run up? I'll stay here for you."

He released a puff of air. "Would you?"

"Sure. What could be easier than watching over a bunch of dead people?"

"*Dude.* Thanks. I'll be right back." He took a few long strides toward the door and then turned. "What floor did you say?"

She hadn't. She wanted him to go far away, but she wasn't sure how many floors the hospital had, so she couldn't shoot too high.

"Fourth."

His brow knit. "*Maternity*?"

"Mater—" She shook her head. "Did I say fourth? I meant *fifth*."

He nodded. "Cool, cool, cool. Thanks."

He jogged out of the room.

Croix grinned.

No problem, dude.

She waited until she heard the elevator ding and then walked across the tile floors to the cold storage drawers. She tried hard not to look at the rib cutters and scalpels lined out on a tray.

What a job.

The silence alone would have driven her crazy. With every creak or tap, she'd think it was one of the bodies trying to claw out of a drawer.

She stood in front of the stainless steel unit and took a deep breath.

Okay, Liam, where are you?

She pulled out the first drawer to find an old woman on the slab.

Nope.

She got lucky on her third try. Liam lay there, much paler than the last time she'd seen him. His bloody shirt looked like it had been run through a meat grinder.

"Holy..."

She found a pair of gloves and put one on to lift the material of his ruined polo out of the way. She counted at least six stab wounds. A couple in his sides, at least three in his chest.

Not an accident.

That was for sure. Not unless he fell on a knife half a dozen times from several different angles. He'd have to be quite the klutz.

She checked his hands and found two, maybe three, defensive wounds. It was hard to tell with all the blood. Someone had come at him in a fury and not let up.

This wasn't a robbery or a hit.

This was *passion*.

She closed the drawer and jogged out of the room. As she stepped into the hall, she heard the elevator ding.

Shit.

Douchy McDoucherson had come back early.

She sprinted in the other direction and found fire escape stairs, which she took two at a time to the main floor. Walking briskly from the building, she kept moving until she was a couple of blocks away.

She didn't think he'd seen her leave, but she didn't want to chance him running after her, all big-lunged and chock full of electrolytes.

She called a car and, en route, called Ethan to check in at the police station.

He hadn't seen any sign of Rowan.

"But I need *food*," he reminded her.

"Soon," she assured him as the car pulled into the driveway of Shee's rental home. "Stop being such a baby."

She hung up and knocked on the door. Shee answered and scowled at her as she entered.

"What are you doing here?" she asked.

"I checked on Liam. Stabbed. I counted six times, maybe more—a *lot* of blood. Defensive wounds on both hands."

"So it was a fight," said Shee, her gaze wandering like it did when she was thinking.

Croix nodded. "It was a *fury*. Big knife, too, jibes with the one we saw in Rowan's hand. Kitchen knife."

Shee snapped back to the present. "Where's Ethan?"

"I left him at the cop shop," she said, opening the refrigerator. She was *starving*. "Looks like they're keeping her."

Shee groaned. "We need to talk to her."

"Why? If she's arrested, isn't our job here done?"

"*No*, because we still have no proof she's Portia."

Croix rolled her eyes. "She walked out of a house covered in blood with a knife in her hand."

"Yes—"

"There was a dead guy inside—"

"Yes—"

"With stabbies all over him."

Shee huffed. "But isn't that what's wrong?"

Croix blinked at her, and Shee sighed like she did when she knew everything and couldn't figure out why everyone else *didn't*.

It was annoying.

Shee proceeded to tell her why she was an idiot.

"This woman is so good at what she does that she's popped up on the FBI's radar. She's gotten away with stuff so many times that it has ceased to be the problem of local law enforcement and is about to go federal."

"So?" asked Croix, unwrapping a package of American cheese. At this point, she knew where Shee was going with her story, but sometimes, it was fun to act as stupid as possible and let her talk.

Shee threw out her hands. "*So*, this *professional* sloppily stabs a man to death and runs outside with the knife in her hand? That doesn't seem weird to you?"

Croix pushed a rolled piece of cheese into her mouth. "It *was* sloppy."

Shee's agitation seemed to drain from her body. "*So* sloppy."

"Maybe Rowan wanted it to look *so* stupid no one would believe she's Portia," said Mason, suddenly appearing behind Shee.

He must have been standing nearby, but Croix hadn't seen him. For a big man, he moved like a cat. It was kind of scary, really.

Shee's head bounced from side to side as she considered his comment. "That's all fine and dandy unless she goes to jail. It only takes one murder charge to ruin your day. Why would she risk it?"

Croix and Mason shrugged in unison.

"Bottom line is we need to talk to her," finished Shee.

"How do we do that if they're keeping her?" asked Croix.

Shee thought for a moment.

"*We* be her attorney," she said.

"But we're not attorneys," said Mason.

Shee chewed her lip. "That *is* the problem, isn't it?"

"How does it work? Who would she have made her one call to? Is that a real thing?" asked Croix.

"Can't you make a sandwich?" asked Mason, motioning to the loose lunchmeat and cheese in Croix's hand.

"It becomes a sandwich in my stomach," Croix explained.

Shee backward-smacked Mason on his chest. "Like *you* don't pick at the meat."

Mason rolled his eyes and looked away. Croix nodded. She'd seen him do it. He was always picking things out of the refrigerator to feed that big *Terminator* body of his.

Shee perked. "Her *mother*. That's who she'd call. She has a mother in Texas."

"Portia has a mother?" asked Mason.

"Do you have a full name for the mother?" asked Croix. "Address? Town? *Mom* doesn't narrow it down. We don't even know if they have the same last name."

"Well, it's a place to start. Call Ethan. Get him to do his computer thing."

"He's a hacker, not a magician."

Shee glowered. "Just *call him*."

Croix wandered away to make the call.

Ethan sounded as agitated as Shee.

"You didn't ask me what I want," he said instead of *hello*.

Croix scowled. "What are you talking about?"

"You didn't ask me what food I want."

"You're *obsessed*. Stop thinking about food for five seconds. Shee needs your help."

She knew he idolized Shee and dropped her name to shut him up.

"What does she need?" he asked.

All business once again. As expected.

"She said Rowan's got a mom in Texas—"

"Misty Riley," said Ethan.

It took a moment for Croix to process.

"That's her mom? Misty?"

"Yep. Lives outside of Lubbock."

"How the hell do you know that?"

"You think I didn't already check her Facebook connections? What do you pay me for?"

Croix scoffed. "I don't pay you shit."

"*Loggerhead* pays me."

Croix looked at Shee. "Are we *paying* him?"

Shee shrugged.

Croix returned to the phone.

"Do you have Misty's phone number?"

"Sure—"

"Text it to me."

"Done," said Ethan. "Hey, seriously, they are going to pay me, right? I never actually asked—"

Croix hung up. "I've got her mother's phone number."

Shee motioned for Croix to hand her the phone and then dialed with the phone on speaker. She set it on the kitchen table as a woman with a voice ravaged by years of smoking answered.

"Mrs. Riley?" asked Shee.

"Story's for sale. I'm not taking less than half a million," said the woman.

"I'm sorry?"

"You're another reporter, right? You want the exclusive? The bidding is at half a million."

Shee pointed at the phone, cocking an eyebrow at both Mason and Croix to silently convey, *getta load of this piece of work.*

"No, ma'am, my name is Shee. I'm a friend of your daughter's."

The woman cleared her throat. "A friend? She didn't tell me about any friends."

"We met pretty recently."

"What do you want?"

"I was wondering if she has an attorney. I wanted to help."

"You want to pay for one, or you *are* one?"

"I had someone in mind—"

Misty Riley coughed. "I got her someone. He's working for free."

"*Free*? You know you can't have a contingency situation on a defense trial. There's no *winnings* for him to take half of."

The woman scoffed. "For the *exposure*. He knows she'll end up on TV or something—big splashy murder in Palm Beach like that. He'll get his piece out of the book deal, probably."

Shee shook her head. "When is he going to see her?"

"Tomorrow."

"Do you know what time?"

"Late afternoon. He couldn't get there any earlier. He's flying in. He's *that* big a deal. Robert Halcyon. Seems like a nice guy, too." She sniffed. "But if you want to hire her someone better, you can send me the money here, and I'll hire him for her."

Shee smirked. "Sure, can you give me your address?"

The woman paused as if even *she* was surprised the line had worked and shared her address.

"Thanks," said Shee. "I'll be in touch soon. You stay strong."

Misty started coughing again.

Shee hung up and let her head fall back to gape at the ceiling.

"Wow. I know where my vote for *Mom of the Year* is going now. She's already selling the rights to her daughter's story, got her a shady free lawyer, and tried to shake me down."

"It's pretty impressive, I've gotta say," agreed Croix.

"Either of you ever hear of *Robert Halcyon*? Is he one of those celebrity ambulance chasers?"

Croix and Mason both shrugged.

"I'm on it," said Croix. She didn't need Ethan for this search—the name was odd enough that she suspected there weren't too many lawyers who had it. She searched on her phone and found a likely suspect.

"I've got him. He's based out of New York."

Shee scowled. "New York? So he's licensed in Florida?

Maybe Texas, too?"

Croix shrugged and gave Shee the phone number. She dialed, setting the phone on speaker again so they could listen.

Halcyon's assistant answered, and Shee asked to speak to the man himself.

"He's traveling and unavailable today," said the woman.

"He's on his way to Rowan Riley?"

The woman paused. "Can I ask who's calling?"

"I'm a good friend of Rowan's. I have information for Mr. Halcyon I think will help her case."

"Mm-hm. I see. If you give me your number, I'll pass along the message."

"If I could talk to him—"

"That's not possible. He'll get back to you if he feels it's necessary. Just one second—"

Hold music played, and Shee hung up.

"That was going nowhere," she said.

She tapped the phone against her chest.

"How do we get him to help us?" she murmured.

"I could *coerce* him, maybe?" suggested Mason.

Shee chuckled. "Thanks, but this is more of a scalpel operation."

Mason straightened. "I *am* a scalpel."

"At war, you're a scalpel. Here, you're a bazooka. We can't walk him to Rowan at gunpoint or with a broken arm."

"Not to mention, I hear threatening officers of the court is pretty illegal," said Croix. "Especially without Mick around to dig us out of trouble."

Shee nodded. "Another excellent point."

"We can dig something up on him? Little blackmail?" suggested Croix.

Shee squinted at her. "Did you say he's from New York? Isn't that strange?"

Croix admitted it was. "I figured he'd be from Texas if he got hold of Rowan's mom that fast."

Shee nodded. "That's what I was thinking. I guess we have

two things working for us—one, we know he's coming from New York, so we can reasonably figure out what plane he took to get to Palm Beach Airport."

"I'll get Ethan to run down the possibilities. He's bored anyway."

"Good."

"What's two?" asked Mason.

"If he isn't local, it's safe to say the cops don't know what he looks like."

"So? You want Mason or Ethan to impersonate him?"

She shrugged. "Well, I can't—"

"And I can't," said Croix. "But Ethan looks like he's thirteen, and *in-the-field* stuff isn't his thing. And Mason—"

The ladies turned to look at him.

"He looks like he *ate* a lawyer," said Croix.

Mason frowned. "I could be a lawyer."

"It *would* be funny to see you squeeze into a suit," said Shee.

Mason snapped his tongue against his tooth. "I'll have you know I look very good in my suit, thank you very much." He sighed. "Still—I'll admit, espionage isn't really my thing. You two are better at that."

"But we've got these damn boobs and stuff," said Shee. She perked at the same moment the answer hit Croix.

"*Ollie*," said Croix.

Shee nodded. "I almost forgot we have a perfectly good conman living half an hour away."

CHAPTER TWENTY-FOUR

Ollie got the call from Shee and packed his most lawyer-like suit. He'd been feeling a little left behind and was happy to be useful.

He'd been showing their latest recruit, Shiva, around the area, but then Angelina swept in and talked the girl into teaching her how to cook Indian food. Shiva was like some kind of brooding wild animal—he'd never dreamed she possessed *domestic* skills—but now the whole first floor smelled like exotic spices, and Angelina had noticed.

Next thing he knew, he was out, and Angelina was in.

He gathered up his case and suit bag and headed to his car. Angelina sat at her concierge desk in the lobby, poking around on her laptop. With Croix away from her station at reception, Angelina had to serve as the Loggerhead Inn's manager, concierge, and check-in. That was on top of her duties taking over for Shee's recently passed dad, Mick—finding them new missions and getting them out of trouble when needed.

Oh, and stealing his new work buddy for cooking lessons.

"Stop goofing around and get to work," he said as he passed her.

Archie, Mason's dog, looked up from his place at Angelina's feet, and Angelina's miniature Yorkie, Harley, popped up from the pillow bed on the desk.

"It's terrible. I don't know *what* to do with all my free time," drawled Angelina as he walked through the front door.

He put his bags in his car and was about to get in and leave when he thought it might be nice to tell Shiva he'd be gone a couple of days.

I mean, she might miss me. Right?

It seemed rude not to tell her...

He went back inside.

"Have you seen your cooking buddy around? I want to let her know I'll be gone a couple of days."

Angelina looked up from her laptop.

"Why? Where are you going?"

"Shee called. They need me to impersonate a lawyer."

Angelina scowled. "Nobody told me that."

"Did you have something better for me to do?"

She shook her head. "No. Things have been slow on the *mission procurement* end of things lately. Thank goodness for Snookie, or we'd be broke." She sighed, seemingly lost in her thoughts.

He imagined she was thinking about Mick. They all missed the old man for various reasons, but Shee, his daughter, and Angelina, his girlfriend, had it the worst.

He gave her a moment, and a few seconds later, she looked up as if she'd forgotten he was there.

"What did you need?" she asked.

"Shiva."

"Oh. No. I don't know. I haven't seen her."

He nodded and made his way down the hall to Shiva's room. When she didn't answer his knock, he walked to the back porch to scan the yard. Their resident *landscaper-slash-sniper*, Trimmer, sat on the step enjoying his mid-morning snack.

It looked horrific.

"What is that brown mess?" he asked.

Trimmer squinted up at him. "Beans on toast."

"It's like a carb nightmare."

Trimmer used his toast to cheer him as if it were a glass of champagne. "You haven't lived, mate."

"Have you seen Shiva?" he asked.

Trimmer nodded. "She's in my shed."

Ollie squinted at the wooden structure by the river. Trimmer lived above it. Below was where he kept all his gardening supplies and occasionally prepared the bodies of enemies for *disappearing*.

If the hotel guests knew half the things that went on at Loggerhead...

"She's alive, right?" he asked, only half kidding.

Trimmer shrugged. "Last I saw her, but I can't make any promises."

Ollie scowled. "What is she doing in there?"

"You wouldn't believe me if I told you."

Certain he'd get no additional information from their taciturn landscaper, Ollie jogged down the porch stairs and walked down the path to the shed. As he stepped inside, he opened his eyes wide to adjust to the dim light.

That's when he spotted her.

Shiva lay on her back in the middle of the cavernous room. Her trademark long dark braid snaked away from her body, stretching across the wooden floorboards. When she'd first arrived, the braid remained wrapped close to her head. In the last few days, she'd let it fall.

Ollie figured that was a good sign.

There were other things that didn't bode as well, though— like the fact she was tossing knives at the ceiling. There had to be thirty silver throwing knives embedded in the wood above her supine body, dangling like Damocles's swords.

"What the hell are you doing?" he asked.

Her eyes bounced in his direction. "Practicing."

"Practicing throwing knives while laying on your back?"

"Yes."

"That a skill that comes up a lot?"

She shrugged. "You would be surprised."

He strolled a little closer—though not *too* close.

"Trimmer knows you're chipping away at his ceiling?"

She tossed another knife, and it stuck. "He doesn't mind."

"And what happens when they fall?"

The corner of her mouth curled, looking dangerously like a smile.

"That's the part that requires skill. That, and the *art*," she said.

"The art?"

She motioned to the ceiling, and Ollie tilted his head to gain something closer to her view. From that angle, he could see she'd thrown the knives in the shape of a smiley face.

He rubbed his temples.

What am I doing with these people?

He thrust his hands into his pockets.

"Cute. Look, I've got to help Shee with a thing. I wanted to let you know I'd be gone a couple of days."

She paused in mid-throw. "Why? Where are you going?"

"I have to pretend to be a lawyer in Palm Beach."

She sat up. "I am bored."

"I thought you were teaching Angelina how to cook?"

Shiva rolled her eyes. "She is maybe better at Italian."

"Hm. Problem is, I don't think Shee needs anyone *pincushioned* for this one. You might as well stay here."

She shrugged. "Or I might as well come with you."

Shiva's leg swept to the left, and the knife appeared stuck into the floorboard where her shin had been.

Ollie hadn't even seen it falling. He shook his head.

"That is the *skill*," she reminded him.

"I can see that now." He glanced at his watch. "I'm packed. You'd have to be ready to go in like five minutes—"

She jumped to her feet. "Give me ten. I want to shower."

She strode out of the shed without another word. Ollie remained, eyeing the knives. One dislodged and fell to the floor, tip embedded in the wood, standing tall like a little silver soldier.

He supposed he had ten minutes to spare.

What was he going to do? Say *no*? Deny a woman who dodged falling knives for fun?

He turned to stroll back to the hotel.

"I see you found her," said Trimmer as he passed him on the porch.

"Yep." Ollie paused. "I wouldn't spend much time in the middle of your shed there for a while."

Trimmer swallowed a bite of toast.

"Noted."

CHAPTER TWENTY-FIVE

Shee and Mason dropped Croix with Ethan at his police station stakeout. The kids could keep an eye on Rowan, work on Robert Halcyon's background check and flight schedule. They had to make a quick detour on the way—Croix insisted they get food first so Ethan didn't whine about how hungry he was the whole time.

"What now?" asked Mason.

"I'm thinking we take a peek at Rowan's and Liam's," said Shee.

"I imagine the cops have already done a number on both."

Shee had to agree. "Yeah, but it's worth a shot."

They reached Rowan's condo to find yellow crime tape crisscrossing the entrance. Mason pulled a small knife from his pocket and cut the tape clean to unseal the door.

"You weren't wrong. Cops were here, all right," said Shee, picking the lock.

The door popped open.

"You do that like you've done it before," said Mason as they entered.

She chuckled. "Once or twice." She turned. "You know what? I also know something the cops don't. Rowan had a book of conquests."

"A *what*?"

Shee headed for the bedroom. "She said she kept a book with all her conquests listed, hidden behind her bureau."

Mason followed her. "And she told you about it? She's only known you for a few days. Isn't it weird she's so loose-lipped about her dirty deeds?"

"In all fairness, I pretended to be cut from the same cloth and got her drunk. Plus, I think it's how she defines herself. She brags about it."

"Still. Doesn't seem very Portia-like."

Shee shrugged. "Could be that's the point. I suspect this book doesn't have any mention of the—"

She stopped. Rowan's bedroom bureau sat shifted away from the wall. Someone had unscrewed and removed the back panel.

"They found it," she said.

"The cops?"

Shee squatted to feel around the back of the bureau to be sure nothing remained hidden.

"Sure looks like it. But how did they know to look *here*? Doesn't that seem a little *thorough*?"

Mason shrugged. "Well, she did kill someone."

"*Allegedly*. Still. They didn't cut her sofa cushions, knock through her walls, or anything else over the top. Why would they think to take the back of the bureau off unless they knew what they'd find?"

"She must have told them."

"Why? That would be *insane* to give them *evidence* she's a predator."

"Maybe someone turned on her." Mason crossed his arms across his chest. "She told *you* about the book. She probably bragged about it to a lot of people."

"You think they already have someone turning evidence against her? How could that be? They *literally* just picked up Liam's body."

"Maybe a jealous friend came forward? A neighbor? Her mom? Liam?"

Shee snorted. "With his dying breath?"

"Seems unlikely. What about that waitress?"

Shee shook her head. "No. She didn't seem to know anything more than what she saw at the bar. None of this makes any sense."

Shee's phone rang, and she answered it.

"Are you still going to break into Liam's?" asked Croix.

"That's the plan. We're finishing up with Rowan's now."

"See if you can get his IP address. Get Rowan's while you're there. Is her computer there?"

Shee looked at Mason. "Look for a computer."

The two of them moved around the small apartment, finding nothing.

"The police have already been here. If she had a computer, they took it."

"Okay. Get the IP of her router, at least. Any username or passwords maybe she jotted down at a desk? Could come in handy."

"Will do."

Shee hung up, and she and Mason spent another fifteen minutes picking through the apartment. Short of cutting open the cushions and walls, there weren't too many untouched places to look. Shee couldn't find a router. Either the police had taken *all* her electronics, or the woman didn't have a computer, WIFI, or—"

Shee turned to scan the living room again.

"There's no television."

Mason looked around. "The police took it?"

"Why?" She scanned the room again. "There's no place that looks like there *used* to be a television."

Mason grunted. "She lives like someone not planning on staying long."

Shee had to agree. "Let's try Liam's."

They drove to Liam's neighborhood and walked through his side gate to the back of the house. From there, they gained access to the attached garage, allowing them time to break into the house through the connecting door without being seen by the nosey neighbors.

Like Rowan's, the house felt picked over.

"I don't think we'll find anything useful here, either," whispered Shee.

"Why are you whispering?"

She cleared her throat.

"It might be them," she said, pointing to bloody footprints on the tile floor leading toward the front door.

She entered the bedroom and stopped at the threshold to point at a pool of drying blood.

"Or that."

Mason came up behind her to peer over her shoulder.

"Looks like we found the scene of the crime," he said.

She moved closer and pointed to the wall.

"Cast-off droplets. Lots of stabbing went on here."

Mason nodded. "Lots of *bleeding*."

Shee stepped over the mess and checked the bathroom. The shower was still wet.

"Seems like Rowan *had* been taking a shower."

"Doesn't mean she didn't get out to stab him."

Shee glanced into a closet and noted one corner had nothing hanging in it. She motioned to it.

"Empty spot. Maybe Joy's clothes were there," she said. She stepped inside for a quick look and noticed an odd lump in a pile of folded shorts. Moving a few pairs aside, she spotted black plastic and pulled out a laptop.

She held it up for Mason to see.

"They missed it?" he asked.

"I guess so. This place doesn't look as turned over as Rowan's. I'm thinking they're coming back to do a better pass."

"Great. I'm glad our hair and prints will be all over the place. We should go."

She nodded and held up the computer. "Let's take this."

His nose wrinkled. "Do we want to mess with their evidence?"

"Just a *little*," she said, pinching the air. "We can return it to them if we find something useful."

They made a quick pass through the house and wiped down the door and knob as they left.

Shee called Croix from Mason's truck.

"We found a computer at Liam's. I'll bring it to you," she told the girl.

"Great. We've got some news, too. Robert Halcyon has worked on other cases."

"I would hope so."

"No, I mean other *Portia* cases. That list Snookie gave us with possible matches? He's worked with the suspects of four we've been able to confirm so far."

Shee's jaw slipped open.

"You're saying he's Portia's personal attorney?"

"Kinda looks like that."

"But he doesn't represent *her*."

"No. The patsies. The ones that didn't survive to make it to trial or otherwise went missing."

Shee felt her blood run cold. "And he's about to meet with Rowan."

"Yep. He's on the way—probably get to her around three."

Shee took a deep breath. "We've got to warn her."

Croix scoffed. "If you like her alive. *Yep*."

CHAPTER TWENTY-SIX

Snookie balanced herself on the seawall rocks as the officer lifted the sheet. She'd come to see what some teenager had found while looking for a place to neck with her boyfriend.

Poor thing was probably scarred for life. After stumbling over rotting human remains on her way to get some lovin', she'd probably throw up every time she heard a love song for the foreseeable future.

"That could be our girl," said Snookie, though what she saw didn't resemble a human at all.

The remains looked more like a soggy loaf of bread. The legs, arms, and head were all missing—the stumps ragged where sea life enjoyed buffets. It seemed odd for all the extremities to be missing, but who knew? Sharks, turtles, sea life—the body had bumped around the ocean floor and bobbed in the sun since Joy disappeared—maybe even longer if it wasn't her.

Was it Joy? Hard to tell. The location of the discovery fit. The sex and size fit, but Snookie wasn't sure she'd recognize her *own* body if all she had to work with was neck to crotch, waterlogged and picked over by crabs. They'd need science to be sure.

The officer with her nodded. "Female, but that's about all we've got to go on at this point. No tats or other markings. No, uh, teeth or fingerprints, obviously."

"Obviously." Snookie nodded and pulled her phone from

her suit jacket to call the closest FBI field office.

She felt a wave of self-awareness, wearing a suit in the South Florida sun. She wasn't an FBI agent anymore—she was something both less than and better—she didn't have to wear the suit.

Old habits died hard.

"I'll see if I can help you speed up the DNA," she said.

The cop nodded.

Snookie wandered away from the torso to make her call. The body stunk. She'd rushed from the Loggerhead as soon as she got the call, but even she couldn't move faster than the sun. It had been early in the morning when she got the call, and she felt bad asking Shee and Mason to wake up when she was only half an hour away. Those two had a lot on their plate, and she thought her *official* presence might move things along.

She cracked her neck as she talked to one of the agents. She could tell this one had heard of her, which was always nice. A little respect. They agreed to have an FBI tech handle the identification.

The problem was there was no guarantee Joy was in the system. In fact, she felt pretty sure they *didn't* have Joy Zabić's DNA on file. She'd looked into the woman, and Joy hadn't been the sort who had DNA on file with the justice system.

They'd need some of Joy's DNA to match it to Torso's. That was the bitch of DNA, wasn't it? You could have forty thousand miles of chromosomes, but all the heads, legs, and torsos were useless unless you had the match.

When she finished the rush job on the DNA, Snookie called Shee.

"Hey, in your travels, have you found anything poor Joy might have touched?" she asked when Shee answered.

"*Joy*? No. Why?"

"We've got a floater. Could be her, but it's hard to tell. I need some Joy DNA for comparison."

"Where'd you find it? Where are you?"

"She's on the rocks. I'm here. Little farther south than you but same general area."

Snookie wiped her forehead with the back of her hand.

And sweating my lady balls off in this suit. What was I thinking?

"Can't you do it with her teeth?" asked Shee.

"No head."

"*No head*?"

"No legs or arms either. Just a torso."

"Yikes. That must be pretty."

"Whoever she is, she's had better days."

Shee paused and then added, "Deliberate? Or she lost limbs to sharks or propellers or something?"

Snookie smiled.

Shee was sharp for a civilian.

She'd been wondering the same thing. It seemed convenient that Torso-Joy was missing everything that could identify her.

"Don't know yet," she said. "It all looks pretty ragged, I can tell you that much. Could have easily been a shark, et al. Could have been an *alien* attack at this point. I'll know more in a day or two."

"Okay. What can we do?"

Snookie thought about giving her the laundry list she had in her head but decided against it. People warned her retirement would bore her to death, and she hadn't believed them.

She believed them now. She didn't want to hand things over to Shee.

I'm having too much fun.

"Tell you what, I'm here. I'll go check Joy's apartment and see if I can find a hairbrush or something."

"You sure? If you give us the address, we can swing by," said Shee.

"Nah. I'll do it *officially*." She paused as a thought occurred to her. "Nothing of hers is at Liam's?"

"No. Just a hole in a closet where her clothes might have been—'well, actually, that's not entirely true. We found a laptop that might be hers. We're not sure yet. I'm going to have Ethan crack it for us."

"You found it at Liam's?"

"Right."

"So you took evidence—*nope*. Nevermind. I'm sorry. You're breaking up. I didn't hear any of that. I'll let you know how the DNA goes."

Shee laughed. "Sounds good."

Snookie hung up, shaking her head, and headed for Joy's apartment. When she reached it, she felt underwhelmed. The building wasn't impressive. She'd expected something nicer. She wasn't sure why—maybe since Joy was pretty and hobnobbed with dermatologists.

Snookie stopped at the office and introduced herself.

"I need to take a look at apartment two-oh-nine," she said.

The woman looked confused. "I can't just let you in there."

"This is an official investigation."

"Okay, but I'd have to get permission from the current occupants."

Now it was Snookie's turn to be confused. "There are new people in there already?"

She nodded. "It was empty. We didn't see the point in leaving it empty."

"Empty?"

She nodded. "Movers came. Then cleaners."

"By cleaners, you mean someone moved out all her stuff, and then *you* had it cleaned? There's no chance of me finding anything interesting in there from her time?"

"No—*she* had it cleaned."

"*Joy* did?"

"No, I guess not *her*, since, *you know*. I guess whoever picked up her stuff did it."

"You don't know who sent the movers?"

The woman shook her head.

"So—and I apologize for being slow, but I want to make sure I got this right. Joy went missing. *The next day*, movers came and took all her stuff, followed by cleaners who cleaned the apartment, and then you rented it to a new customer."

"Yes. I don't know if it was the next day—I don't know when exactly she went missing and when I read about it in the paper."

"That's how you found out about her?"

The woman nodded. "They cleaned out the place the same day I saw it in the paper."

Snookie frowned.

That had to be the day after she went missing.

"Who let the movers in?" she asked.

"I don't know. No one asked me."

"You were working that day?"

She nodded.

Snookie scowled as she tried to think what was left to ask and then perked with an idea.

"Ooh, was there a damage deposit? Who picked up that? Who signed off? Anyone?"

The woman shook her head. "No one."

"And you're sure? Maybe someone else processed that paperwork?"

"I'm the owner. I'd know."

"Hm." Snookie chewed on her lip and glanced up at the apartment building through the office window.

"So, if I was looking for Joy's DNA, I'm not going to find it anywhere. No storage unit left behind, nothing in the apartment."

"Nope." She chuckled. "It was the cleanest apartment we've ever had vacated. It was great—I mean, I don't mean to be rude, but this is how we make our living. Empty apartments cost us money."

Snookie sighed. "I got it. Okay. Thanks."

She stepped outside into the sun and slipped on her glasses.

She wasn't sure where to go next.

"Where can I find a little Joy?" she murmured.

CHAPTER TWENTY-SEVEN

Croix stood in the airport holding up the sign with *Robert Halcyon* written in large block letters. She felt confident the lawyer's flight from New York had landed safely, but she'd feel better when the guy *appeared*.

And then he *did*.

A chubby man with a goatee glanced at her as he rode the escalator to the luggage area. He did a doubletake on the sign.

Gotcha.

This Halcyon, the one riding the escalator to retrieve his luggage, barely looked like the photos Croix and Ethan had been studying. This version was exasperated, agitated, and older because, like everyone, he'd taken one decent photo ten years ago and left it on his website for life. Croix knew local real estate agents who looked thirty in their ads and like *mummies* in real life.

She held the sign a little higher. Halcyon toddled to her, a deep scowl on his face.

"Robert Halcyon?" she asked as he approached.

"Yes?"

"I'm your driver."

He shook his head. "I didn't request a car."

She shrugged. "I guess someone ordered it for you?"

He shook his head. "I *rented* a car."

"Well, now you don't have to," said Croix as perkily as possible.

He waved her off. "No, this isn't right. I don't want a ride. I want a *car*. Thank you, anyway."

Croix watched him walk away, her sign lowering until it touched the ground.

Crap.

She called Ollie.

"It didn't work."

"What do you mean it didn't work?" he asked. "Failure is not an option."

"Failure is all I got. He doesn't want the free ride. He wants his own car. He rented one."

"You couldn't talk him into going with you," said Ollie, the disappointment thick in his voice. A statement—not a question.

Croix scowled. "*No.*"

Ollie clucked his tongue.

"*Shut up.* He'd already rented a car. There wasn't anything I could do."

"Okay. Plan B. *Follow him.* He'll want to check in at his hotel before he goes to Rowan. We'll figure it out from there."

He hung up, and she jogged after the lawyer, watching him from a safe distance until she saw from what company he'd rented his car. She called Ethan and told him to meet her at the car lot exit. She shadowed Halcyon to the lot and then jogged out to find Ethan.

"He picked a white BMW. Should be coming out any second," she said, climbing into the Jeep.

They waited until the BMW pulled out and followed him to his hotel. Ollie had guessed that bit right—the man *did* want to check in before he headed to his new client.

Ethan parked, and she called Ollie, who'd been waiting near the police station to start his career as Robert Halcyon.

"He rented a white BMW," Croix said after letting Ollie know Halcyon's hotel.

"Sit tight," said Ollie. "We'll be there in a second. Don't let him get back in his car. Think you can handle that?"

Croix growled and hung up.

Smartass.

"What's wrong?" asked Ethan.

"Ollie's effing with me."

She scowled at the BMW. They'd parked nearby, where they could see through the glass entryway and down the long hall leading to the hotel elevators inside. As soon as Halcyon stepped off the elevator and headed for the parking garage, they'd see him coming.

"We can't let him get back in his car," said Croix.

Ethan looked at her. "Ollie said that?"

"*I* said that."

"Okay, so how do we stop him? Tackle him?"

Croix sighed. "I'll worry about that if it comes up. I'm hoping Ollie will be here before that." She paused and cocked her head. "He said *we.*"

"Hm?"

"He said *we'll be there. We.* He's with someone."

"Snookie?"

"Maybe."

She didn't think it was Snookie, though. She suspected Shiva was coming with him—that's why he was acting like a tough guy on the phone. He was showing off. He'd taken stupid Shiva under his wing—

She looked away.

Stop it.

She felt like a jealous woman, and that wasn't it. Ollie was twenty years older than her. She didn't have a crush on him *that* way—which was good because she'd accidentally caught a glimpse of those scars on his abdomen—and he'd all but said *that* kind of relationship wasn't in the cards for him anymore anyway.

She didn't know.

She didn't *want* to know.

She just kind of *missed* him—as a friend.

She glanced at Ethan, who had pushed his seat back to work on the laptop Shee'd found at Liam's.

She had Ethan to pal around with now, she supposed. Something was maybe going on between them, but she wasn't sure about that yet, either.

He *was* cute...

"Making any progress?" she asked.

He nodded. "I'm in. It's weird, though."

"The computer's weird?"

"It's empty."

"Empty? Like, wiped?"

"No. There's the bare minimum here, and I found some emails Shee will want to see, but there's no *life* to it—no saved docs or evidence it's been used on a regular basis.

"Maybe she just used it for email?"

"That's another thing. The emails are saved as files in a directory called *Rowan*. They didn't originally come to this computer at all—they were moved here and saved."

"Like someone wanted them found."

"That's what it looks like. I'm not finding anything else hidden." He sighed. "It's weird."

A car crept up the aisle toward them.

"Flash the lights," said Croix.

Ethan did.

The car pulled into a spot and parked. A moment later, Ollie appeared, and Croix got out to meet him. By the time she had, Shiva had appeared next to him.

Croix scowled.

I knew it.

Shiva wore camo pants, boots, and a tank top that exposed a collection of scars scattered across her long brown arms.

Psycho.

She looked like she'd just stormed a desert bunker.

Croix rolled her eyes and, skipping the niceties, pointed to the lawyer's rental.

"This is his car," she said.

Ollie held out his arms. "What, no hug?"

Croix felt her face grow hot.

"Shut *up*," she muttered.

He lowered his arms to put his hands on his hips.

"Really? Seems like you might need one since you failed to get Halcyon into your car."

"Oh *snap*," said Ethan, who'd lowered the driver's side window to listen.

Croix shot the hacker a look and turned back to Ollie.

"Okay, smart guy. What are we going to do? He's been gone for about twenty minutes. He could be back any second."

Ollie pulled at his ducktail beard. "First off, we make sure no matter what happens, he's late to his meeting with Rowan. *Very* late."

"How do we do that?"

Ollie looked at Shiva and nodded back at the lawyer's car.

"Do your thing," he said.

Without comment or a ripple of human emotion, Shiva pulled a throwing knife from—Croix didn't know where. It appeared in her hand like a magician's card trick. With a flick of her wrist, she tossed the dagger into the sidewall of the man's rear tire.

The tire deflated, picking up speed when Shiva plucked the blade from the rubber.

Croix felt her mood darken. Stupid Shiva was so damn *cool*—and strange AF.

Total freak.

"Uh oh, looks like he's got a flat. He's going to need a ride," said Ollie, picking up the slack because, *obviously*, Shiva was too *weird* to talk.

He looked at Croix. "Wouldn't it be fantastic luck if—the moment he realizes he has a flat—the driver who tried to pick him up at the airport appeared, dropping off another customer?"

He motioned to Ethan.

"Don't you think that would be great, Mr. Customer?"

"What luck!" agreed Ethan, grinning.

Croix glowered at the two of them.

"So, I offer the ride again?" she asked.

"Yes, and this time, make sure it works."

Ollie smiled.

She didn't change her expression.

He continued.

"Then, like we planned to do the *first* time, you drive him *far* in the wrong direction to give me the time to do my thing."

Croix nodded. "Got it."

"He's coming," said Ethan.

Ollie tapped Shiva's arm with the back of his hand.

"Take the car. Meet me out front."

She nodded and headed back to their vehicle.

"What are you doing?" asked Croix.

"Get in the car. Pretend you're dropping Ethan off."

Ethan scrambled into the passenger seat as Ollie jogged to the door leading into the hotel.

Croix hopped in the driver's seat. From there, she saw Ollie heading down the hallway toward Halcyon. Ollie's head hung down as if he were looking at his phone.

The two men collided.

"*Oh!*" yipped Ethan at the collision. "That looked like it *hurt.*"

Croix maneuvered out of the parking spot to make it look as if she'd just arrived. By the time she had a clear view of the hallway again, Halcyon was almost to them.

Ollie was at the far end of the hall, grinning, holding up something, and pointing at it.

Croix squinted.

A phone?

Ah. It hit her.

Halcyon's phone.

Ollie had pickpocketed the man.

As Halcyon entered the garage, Croix and Ethan waited. The lawyer opened his car, got inside, turned it on, and began to pull out of his parking spot.

He hadn't gone three feet before his brake lights flared to life.

He'd felt the flat.

Halcyon lumbered out of the car to stare at the tire.

He swore.

"That's our cue," said Croix.

Ethan got out of the car and walked into the hotel like he'd just been dropped off.

Croix crept the Jeep forward and lowered her window.

"Hi again," she said. "Fancy meeting you here. I just dropped someone else here."

The fuming lawyer blinked at her and then pointed. "I know you. You were my ride at the airport, right?"

She reached into her back seat to retrieve the sign she'd had when he last saw her.

"Me with the sign. I see you got your car."

He scowled. "I did. And now it's got a flat tire."

"Really?"

He nodded and then cocked his head, eyeing her Jeep.

Croix fought not to look smug.

That's it. You can do it...

"Can I still get that ride?" he asked.

Ding ding ding! We have a winner!

Croix felt her nerves tingle with excitement. Damn... Ollie had made completing this mission seem like winning the lottery.

"Sure. Where do you need to go?"

"The police station downtown."

"No problem," said Croix, grinning. "Hop in."

The man inched his lame car back into its spot and clambered into the back of the Jeep.

"You know the way?" he asked as they left the parking garage.

"*Sure*," she said, turning toward parts unknown. Without his phone, Halcyon wouldn't be able to check her progress.

She smirked.

Thanks, Ollie.

CHAPTER TWENTY-EIGHT

"Look what I have," said Ollie, shaking Halcyon's phone as he hopped into the car.

"It is a phone," said Shiva.

"Ah, but not just *any* phone. It's *Halcyon's* phone, and look what he has tucked into the case."

He held up Halcyon's driver's license.

Shiva nodded. "Very nice. You are a very sneaky man."

"Thank you. I don't know if I love the word *sneaky*, but I'll take it as a compliment."

"That is your prerogative," said Shiva.

Ollie side-eyed her.

"Do you want me to come with you inside the police station?" she asked.

"Looking like an extra from *Commando*? No, thanks. I've got it."

Shiva looked down at her clothes but didn't say anything.

Ollie drove to the nearby police station, left Shiva in the car, and entered the Spanish-style building.

He'd worn what he thought was a very lawyer-y suit and *felt* like a lawyer. He approached the attending officer and let him know he was there to see Rowan Riley.

The man nodded without looking up at him.

"We were expecting you. We've got her in the interview

room. Can you confirm your name?"

"Robert Halcyon."

"ID?"

Ollie produced Robert's license. They didn't look much alike—Ollie was thinner, tanner—more handsome by far, in his opinion—but the fact that Halcyon was overweight and Ollie had a beard would work in his favor.

The cop glanced at the license and went to hand it back before pausing to check it again. He squinted one eye at Ollie.

"I've lost a lot of weight since then," said Ollie with a chuckle. "And the beard—what do you think? Pretty slick?"

He took a step back to let the officer get a good look at him, and the man thrust the license at him.

Perfect.

Ollie put the license away, and the desk clerk had another officer lead him to an interview room where Rowan sat looking puffy-eyed and morose. She glanced up at him. Her expression didn't change.

Whew.

That was the part he'd been worried about. If Rowan knew Halcyon, she'd raise the alarms. Apparently, the two had never met.

"Hello. How are you doing?" he asked as he sat across from her, and the officer closed the door.

"I've been better," said Rowan. "Who are you again?"

"I'm Robert Halcyon. Your lawyer."

"Are you court-appointed?"

Ollie shook his head. He knew Halcyon wasn't court appointed—courts didn't reach to other states for lawyers, but that's all he knew for sure. The man had contacted her mother with some nonsense about wanting to work for free for the exposure, but the story didn't add up. He was up to something, or, at the very least, he knew something Ollie didn't.

"Let's take it from the beginning," he said.

Rowan nodded without looking up.

He reconsidered. "In fact, let's back it up and start with

Joy."

That caught her attention. "Joy? Why? What does she have to do with this?"

"You don't think it's odd both Joy and Liam ended up dead within a month?"

She blinked at him. "I guess. You think someone killed Joy?"

"You tell me. Do you think so? They both died within a month of meeting you."

Rowan held up a hand. "Hold on a second. She *drowned*. How could I have killed her in the ocean?"

Ollie shrugged. "They haven't found her body. Are you sure she drowned? All we know is that she told Liam she was going swimming and never came back."

"They found her bag on the beach, didn't they? The bag she had with her towel and stuff in it?"

"Did the police tell you they found her bag?"

Rowan scoffed. "*No*, they've been pretty busy asking me about Liam. They haven't mentioned Joy."

"So, how do you know about the bag?"

Rowan hemmed, and Ollie leaned forward.

"I'm your lawyer. I'm here to help you, remember? Just be honest."

She sighed. "I *saw* it. I saw her that morning on the beach, I think."

"The morning she died? Before her last swim?"

She bit her lip. "That's not good, is it? If I was the last one to talk to her before she went swimming, and now Liam—"

"It's not great." Ollie wasn't sure if a real lawyer would be that honest, but the answer to her question seemed tragically obvious. "It would have been better if you'd been in *Kansas* that morning, but let's work with what we've got. When you saw her that morning, did Joy seem odd? Sick? Troubled? Anything strange?"

"No..." Her eyes floated up to the left as she accessed the memory. "I was jogging and happened to see her—"

Ollie suspected his face twitched at the coincidence because Rowan scowled.

"*Honestly*. I *know* it sounds crazy to have bumped into her *that* day. I jog most mornings, and I'd never seen her there before."

"Same time?"

Her eyebrows raised. "Hm?"

"You always jog at the same time?" he clarified.

Rowan nodded. "More or less."

"Okay. Go on."

She picked at her fingernail as she continued. "I stopped and talked to her, of course. We made plans to meet later in the day, and she never showed up, obviously."

"Did you find it strange that she didn't show up at the time? Did you call her?"

"Yes. I called her from the restaurant, and then after that— it was like she fell off the planet." Her mouth pinched. "I thought I pissed her off or something. I thought she dumped me as a friend."

"Why would she have done that?"

"I don't know. I figured we weren't getting along as well as I thought, is all. I hadn't known her that long."

Ollie nodded. "Okay. What did you talk about on the beach? Something that pissed her off?"

"No. Not at all. Like I said, we made plans. She said her orange juice tasted funny—"

"Tasted funny? Like what?"

"She didn't say. She said it was a bottle she'd been reusing. You know those little shot-glass OJs? She'd been refilling from a big bottle—she said she thought maybe she'd reused it too many times, and that's why it tasted funny."

"So, it was an opened bottle..." murmured Ollie.

Her head cocked. "I talked about this to another friend of mine. She thought maybe someone poisoned the bottle. Do you think so? Do you think the police will think *I* put something in it?"

Ollie pulled at his chin. "I'm a lawyer. I don't *think*."

She opened her mouth and shut it again.

He continued.

"Bottom line is you were there—you *could* have put something in her juice. But so could Liam or anyone else. Do you know what happened to the little bottle?"

"She finished it, and I took it to throw it out for her."

"Did you?"

"Yes. In one of those big cans by the beach stairs."

Ollie nodded.

"Is that bad or good?" she asked.

He shrugged. "Both. We can't prove it wasn't poisoned, but on the other hand, we also don't have a poison-laced bottle with your fingerprints all over it to worry about."

Rowan dropped her head into her hands, propping it up with her elbows on the table.

"I'm going to die in here, aren't I?"

"No."

She looked up. "You don't think so?"

"No. You won't die in *here*. This is jail. You don't stay here. They transfer you to *prison*. That's where you'll die."

She gaped at him, and her eyes grew wet with tears.

He reached out and patted her arm. He shouldn't have teased her. He didn't want her making a scene.

"Bad joke. I'm sorry. You're not going to die in *prison*, either," he assured her. "Don't worry about Joy. She probably got caught in a rip current. Her disappearance didn't have to be murder at all."

Rowan sniffed. "Right."

"Our problem is Liam. Tell me everything that happened."

Ollie glanced at his watch. He needed to get moving.

Rowan sat up and spoke in a monotone that implied she'd already told the story to the police a hundred times.

"I was in the shower. When I turned off the water, I heard something out there—outside the bathroom door."

"Which was closed."

"Right."

"What did you hear? What did it sound like? A thump, voices—?"

"I don't know. Like a thump—maybe a couple of little thumps in a row."

"Okay. Go on."

Rowan pulled at a strand of her hair. When it gave way, she worked on singling out another.

"I didn't think about the noise at first—I figured it was Liam doing *whatever*. Then I thought of something I wanted to ask him—I forget what. I figured he was right outside, so I called him, but he didn't answer. I did my thing for a bit—dried off, combed my hair—then poked my head out of the bathroom to look for him."

She fell silent, her eyes locked on the empty table as she pulled another hair from her head.

"That's when you saw him?"

She nodded without looking at him, her eyes wide and haunted as if she were watching a broadcast of the moment on the tabletop.

"He was on the bedroom floor?"

She nodded. "At the end of the little hall between the two closets. Just laying there, on his side, like a baby—" She looked up at him. "What do they call that? When you're curled up like a baby? There's a name for it."

"Fetal position?"

She nodded. "That's it. He was in the fetal position. I couldn't see his face."

"You had a towel wrapped around you, and you went out to check?"

"Right. At first, you know, I think I kind of laughed—even with all the blood. Is that weird? It was like my brain couldn't process it. I thought he was kidding—being *silly*."

"Was he a silly kind of guy? Did he play tricks like that?"

"No. He wasn't silly at all, but..." Her expression pinched. "It just didn't make sense, you know? I figured it had to be something stupid. Like I was seeing it wrong?"

She sat back and ran her hand through her hair before continuing.

"I guess I said his name a few times. I think I pushed him with my foot—" She held up a finger. "Didn't kick him, like *nudged* him with my foot, you know?"

He nodded.

"When he didn't move, I got down on my hands and knees and turned him over, thinking I should, I don't know, *clear his airway* or something like I've seen on television, and that's when I really saw the blood." She looked away. "There was *so* much. I don't know how I didn't see it until then."

"That must have been awful."

"It was. I mean, I *guess*—I don't know. I freaked out." She looked up. "No, *blanked* out. Next thing I know, I'm in the front yard screaming my head off."

"And you had the knife in your hand."

"That's what they told me."

"You don't remember picking up the knife?"

She shook her head but didn't make eye contact.

"No."

"You don't know where you got it? Was it on the ground?"

"I don't know."

"Was it in his body?"

"*No.*" Her head snapped up. "No. It couldn't have been. I can't imagine a world where I pulled a knife out of him—no matter how freaked out I was."

Ollie sat back in his chair. Her story had been pulling him closer with every new revelation, and he needed to back up before he crawled into her lap.

"Best you can remember, you picked up the knife and ran outside to get help?"

She nodded and looked into his eyes without speaking.

"What is it?" he asked.

She swallowed. "I remember thinking I needed to get it away from him. The knife. Like it could still hurt him if I left it there."

Ollie held her gaze as her eyes rimmed with tears again.

Damn.

He either believed her or she was a *fantastic* liar.

He nodded and looked away to break the trance. "Okay. That makes sense on some level. What about the message on the garage door? *I know you killed her.*"

She cocked her head. "How do you know about that?"

"Just assume I know everything."

She scowled. "Now that you mention it, *what about that*? It had to be the killer, right?"

"You think the person who left that message is the same person who killed Liam?"

She shrugged. "It makes sense, doesn't it? They think Liam killed Joy, so they killed him."

"You think the message was about Joy?"

She laughed. "Who else could it be about? How many people could Liam have killed?"

"Did you talk to Liam about it?"

Her eyes popped wide. "About how many people he's killed?"

Ollie sighed. "*No*, about the spray paint."

"Oh. Yes. He thought it was his neighbor."

"Which one?"

"I don't know. An older guy. Around the corner to the right, and then hang a left. He lives down there with his little white dog. Liam thought he did it because he yelled at him for putting his dog poop bag in his trashcan."

"Seems extreme, doesn't it? To accuse someone of murder in two-foot-high red letters because he yelled about poop bags?"

Rowan nodded. "I thought so. That's what I'm saying. I think Liam was wrong. Someone else did that. Someone who thought he killed Joy."

"Did Liam ever say anything that led you to believe he killed Joy?"

"*No.* I wouldn't have dated him if I thought he killed his

last girlfriend. He still has her stuff in the closet, for crying out loud. He was *sad*."

Ollie arched an eyebrow. "So was so sad he was dating you?"

She huffed. "He had to get on with his life at some point, and anyway, Joy told me to take him."

Ollie sat up. "What?"

"Joy. It was a joke. I was telling her about how I..." She paused to squirm in her seat and then continued, "...how I date rich old men. Liam was a rich, *younger* man. I was kidding with her that I was jealous, and she said if anything happened to her, I could have Liam."

"Do you think she might have killed herself?"

She grimaced. "No. That's not her. She seemed strong and pretty happy, really."

"Did she think something was going to happen to her?"

"No—I assumed she was kidding about me taking Liam."

"But you did date him once she was gone."

She sighed. "By accident. I didn't even know it was him— *Joy's* Liam. Total coincidence."

He nodded. The tremendous strides Rowan had made convincing him she was innocent didn't seem as wide anymore. He didn't like the feel of everything. Too convenient. Too many coincidences.

He looked up to find her glaring at him as if he had hieroglyphics on his forehead.

"What?" he asked.

"They left me a message, too," she said. "Whoever spray-painted Liam's garage. It had to be the same person."

"They spray-painted your door, too?"

"No, they slipped a note under my door. It said, *don't trust him*."

"You took it to mean Liam?"

She nodded.

"Could it mean anyone else?"

"I don't think so." She looked away as if she were thinking

and then refocused. "Believe it or not, I'm pretty loyal once I start with someone. And it happened right after he left my apartment, too—like they'd been watching us. Which is pretty creepy, now that I think of it."

"Any idea who it could have been? Do you know anyone else who knows him?"

"I looked on his phone. He'd gotten a couple of calls from someone he had labeled as just K—the letter, not the name. I think he was cheating on Joy with her."

"So you think this K did it?"

"Maybe." She crossed her arms against her chest. "All I know is it wasn't me. You have to look into her."

"We will. Why were you looking through his phone?"

She shrugged. "Joy had said he was cheating on her, and I started...*worrying*, I guess. Also, I thought if this other woman killed Joy, it meant he didn't."

Ollie squinted at her.

"So you *did* wonder if he killed Joy?"

She rolled her eyes. "Not *really*. The message on the garage—and then I had some half-drunk conversation with my friend that got me all worked up—plus, if there was another woman and she killed *Joy*, she might try to kill me, too, right?"

"Makes sense, I guess."

She nodded. "Plus, he got a couple of weird calls."

"Liam? Weird, how?"

"You know that thing where someone gets a call while you're with them, and they walk away to take it? Like they don't want you to hear?"

Ollie nodded. He didn't have a fraction of the drama in his life this woman seemed to, but he'd seen enough movies with cheating spouses to know the look.

That was one good thing about having a 'war wound' that ended sexual activity. It removed a lot of drama as well.

"So it's possible Liam had another girlfriend. Or at least, an *old* girlfriend. Maybe someone jealous enough that they killed both Joy and him?"

Rowan pointed at him. "Oh, I *like* that," she said. "That's reasonable doubt, right?"

He had to agree. For her sake, that theory made a good option.

"Not out of the realm of possibility that Joy killed herself because, like you just confirmed, she knew he was cheating on her."

Rowan nodded. "I guess."

Ollie's phone rang, and he held up a finger to put Rowan on pause and answer it. It was Shee.

"I'm in with her now," he said.

"How's it going?"

"Fine. I don't have a lot of time. I need to go."

"Right, sorry," said Shee. "There are some things you need to know. She told me about a book she had—a book of conquests."

"Conquests?"

Rowan glanced at him.

"*Men*," said Shee.

"Ah."

"The cops found it. At least, I assume it was them, but they found it behind her dresser—they had to unscrew the back to get it. They had to *know* it was there."

"You want to know how they knew?"

"Yes. Also, Snookie's got a floater. Probably Joy."

"Probably?"

"Just a torso. A mess, apparently. It'll take a little time to positively ID it. No prints, no teeth—seems convenient."

"There's a lot of that going around."

"Missing teeth?"

"Convenient coincidences."

Rowan scowled at him, and he realized she'd have to be an idiot not to know he meant her.

He put his hand over the phone.

"*Not you*," he whispered.

She looked away.

Ollie returned to his call.

"Okay. Let me get back to this."

He hung up.

"Who was that?" asked Rowan.

"They found Joy."

Rowan's eyes saucered. "On the beach?"

"I don't know the details." He cocked an eyebrow. "Unless you'd like to fill me in so I don't get blindsided?"

She shook her head. "I told you. I don't know anything more than what I told you."

Ollie thought for a moment. The sound of Shee's voice reminded him of something she'd mentioned before.

"One of Liam's neighbors said they saw you sneaking around outside not long before the murder," he said.

Rowan squinted. "Saw *me*? Sneaking around outside? What does that mean?"

"I don't know. You said you were in the shower."

"I *was*." She shook her head. "I don't think I've ever been outside his house except to walk from the door to the car."

"What about your book? The one in the bureau?"

Rowan paled. "What?"

"The cops found it. They knew to look behind your dresser."

She remained silent.

"How did they know to look there?" he asked.

"I don't know."

It sounded as if all the strength had been sapped from her voice.

"Are the police going to be upset by what they find in that book?"

She wrapped her arms around her chest as if she'd caught a chill.

"No. *Maybe*. It's in code—*kinda*—and it doesn't matter. It doesn't have anything to do with Liam."

"Is it a list of men? Maybe a list of what you got from them?"

She stared in stony silence.

"Liam was one of your marks. Is *he* in the book?"

She shook her head, and her eyes teared again. "He wasn't a *mark*. Not exactly. I was hoping he'd be different."

Ollie sighed. "I suppose, in a way, he was."

He checked his watch.

"I've got to go."

Rowan sat up. "Where? Why? What am I going to do?"

"I'll be back," he said as he stood and then, suffering a pang of conscience, added, "Or one of my associates will."

One with the same name, oddly enough.

He knocked on the door before she could complain, and an officer let him out.

Ollie left the station and called Croix upon returning to the car.

"I'm done," he told her.

She sounded relieved. "Good. I was just about to call you. Halcyon figured out I didn't know where I was going, and I couldn't stall him any longer without getting dragged in for kidnapping. He demanded I let him out at a convenience store. Looks like he got something—maybe a burner phone? He's got himself another car, so he'll be on his way soon."

Ollie nodded.

"Good. She could use a lawyer."

CHAPTER TWENTY-NINE

Getting everyone together at Shee's rental took a while, but the group gathered. Shee, Mason, Croix, Ollie, Shiva, and Snookie found places around the living room. Ethan remained watching the police station, though Rowan wouldn't leave any time soon.

Shee looked to Snookie to start the meeting, but she declined.

"You've got a better handle on the big picture than me," she said.

Shee nodded and stood before the group, gathering her thoughts.

Croix raised her hand, and Shee glanced at her.

"What?"

Croix cocked her head.

"Will there be a slide show?"

Shee glowered. "No. *Sorry.*"

Croix snickered. "*Amateur.*"

Ollie winked at her, and they tittered like schoolchildren.

Shee shook her head. "All right, here's what we've got. Joy goes swimming and never comes back. Is she part of Portia's plan or just unlucky?"

"Officially, we'll have to stay TBD on that," said Snookie. "We're having trouble finding DNA to match her to the floater."

"She's got clothes in Liam's closet. Maybe you can pull something off of them," suggested Ollie.

Shee looked at him. "How do you know?"

"Rowan mentioned it. Used it as proof Liam missed her and wouldn't have killed her, no matter what people spray-painted on his garage."

"But there *weren't* any clothes there—just a space where clothes used to be—" Shee locked on Ollie. "Rowan thinks they're still there?"

Ollie nodded. "That's my impression, though it wasn't something I thought to grill her about." He frowned. "They've only been dating a few days, right? If they went missing, it had to have happened today? Yesterday, *maybe*?"

"Do you think *Liam* threw them out?" asked Croix. "Maybe he decided keeping them was creepy—especially with Rowan floating around?" She covered her mouth. "Sorry. I shouldn't say *floating* when it comes to Liam's girlfriends."

Ollie snorted a laugh, and Shee frowned. She'd have to move things along to keep those two idiots from feeding off of each other.

"It must have been Liam," said Shee. "That makes the most sense. I haven't heard anything about Joy having family? Someone to collect things?"

Shee noticed Snookie's expression had squinched into the center of her face.

"What's wrong with you?" she asked.

Snookie scratched her head as if the action would help her brain process faster.

"I've got some issues," she said, standing. "Let me make a call."

She opened a slider and walked into the back yard.

"What's that about?" asked Croix.

Shee shrugged and noticed Mason had a similar look on his mug.

"What's wrong with *you* now?" she asked.

"You found that computer in there," he said.

She nodded. "It was between *his* shorts, though. It wasn't like he was trying hard to hide it. If it is hers, maybe he threw out her stuff and put the computer aside."

"You wouldn't throw out a computer," agreed Croix.

"Right. Not until you had a look—maybe keep it for yourself."

"Ethan said it was both suspicious and *not* suspicious," said Croix.

Shee chuckled. "I'm glad he cleared that up for us."

"He said it was clean—not even locked."

"Which itself is weird," said Ollie.

Croix nodded. "He wasn't done looking last I talked to him, but he said there's almost nothing on it except saved emails between Joy and Rowan."

"Anything in there we need to know?" asked Shee.

"A lot of Rowan bragging about duping old men."

Shee nodded. "That's kind of her thing."

"Joy told her to take Liam," said Ollie.

Shee straightened. "She did?"

"That's what Rowan said."

"Like Joy gave her the idea for bumping her out of the picture?"

Ollie shrugged.

Shee paced. Something about the laptop felt wrong.

"We took the laptop before the cops could find it."

"Against my advice," muttered Mason.

"If the thing is empty except for some email string between Joy and Rowan—it's like someone wanted the cops to find that and only that."

Ollie frowned. "It doesn't put Rowan in a good light. Makes you think of her for Joy's death and maybe Liam's, too."

Shee turned to Croix. "Have Ethan send me the emails, and after, we'll give Snookie the laptop, let her figure out the chain of custody—or, if she wants, we'll put it back for her. I'll leave it up to her."

As she finished her sentence, Snookie entered from out back.

"We were just talking about you," said Ollie.

Shee shot him a look.

"My ears were burning." Snookie lowered her phone. "So, the floater *isn't* Joy."

"How do they know?" asked Shee.

"When she went missing originally, Liam reported she has a birthmark on her right shoulder shaped like an upside-down heart. This one doesn't have that."

"Could it have worn off? Been nibbled off?" asked Shee.

Snookie shook her head. "No. If she had it, it would still be there."

"Maybe he remembered it wrong?" suggested Mason.

Snookie shrugged. "Always a possibility, but wasn't he a skin doctor? I imagine he notices things like that."

Shee nodded. "So, who is she? Do your people have any ideas?"

"No, but who the torso is isn't what has me curious right now. I went to Joy's apartment today. Someone cleaned out the place the day after she went missing, and I mean *cleaned out*. The owners of the apartment building were thrilled. Movers packed everything, and a cleaning crew pretty much bleached the place."

"So you couldn't get any DNA," murmured Shee.

Snookie nodded. "When you started talking about the cleaned-out closet, it reinforced my suspicion—"

Shee pointed at her. "But maybe they *did* want us to find that body."

"Convenient it popped up when it did," agreed Ollie. "No pun intended."

Mason scowled. "They'd have to know we'd identify it eventually."

Snookie shrugged. "Maybe, but maybe it would take a while."

"Long enough for Portia to get away," said Shee.

Mason cocked his head. "So, you think someone wanted to hide the fact Joy was *murdered* and didn't drown? So much so, they gave us another body to look at?"

"I don't think they're hiding Joy's murder..." said Shee as her thoughts gelled.

Snookie followed her thread. "You think they're hiding that she's still *alive*."

Croix gasped. "*Joy* is Portia? She's been pulling the strings while we've been hung up on Rowan?"

"Worse, she's been setting up Rowan while we *concentrate* on Rowan." Shee dropped her head into her hands. "We came into this knowing her whole game was pinning murders on others, and we *still* fell for it."

"If it makes you feel any better, she hasn't faked a death before," said Snookie. "Not as far as I know."

"Where is Joy now?" asked Mason. "Is Liam's money already gone? Is she already jetting to Europe?"

Croix's phone rang, and she answered it. She listened and then looked at Shee, her eyes wide.

"What is it?'" asked Shee.

"Rowan's been released."

Now, it was Shee's turn to go wide-eyed.

"*What*? How?"

"She walked out of the police station with her lawyer. Halcyon left her at the curb and, before Ethan could call us, reappeared to pick her up in a rideshare."

"In a *rideshare*?" echoed Shee.

"We flattened the tire on his rental," interjected Ollie.

Shiva confirmed with a head nod.

"Is Ethan following them?" asked Shee.

Croix nodded. "Looks like they're headed for her apartment."

Ollie shook his head. "I'm not a lawyer—I only play one on TV—but I don't know *how* Halcyon got her released already."

"Doesn't matter. She's in danger. Halcyon must work for Joy."

Shee headed for the door.

"He got her out to disappear her."

CHAPTER THIRTY

Rowan stood behind Robert Halcyon as he went through the paperwork to have her released. The whole process took much longer than it should have because the guy had lost his ID—to the other lawyer, apparently. The handsome, fake one.

"You're a total lifesaver," she said. She wanted to hug the big, sweaty lug, but...*no.*

"Uh-huh," he grunted without looking up.

Rowan rocked on her heels. She felt horrible. Tired, vaguely nauseous, excited, numb, all at the same time. She'd never been arrested before—certainly never for murder. She couldn't say she'd recommend it. Somehow, knowing she was innocent didn't make it any easier.

She couldn't *wait* to leave.

"I don't know how you got me out. The last guy didn't," she said.

Halcyon handed the clipboard to the officer and turned to her, his skin glistening. The station was muggy, especially inside the front doors, where the last of the day's sun blasted through the glass.

Halcyon scowled at her. "*I told you*, that guy wasn't a lawyer. He was some kind of scam artist."

She shrugged. "Yeah, but he seemed like a lawyer."

"He told you his name was Robert Halcyon, didn't he?"

"Yes."

He slapped his hand against his chest. "*I'm* Robert Halcyon."

She frowned. "But why would someone come in here pretending to be you?"

"To talk to you."

"But why?"

He huffed. "I don't know. Believe me, I'll look into it. For now, let's get you out of here."

The officer handed over a bag with her phone—the one thing Rowan had insisted the officers gather from Liam's for her before they left.

She noticed it was dead and swore under her breath.

Halcyon walked through the front doors, and she followed, glancing over her shoulder to be sure none of the officers were chasing after them, guns in hand.

It's true. I'm free.

She took a deep breath. Clouds rolled overhead, offering some relief from the heat. Rowan heard thunder grumble in the distance.

"He seemed kind of nice," she mumbled, still thinking about that handsome, fake lawyer.

Halcyon kept walking.

"He had a thing about him that made me trust him," she added, loud enough for him to hear.

The lawyer glanced at her. "That's probably how you ended up in here."

"Him? You think he set me up?"

"*No*, I mean because you're *gullible*—" He sighed and raised his phone. "Nevermind. I'm calling a car. Let's get you home. You can get a shower and go to sleep. Doesn't that sound good?"

"It sounds *great*." She eyed his phone. It was strange and cheap-looking. "What kind of phone is that?" she asked.

"Someone stole mine. I got this one."

"That's a shame," she said. "You didn't explain how you got me out?"

He shrugged. "They didn't have enough to hold you, and I

pointed out a few discrepancies."

"So this is over?"

He patted her on the arm. "Sure. It's over. Go live your life."

His smile was off. *Sneery*, maybe. She trusted the fake lawyer more than this guy. She was grateful he'd gotten her out, of course, but something didn't make sense.

"*Why* are you my lawyer?" she asked.

"What?" He glanced at her. "Can I use your phone to call the car?"

She held up her phone. "Dead."

He scowled at her.

"People like you deserve everything they get," he said.

She gaped.

"*What*?"

He grunted and returned to figuring out his burner.

She felt her anger building and tried again to get an honest word out of the man.

"Why are you my lawyer? How did you show up if you're not court-appointed?"

"Your mother hired me."

Rowan laughed. Now, she trusted the man even less.

"My mother doesn't have two pennies to rub together, and she wouldn't trust a lawyer as far as she could throw one."

He huffed. "It's *pro bono*. I need to do X amount of charity work each year."

She hooked her mouth. She'd heard those words before—*pro bono*. That part might be true.

"But why *me*?" she asked.

He shrugged. "I'm trying to raise my profile in the Palm Beach area. I got us a car." He glanced down the block. "We need to go down to the corner."

He turned his back to her and walked down the street as a light rain fell. Rowan squinted up at the sky.

I need cash.

She didn't know what was going on, but she needed money. She knew that much.

Her mother had taught her whenever things felt weird, *get cash*. It was probably going to come in handy real soon.

She had her bank card tucked in her phone case, but she wasn't sure she had enough in her account for anything useful. She spotted an ATM at the bank next door.

"I'll catch up," she called to Halcyon.

He turned. When he saw her approach the ATM, he waved her off and walked on.

She punched in her code and took out sixty dollars, wincing as she pressed *enter*.

Please let me have sixty dollars.

She heard the gears spin and clack.

It *worked*.

The machine rattled out the bills.

"Hop in," said a voice behind her.

She grabbed the cash and the receipt and turned to find Robert Halcyon in the car's back seat.

"I'll drop you off on the way to the airport," he said through his open window.

She nodded and hustled to the car. She hated Halcyon but didn't want to use her last sixty dollars on a taxi.

She stuffed the money in her pocket, and they drove the short distance to her apartment. Halcyon didn't say a word. He seemed even more distracted and annoyed than he had the entire time they'd been together in the police station, which was saying something.

The driver pulled up to her building, and she turned to offer Halcyon one last smile. She might need him later—no reason to make an enemy out of him—even if he was a total *prick*.

"Okay, well, thanks for this, and thanks again for—"

"Yep," he said, cutting her off.

Asshole.

She got out of the car and then leaned back in.

"I didn't get your number in case they arrest me again?" she said.

He shook his head. "You won't be arrested again."

"How can you be so sure?"

He shrugged. "I've been doing this a long time."

She shut the door and watched the car pull away. She still didn't understand why he went out of his way to represent her, just to be the rudest human being on the planet.

Rowan went upstairs, each step heavier than the last. She reached her door and stared, dismayed at the yellow police tape.

What am I doing with my life?

She took a deep breath, bracing herself for the mess she'd find inside. She wasn't sure she had the energy to deal with it today. Maybe tomorrow. Of course, tomorrow, she had a lot on her plate. She needed to rethink her life, for one—

She noticed someone had cut the tape. Was that a good thing? She recalled Fake Halcyon mentioning the cops had found her book. How did he know that? He knew *where* they found it, too. She'd assumed the cops told him that, but he wasn't even a real lawyer—at least, not *her* real lawyer.

Had *he* gone through her apartment?

She walked inside.

It was a mess, as suspected. Nothing looked broken, though. It wasn't like on television, where the police broke everything because they could.

She dropped her keys on the table and pulled the cash from her pocket. The receipt had wrapped itself around the bills, and she glanced at it to check her balance.

Twenty-five thousand dollars and change.

Rowan's cheeks tingled.

What the...

She didn't have twenty-five *thousand* dollars in her checking account.

She'd *never* had that much money in her checking account.

She scanned the room as if someone were hiding behind the sofa or under a table, waiting to jump out and laugh at her.

There had to be a mistake.

A good mistake, maybe, but a *mistake*.

She shook her head.

How could she have such unbelievable bad luck *and* good luck on the same day?

She squinted at the ticket again and set it on the table, afraid handling it would make the total change. She'd have to check her online banking. It was probably a misprint with the receipt. Or maybe she'd accidentally accessed someone else's account?

She chuckled.

I should have taken out more money.

She felt *crazy*.

Her day had been like one long fever dream.

She wandered toward her room. She needed a shower and a long sleep. She couldn't figure it all out now—

"Hi, Rowan."

Rowan gasped.

A dark-haired woman sat on the edge of her unmade bed.

She recognized her.

"Joy?"

Joy smiled as if nothing had ever happened—as if she hadn't gone missing—as if her boyfriend hadn't been brutally stabbed to death.

"You're *alive*?" asked Rowan, though the answer seemed readily apparent.

Joy nodded. "Very much so."

"That's, *gosh*, that's *great*."

Rowan threw out her arms and stepped forward to wrap Joy in a bear hug, her mind racing. Did Joy know about Liam? Did she know about *her* and Liam?

Before she could reach her old buddy, Joy stood and raised a gun from her side.

Rowan stopped.

Oh.

She lowered her arms.

"What are you doing?" she asked, her gaze locked on the gun.

"I need a favor," said Joy.

"Sure. Of course. You don't need a gun to ask me for a favor."

Rowan forced a smile. She didn't like the look in Joy's eyes.

"What do you need?" she asked.

Joy took a deep breath and released it.

"I need you to kill yourself," she said.

Rowan swallowed.

"What?"

Joy rolled the hand *not* holding the gun to point her palm to the ceiling. "You know the drill. You can't take the stress. Killing yourself is the only way out, blah, blah—" She snickered and waved the gun at the room. "I've seen your apartment. It's not like you have anything to live for."

Rowan's jaw worked, but she couldn't find the words. "I don't—"

"You know, all the bragging you did about tricking old men out of their money, I imagined you'd have a better apartment than this."

Rowan's face felt hot. "I'm not usually here—"

"Oh, you mean you're usually at Liam's? Or, that was the plan—before you killed him?"

Rowan shook her head. "Is that what this is about?" Though her situation hadn't changed—Joy still held the gun—she almost felt relieved. "You've got it wrong. I didn't murder Liam—"

Joy smirked. "I know."

She remained staring with the same smug look until it made sense.

Rowan's eyes widened as the truth smacked between them.

"Because *you* murdered Liam?"

"*Ding, ding, ding,*" said Joy. "For such a crafty girl, you're a little slow on the uptake."

"But that message on his garage and—"

"From me. Just dropping nuggets to be sure everyone investigating looks somewhere other than *here.*" Joy tapped her chest.

Rowan reached behind her to feel the bureau and use it to help her stay upright. Her knees felt wobbly.

Will this day never end?

She swallowed. Maybe that wasn't the right thing to wish for right now. She might get what she wanted.

"Why are you doing this to me?" she asked.

Joy cocked her head. "You don't see it?"

"See what?"

"Look." Joy motioned behind her. "Look at us. *Twinsies.*"

Rowan glanced at her bureau mirror. She saw Joy in it.

She'd never noticed how much they looked alike.

"Liam has a type. Dark hair. Fine features. Small-boned. That's why I picked him, and that's why I picked you. You looked familiar to me at the art fest because you looked like *me.*"

Rowan recalled their first meeting. Remember feeling in charge of the exchange—Joy was quiet, seemingly in awe of her. It drew her in.

She'd done it all on purpose.

"But why?" asked Rowan. "You saw me shopping and thought, *I can destroy this girl's life*?"

Joy laughed. "Oh, *please.* Your life was already a trainwreck. Either way, I couldn't care less about your life. This was always about Liam."

"You hate him that much?"

"*Hate him*? Not at all. To hate him, I'd have to acknowledge he's even a *thing.* I don't. He served a purpose."

"You killed him to frame me?"

Joy shook her head. "You're still trying to make this about *you.* Framing you was a tiny part of the bigger picture, but there's—" She looked away and then refocused. "There's too much going on here. Someone's after me this time. I can't leave you in the wind."

"You sent Robert Halcyon? To get me out so you could kill me? "

Joy nodded. "You didn't think it was strange he didn't give

you any instructions?"

Rowan blinked at her. She didn't understand.

Joy rolled her eyes. "You think they just let you walk out of there? No bond? No instructions about where you can go or what you can or can't do?"

Rowan scowled. She'd been thinking about skipping town. No one had told her she couldn't.

"He didn't bother because he knew you were about to kill me," she said.

Joy nodded. "He knew you were about to kill *yourself*."

Rowan shook her head. "No one will believe I killed myself."

"Who is there to convince? Your drunk-ass mom in Texas? She's all you've got."

"I have friends."

"No, you don't. Women like you don't have friends, Rowan. Women don't like women like you. You're a man-stealing whore."

Rowan straightened. "I am *not*."

"Yes, you are. It's what made it so easy for me to slip myself into your life. It made you predictable, too. And boring, *so* boring."

Rowan felt tears banging at her eyes. She didn't want to cry.

"My mother—"

Joy held up a hand to stop her. "Once your mother gets her little inheritance from you, she'll move on, no questions asked."

The words struck Rowan funny.

"*My inheritance?*"

Joy nodded. "You probably haven't checked your account yet. You're *rich*." She smirked. "Well, what *she'd* consider rich."

Rowan gasped.

"The twenty-five thousand?"

Joy's eyebrows raised. "Oh, you *did* see it. Know where it came from?"

"No—"

"*Liam.* Direct transfer from Liam's now empty account. It all went to you, and then most of it bounced to my offshore account. Just enough stayed behind."

"To make people think I robbed him?"

"Yes. My goodness, Rowan, you're really piecing things together like a *genius* now. I didn't give you enough credit. You robbed him, killed him, and then killed yourself. Got it?"

Rowan *seethed*. Joy's demeaning tone had shifted much of her fear and confusion into pure *rage*. She hadn't clawed her way from her mother's trailer to Palm Beach by being a shrinking violet. Maybe she'd gotten older and softer, but there was still plenty of that Lubbock, Texas girl left in her veins.

She wanted to *kill* this bitch.

She jabbed a finger at her. "Why would I take all his money and then kill myself? That doesn't make any sense."

Joy shrugged. "Guilt is a weird thing. And, hey, it's not like you don't have a history of taking money from men. The police have your book to prove it."

"*You* told them about the book."

"Anonymous tip." Joy smiled. "You've got a big mouth."

Rowan looked away, listening to the soft rhythm of the rain on the awning of her back porch. She used to like that sound. Now her breathing came faster, each breath shorter than the last as her anger shifted to panic. The conversation was coming to an end. She knew once Joy stopped talking, *she'd* stop breathing. She didn't know what Joy planned to do, but every option ended with her dead.

She needed to delay what was coming until she could think of a way to escape.

She glanced toward the living room.

She could *run*. Take her chances. Hope if she were shot, she'd survive long enough—

"*Don't*," said Joy, as if she could read her thoughts.

Rowan turned to Joy. She wasn't sure why, but it felt like a tiny bit of control had swung her way.

"If you shoot me, it won't look like a suicide. It'll mess up everything for you."

"I'm nothing if not resourceful," said Joy. "I'd figure something out."

Someone banged on the front door. They didn't *knock*. They were using fists.

Rowan spun toward the sound as if it were the entire 7th fleet, complete with battleships, arriving to save her.

"Rowan," called a voice. "It's Shee—"

Not the Navy. Shee.

That'll have to do.

Rowan saw her moment.

She dove into the living room like a desperate baseball player reaching for home. She hit the ground and rolled away to remove herself from Joy's line of sight. She didn't hear a gunshot.

That had to be good.

"I'm in here!" she screamed. "She's got a gun!"

Her front door *exploded*. Shee and an enormous man with a gun entered the room. Behind them, she spotted Fake Lawyer and a woman wearing camo pants.

Her mind swam. She tried to speak and then curled into a ball.

Is Shee with Joy? The guns—

Peeking through her crossed arms, she saw the big man stride into her bedroom, moving like some kind of action hero. The tall, dark-haired woman in camo shadowed him.

Rowan felt like she'd been tossed into the middle of a video game.

What is going on?

"*Clear,*" the man called out from her bedroom. Then, "*Fire escape!*"

The woman in camo disappeared into the bedroom.

Shee came to Rowan, kneeling beside her.

"Are you okay?" she asked.

Rowan focused on her new friend. Behind her, she recognized a handsome face.

"Fake Lawyer," she said.

The man smiled. "Good to see you again."

The room spun. Rowan closed her eyes.

Nothing made sense.

CHAPTER THIRTY-ONE

With Rowan secure, Mason moved into the bedroom with his gun drawn.

He found no one.

"Clear," he barked, as much out of habit as to be useful.

Long curtains undulated with a breeze generated by a storm passing overhead.

He heard a noise outside and moved that way.

"Fire escape!"

Feeling a presence behind him, Mason glanced over his shoulder to find Shiva following, her eyes scanning the room.

He nodded to acknowledge her support. She nodded back. They stepped through the oversized window onto the small balcony, and Mason swept his gun toward the attached stairs. Seeing no one, he glanced over the side. They were five stories up.

A dark-haired woman glanced up at him from the ground. She pointed a gun and then thought better of it.

She ran.

"She's there," said Mason.

He moved to the stairs and reached the second step when he saw Shiva flip over the balcony railing.

What the—

He paused, gaping, doubting what he'd seen.

There was no way she'd survive a five-story drop unscathed. He didn't know much about their latest recruit, but he'd *assumed* she hadn't been bitten by a radioactive spider or sent from another planet.

He hit the next balcony and leaned over to look. Shiva hung from the railings of the terrace below him. She released and dropped to the next, and then the next until she'd reached the ground.

Holy hell.

He'd have to remember not to piss that one off. The girl had *skills*.

Neither his bulk, one remaining leg, nor the miles on his body would support him trying such a trick. He'd have to do things the old-fashioned way. He continued down the stairs as fast as he could go.

Shiva and Joy were distant memories by the time he reached the ground. He jogged in the direction he'd seen Shiva go. He'd gotten pretty good at running with his fake leg—his daily beach runs made running on the flat cement around Rowan's apartment a breeze.

Still, he wasn't flipping down balconies like some spider from Mars.

He glanced into an alley and spotted Shiva walking toward him.

"Got away?" he asked.

She nodded.

"Car," she said.

"You couldn't monkey your way onto the roof or something?"

She scowled. "What?"

"The way you went down those balconies..."

She shrugged. "You were blocking the stairs and slowing me down."

He put away his gun. "My bad."

"Did you get a license plate?"

She nodded.

"Good. We'll get that to Angelina and see if she can tap into Mick's contacts at the police station. Can you identify the car?"

She nodded again. "It has a knife in the trunk."

He smiled. "I was thinking more *make and model*."

"I have that," she assured him.

He motioned to the fire escape. "You want to take the elevator or climb?"

She rolled her eyes, and they took the elevator back to Rowan's apartment together.

"You're back. No luck?" asked Shee when they entered.

Rowan sat in a chair, her knee bouncing with nervous energy.

"She drove off. Shiva's got her car and plate number. I told her to get it to Angelina."

Shee nodded.

Ollie handed Rowan a glass of water, and she took a shaky sip.

"I don't mean to rush you, but I need to know *everything*," Shee told her.

Rowan looked at the others.

"Who are these people with you? Are you with the police?"

Shee shook her head. "We're on loan from the FBI. We're investigating a black widow—she steals from rich men, sets another woman up for the crime—everyone goes missing in the end."

Rowan swallowed. "Joy was going to kill me—*no*—she wanted me to kill myself."

"That tracks," said Ollie. "Liam's dead, Rowan kills herself from the guilt. No one asks any questions."

"She said she took his money," continued Rowan. "She gave me twenty-five thousand."

"Gave you?" asked Shee.

Rowan pointed toward her front door. "There, on that table, is my ATM receipt. It should be empty, but there's all that money in there. It's Liam's—she did it to frame me."

"Twenty-five thousand doesn't seem like enough for all this trouble," said Mason.

Ollie had the receipt in his hand. "I'm sure there's more.

She probably transferred it from Liam to Rowan and then sent the bulk offshore. She left some behind to help frame Rowan."

"*Yes*," said Rowan, pointing at him. "*Yes*—that's what *she* said."

Shee focused on the brunette. "Do you have any idea where she might have gone? Where she may have been hiding for the last month? Did she say anything that would help us trace her?"

Rowan shook her head. "I don't think so. Give me a second to think—my brain feels like it's in a blender." She looked up at Shee. "You knew Joy was going to kill me, and you didn't tell me?"

Shee touched her hand. "We didn't know Joy was going to kill you. We thought Joy was dead, same as you."

"Then why—" Rowan gaped. "You thought *I* was this black widow?"

Shee's mouth hooked. "You have to admit, the shoe fits..."

Rowan's shoulders slumped. "That's all about to change. I can promise you that."

"You should try real estate. I think you'd be good at it," suggested Ollie.

Rowan blinked at him.

He put his hands in his pockets. "But you know, think about it. Take a minute."

Shee stood and ushered the rest of them into the hall.

She lowered her voice.

"Joy's in the wind. We've got to move before she gets set up somewhere else."

"Just tell us what you want us to do," said Ollie.

Shee put her hands on her hips and stared at the floor before continuing.

"Planes, trains, and automobiles," she muttered. "How is she going to move to her next stop? We can't cover the airport. I'll call Snookie and see if she can get the FBI to handle that now that we've done all the heavy lifting. They'll probably want to sweep in and take credit anyway." She turned to Shiva. "You call Angelina and give her the information you have on the car so she can work our police contact—maybe track down that vehicle."

Shiva nodded, and she and Ollie strolled off to make their call.

"Can't the FBI look up a license plate?" asked Mason.

Shee shrugged one shoulder. "I'll see if Snookie can swing it, but the red tape—remember, they haven't officially taken this case. I don't mind having Angelina as a backup. We'll be lucky if we can mobilize the FBI to cover the airport."

Mason and Shee returned to the living room, where Rowan stared blankly at the floor.

Shee approached the woman. "Rowan, you're coming with us. We can't leave you here."

She peered up at her. "Damn straight, you can't leave me here."

Shee looked at Mason. "We'll take her back to our place and get her working with Ethan."

Ollie and Shiva reentered.

"Angelina's going to give us a call back in a bit. What do you want us to do in the meantime?" asked Ollie.

"*Trains*," said Shee. "Go keep an eye on the train station. There's one in West Palm."

Ollie motioned to Shiva to follow him outside.

"What are we going to do?" asked Mason.

"We get Rowan safe and hope someone thinks of something to give us direction. Joy had to be *somewhere* for the last month. Wherever that was, she's probably headed there now to wrap up."

Mason nodded and pulled out his phone as he headed toward the elevator.

Shee turned in time to see Rowan's eyes suddenly pop wide.

"What is it?" she asked.

Rowan stood. "You said Joy's been staying somewhere?"

"We can only assume," said Shee.

Rowan nodded.

"I think I know where."

CHAPTER THIRTY-TWO

Angelina shoved her boobs together and took a deep breath.

Sure, she could have *called* Officer Artie Janket, but she suspected things would go faster if she asked in person.

She'd stopped at the police station and asked for Artie, only to be told he was next door at the coffee shop.

That worked.

She went next door. Officer Artie Janket sat in the corner window seat, reading.

She approached his table.

"Officer Janket, I was looking for you, and here you are eating donuts."

Artie looked up.

"*Angelina*," he said, swallowing his bite of croissant. "Come on—I don't eat donuts. You're better than that joke."

She smiled. "Sorry, you got me. That was a cheap shot. Mind if I sit down?"

He cleared a stack of papers so she could sit without feeling buried.

"Do you come here a lot?" she asked.

He nodded. "I like to do my paperwork here."

She slid into her chair.

"Can I get you some coffee? No, tea, you like tea. Tea?" he asked.

She smiled. "That's sweet of you to remember. I'll get some in a second. I have a favor to ask first. Time is of the essence."

She grinned at him. It wasn't hard—she *was* impressed he remembered she preferred tea. He was a sweet man.

Not really her type.

"I don't have any jobs for you," he said. "I've been keeping an ear to the ground, but I've got nothing that fits you guys."

Angelina shook her head. "It isn't that. I mean, it *is*, but what I need right now is for a job Snookie got us."

Artie's brow knitted. "Your sister still in the FBI?"

"Retired, consulting."

He nodded. "Cool."

She pulled the paper from her purse with the make, model, and plate number Ollie had asked her to trace.

"Can you run this for me?" she asked, handing the information to him.

He read it and looked up at her. "A plate number? I don't know—"

"You did it all the time for Mick."

He frowned. "Yes, and when he died, it was a relief—" He stopped and held up a hand. "That's not what I meant."

"I get it," she said, sliding her hand over his. "But a woman's life is at stake."

He sighed.

"That's how Mick got me to do it the first time. Always someone in trouble."

She shrugged. "That's what we do. We help people." She reached out and put her hand on his. "And so do you."

He nodded, staring at their hands. With his other hand, he rubbed the stubble on his chin. Angelina noticed he'd let it grow in.

"Are you growing a beard?" she asked.

"No. Not really. Just, you know, a five o'clock shadow."

She nodded her approval. "I like it. You look *manly*."

He blushed. "You're messing with me."

She shook her head. "*No*, I'm serious."

"I figured it might balance out my head," he said, rubbing his bald pate.

She smiled at him without speaking, and his shoulders slumped.

"Alright, *fine*. You know I can't say no to you."

She grinned. "It goes both ways."

"I wish that were true," he muttered. "Give me a second."

He slid his laptop to him and logged in.

While he worked, she flipped over the book he'd been reading when she walked in. It was a history of Benjamin Franklin.

"I read this," she said, surprised.

He looked up. "Yeah?"

"*Yes*. He was fascinating, wasn't he?"

Artie nodded. "I like that bit about his daily routine—how he started each day with the question, *What good shall I do this day?* and ended with, *What good have I done today?* It's so simple but—"

He stopped. "Why are you looking at me like that?" he asked.

Angelina shook her head. "Hm? Nothing. I just never—" She shrugged. "It's nice to have a friend with such a curious mind."

"You inspire me," he said.

They held each other's gazes for a moment.

"So, that number? I need to get the info back to Shee *yesterday*."

"Oh right, right. Hold on." He looked at his computer, poking keys.

He wrote down some information and handed it to her.

"Remember, you didn't get this from me."

She grinned. "Of course not."

She stood, and he looked up at her.

"I don't suppose you'd be interested in dinner this week?" he asked. He shook his head. "I mean, not because you owe me for the favor—I mean, because it might be nice?"

Angelina studied him. There was something attractive to the earnestness in his eyes. The jawline wasn't bad...

"Sure," she said. "I've got to go, but give me a call later?"

His eyes widened.

"Sure, yes. Will do."

She turned and left the café, feeling his eyes on her as she moved.

It wasn't a terrible feeling.

CHAPTER THIRTY-THREE

"So where's the *pen*?" asked Shee for the third time since they started the drive from Rowan's apartment to their rental house.

Rowan moaned. "I don't *know*. I'll think of it."

They'd spent twenty minutes of wasted time tearing Rowan's apartment apart, looking for a pen she'd borrowed from Joy. Rowan swore she'd seen the name of a hotel on it, but she couldn't remember *what* hotel. She thought Joy might be there, which was great—*except she couldn't find the pen.*

"She told me she lived in Shoreline Ocean but never had me over, so I think that was a lie."

"Gosh, not like her to lie," muttered Shee.

Rowan sighed. "*Everything* she told me was a lie."

"Well, we know the bit about Shoreline is a lie because we know about an apartment she ditched," said Shee. "And that wasn't in Shoreline."

"But my theory is good, though, right?" asked Rowan. "That the place on the pen is probably her real home base?"

Shee shrugged. "It's not a terrible theory—it's just a *useless* theory if you can't remember where the damn pen is."

Rowan grunted. "I don't know where it went—but I can almost picture it—"

She closed her eyes, grimacing like she was trying to complete a bowel movement.

"—something to do with *clowns*."

Shee twisted so fast she nearly pulled the car off the road. "*Clowns*? You think she's staying in a clown hotel?"

Rowan's eyes opened. "Something like that."

"Pay attention before you kill us," said Mason.

Shee muttered under her breath as she pulled into the driveway of their rental. She parked and found herself staring at the house next door.

"Did you notice our creep neighbor left?" she asked Mason.

He glanced that way. "Yeah?"

She cut the engine. "There was a guy next door with a bad vibe. I caught him screaming at a woman—his mom, maybe—and he sneered at me when he saw me watching. No shame."

"Sounds like a winner," muttered Rowan. "I'm surprised I'm not dating *him*."

"There were movers there this morning," added Shee.

Mason perked. "Yeah?" Shee thought she saw him smile as he turned away.

Hm.

Something up there.

She was about to ask him why he looked suspicious, but Rowan, who hadn't stopped talking since they got in the car, started anew as they headed into the house.

"*Red* clowns," she said. "Something to do with *red clowns*."

Shee glared. "There are no Red Clown Hotels in the area. I promise you. I'm not even going to check."

Rowan pouted. "You only made friends with me because you thought I was Joy, didn't you?"

Shee winced. She hadn't expected that question, but there was no point in lying.

"I'm afraid identifying Portia was the point, yes."

Rowan frowned as they entered the house. "Maybe we could stay in touch."

Shee flashed her a smile.

Yeah, *no.*

Rowan wasn't someone she hoped to stay in touch with.

From the living room, Shee saw Snookie outside on the

phone, pacing. Croix and Ethan sat at the kitchen table on their laptops with papers and scratch pads nearby.

"Anything?" asked Shee.

Croix shook her head.

"What are they doing?" asked Rowan.

Shee pinched the bridge of her nose. All the *questions.* It was like hanging out with a toddler.

"Trying to find Joy, trace the money, anything that will lead us to her," she explained.

"Try the Red Clown Hotel," Rowan told them.

Ethan and Croix looked at Shee, who rolled her eyes. "Sure. Why not."

Shee's phone rang. *Angelina.*

Good. Maybe they'd get a lead on Joy's getaway car, anyway.

"Did you get it?" she asked.

"Got it," said Angelina. "The car is registered to a *Rowan Riley*—"

"*What*?" Shee lowered the phone and counted to ten. When she'd finished, she looked at Rowan.

"She took *your* car," she said.

"Who?"

"*Joy*. What kind of car do you have?"

"A Mercedes."

"Old?"

"1996 203 C-Class." Rowan sniffed. "It was a gift."

"I'm sure it was. Why didn't you tell us you had the same car Shiva saw Joy take off in?"

She shrugged. "I didn't know."

"In her defense, Ollie and Shiva stepped outside to call Angelina," said Mason. "She wouldn't have heard."

Shee sighed and returned to her phone call. "Thanks, Angelina. We've got to go." She hung up and tapped the phone against her skull. "She's in the wind, and we've wasted half an hour looking for a pen and researching a car we already know."

Snookie reentered. "I've got the wheels in motion for

FinCEN to trace the money in and out of Rowan's account."

"I guess that means I don't get to keep the twenty-five thousand," said Rowan to no one in particular.

Shee ignored her. She noticed Ethan staring.

"What's up with you?" she asked.

"I wasn't paying attention—but did you say Joy has *Rowan's* car? The old Mercedes?"

"It's not *that* old," whined Rowan.

Shee nodded. "Apparently. Why?"

Ethan made a palms up *ta-da!* movement with his hands. "Because I have a tracker on it."

Croix gasped. "You *did* put that tracker on her car?"

He nodded. "*Yes*. I told you I would. You never checked the app?"

She shook her head. "*No*, I was always staring right at her until they took her to jail—I thought the tracker was overkill."

Ethan grinned as he pulled out his phone. "Well, how you like me now?"

"Wait. What are you two saying?" asked Shee. "Are you saying we can track the car she took? Because, at this point, that kind of luck doesn't seem possible."

Ethan tapped and swiped around his phone. "That's what I'm saying. I put a tracker on Rowan's car in case she gave us the slip."

"So you can tell us where she is?"

He stared at his screen. "If she's still in the car—*got her*. The car's parked near the Coral Crown Suites, about five miles south of here."

"That's it!" yipped Rowan, pointing at him. "*Coral Crown*. That's what the pen said."

Shee shot her a withering glance. "Not *red clown*?"

"No." Rowan shook her head. "No, that was wrong. You can see how I made that leap, though."

Shee stared at her. "Does this airhead thing work with rich old men?"

Rowan nodded.

"Really well, actually."

Shee turned to Snookie. "Can you send agents?"

Snookie already had her phone against her ear.

"On it, but you'll get there faster."

Shee nodded and looked at Mason.

"Let's go."

CHAPTER THIRTY-FOUR

Joy tapped her fist against her teeth, thinking.

Palm Beach is cursed.

She'd been through town once before and had *no* problems. That time, she'd taken close to three hundred thousand from an art dealer and pinned the whole thing on his cousin. Easy peasy. This time—who were these people after her? *Police?* They weren't wearing uniforms. *FBI?* The woman who'd chased after her looked like she was in the army.

Would they send the army after me?

No. It was too ridiculous.

And how did anyone know about her anyway? All her murders were *solved*. The obvious perpetrator was always dead or missing. There was no reason for anyone to look for other options. No reason for them to look for *her*.

So how?

Was it her pattern? Had she done it too many times?

Maybe. She was getting awfully prolific.

It was just so much *fun*.

Too bad, too, because it had never seemed so easy as it did with Rowan. She couldn't have *built* a better person to pin things on. But then Liam had to start cheating on her, and these people came out of nowhere—she had to bump up her timeline—

She huffed.

Total cluster.

Okay. No time to dwell on mistakes.

Think.

She had enough money to disappear. She'd take some time off. Start again later. Maybe go international?

Hm.

Food for thought.

First things first. She had to get the hell out of Palm Beach. She'd explained everything to Rowan like some stupid James Bond villain and then had to leave without her *dead*.

Maybe she'd keep her mouth shut, hoping to keep the money in her account? *Nah*. That idiot would spill everything to those people who broke into her apartment—

Those *people*.

Who were they?

No. Stop thinking about them. It doesn't matter.

She needed to *go*.

She threw her suitcase into the trunk of Rowan's old Mercedes and hopped into the driver's spot, leaving her gun on the seat beside her, just in case.

She headed west. She was thinking about Texas—maybe because of Rowan—and then changed her mind. If she was being watched and the odds were better than usual that she'd be caught, maybe a death penalty state wasn't the *best* choice. Maybe she should head to California and put as much space between her and Florida as possible. Maybe stop someplace like Nebraska—some place no one would ever expect her to pop up. Maybe just lay low for a while.

Maybe it was time to crack into her overseas accounts. She hadn't planned on retiring for a few more years, but maybe it was time. She had plenty to live like a princess in Portugal.

She checked her gas gauge and found it wanting. *Figures*. Rowan was such a dizzbang—of course, she'd only have a few gallons of gas left.

She spotted an enormous rest stop. One that catered to truckers and families alike and pulled up to one of the seven gazillion gas pumps there.

She reached for her credit card and then shook her head. Nope. No using the card, even if it was in one of her other names. Maybe because it *was* in one of her other names.

Who knew how much they knew?

Whoever they were.

Cash *only* from here on out.

She slipped out of the car and went to the trunk to open her suitcase. She had about ten thousand in cash there. It would be plenty until she figured out her next move, even though it was hard to find someone willing to take cash for anything these days.

Things must have been so much easier for grifters back in the day, back when her parents ran their scams. No cameras, no Internet educating people about scams, no network shared between law enforcement—

Those were the days.

She headed into the Cluckie's *'Cross-the-Road* Road Stop, walking beneath the giant bucktoothed chicken and his slogan:

Because clean rest stops are rare as chicken's teeth!

To even be walking into that place—something had gone terribly wrong in her life.

The air felt good, though, and smelled vaguely like caramel popcorn. The place was enormous. Aisles and aisles of utter crap. Tee shirts, mugs, candy, stuffed chickens, and cameras—lots of cameras hanging from the walls, dangling from the ceilings...She kept her head down and approached the counter to pay, grabbing enough snacks and water to keep her alive until she ran out of gas again. Next time, she'd switch cars. For now, she'd keep Rowan's. She needed to put some space between her and Palm Beach first.

"Which pump?" asked the kid behind the counter.

Shit.

Joy looked out the window and pointed. "Right there, that Mercedes sedan—"

A truck had parked at the pump behind hers—inches from her bumper.

Too close.

A very large man hovered near her car, peering inside.

No. It isn't possible.

She recognized the giant. She'd caught a glimpse of him as she drove away from Rowan's—he was hard to miss.

How?

How could they have found her so fast?

Joy stomped her foot.

"Who are you people?"

The mood around her changed, and Joy turned to the kid behind the counter. He was staring at her. She realized she'd voiced the screech she thought she'd only heard in her head.

"Pump twelve?" asked the kid.

"I, uh, I have to get something else," she said, melting back into the store. "I forgot."

He watched her go without comment.

She turned and ran.

CHAPTER THIRTY-FIVE

"She's *got* to be inside," said Shee, eying the old Mercedes.

Mason nodded. He reached into the truck, found his gun, and tucked it into his waistband. He fluffed his untucked shirt to hide it.

She looked at her shirt in dismay.

"If I try to hide a gun on me, the guards will tackle us the second we walk in the door.

He nodded. "Don't risk it. Just stay close to me and remember—she had a weapon."

Reaching behind his seat, he pulled out one of his SOG folding knives and approached the Mercedes. Checking to be sure no one was watching, he stabbed the back driver's side tire. Crabbing to the front of the vehicle, he flattened that tire as well.

The Mercedes slowly listed.

"We're hell on tires this week," said Shee as he put his knife in his pocket.

"At least, we know she won't be going anywhere."

"Not in that car—but if she grabs a different one, it won't have the tracker on it."

Mason grimaced. "Shit. I didn't think of that."

She shrugged. "Well, let's just make sure she doesn't leave this place without us."

They went into Cluckie's and scanned the place. She had never seen anything like it. She'd been in a lot of rest stops over the years, but none that could fit a football stadium inside of it.

"This place is ridiculous," she said, eyeballing "'chicken 'feed" candy sacks stacked higher than her head. "I know you said to stay close, but we'll have to fan out. This place is too big."

He nodded. "Go right. If you see her, come get me. Don't be a hero."

She shook her head. "Never."

He wrapped his fingers around her arm to hold her in place, and she looked at him.

"I'm serious," he said, a grim look on his face. "She has a gun. I saw it back at Rowan's. Don't do anything *stupid*."

She nodded. "She has a baggier shirt than me. Got it, Commander. Sorry."

He scowled at her, and she blew him a kiss.

"Of course, I'll be careful," she said to put his mind at ease.

He grunted.

She headed to the right side of the store, moving quietly but fast. She didn't have time to stalk around. She surprised a few startled families, peering around corners at them before hearing Mason's voice boom from the opposite side of the store.

"Hold it, there!"

Shee bolted in that direction.

"Freeze!" said another male voice.

She stutterstepped to slow down.

Who was that? Had Snookie's agents already found them?

She peeked around a corner to see a store security guard holding a gun on Mason. The SEAL had his massive arms in the air, his hands behind his head. He still had his gun in his hand.

Shee saw the guard was panicking.

"Drop the gun! Drop the gun!" he said on repeat.

Someone a few aisles over screamed. She heard the door ding as shoppers started pouring out of the store.

Shee took a few steps forward, hoping the guard would see her and be less likely to shoot at Mason for fear he'd hit her instead.

"I'm putting the gun down," said Mason, moving slowly.

"Ma'am, get out of the way! Get away!" barked the guard. His fear had rendered him incapable of communicating without screaming.

"I'm the good guy. She's getting away," Mason said as he bent to place his gun on the ground.

"Put down the gun!" screamed the guard moments after the gun touched the ground, and Mason was already straightening without it in his possession.

The kid was a mess. Young and terrified. He wouldn't be taking Mason's word for anything, and they'd be lucky if someone didn't end up shot.

Mason had his back to Shee but turned his head to the side so she could see his profile.

"She ran toward the southwest corner. There's probably a door there," he shouted.

She could tell he was talking to *her*. Giving her directions.

"Kick the gun away!" yelled the guard.

Mason stepped on the gun with his good leg, balanced on the prosthetic, and pushed the weapon *backward*. The Beretta spun across the tile floor before stopping at Shee's feet.

Nice.

"Lay down on the ground!" screamed the guard, moving toward Mason.

This was her chance to grab the gun—while the guard wasn't looking. She didn't want to make a move for it too early, have him freak out, and shoot Mason in a panic. She was already half-hidden by the endcap display. It could work.

She squatted to snatch up the weapon and then dodged away, running for the southwest corner as Mason suggested. The screaming had stopped behind her. All the people who could get out had left.

Best of all, the guard didn't shoot.

She guessed he felt like Mason was under control and hadn't noticed the missing gun yet.

She passed a young couple cowering behind a stack of beer cases. They gasped when they saw the gun in her hand.

"Go toward the front of the store," she told them. "Did you see a dark-haired woman run this way?"

"Are you a cop?" asked the young man.

The girl didn't care. She just nodded and pointed at a glowing exit sign at the back of the store as her boyfriend pulled her toward the front.

As if on cue, an alarm blasted through the store and then cut short.

Joy had opened the emergency exit.

Shee sprinted toward the door, using her free hand to pull her phone from her pocket.

She hit Snookie's saved number.

"What's up?" answered Snookie as she paused at the emergency door.

"We're at a Cluckie's off of ninety-eight. Joy is here with the car—Ethan can track the exact location, though I imagine you can just follow the active shooter alerts."

"We've got you," said Snookie. "You've got her?"

"She's here and on the run. Mason had her, but a rent-a-cop took him for the bad guy. The guard is jumpy. I'm a little worried someone will get shot—probably Mason."

"Tell him to comply."

"He is, obviously, or the guard would be fifty shades of *dead*. But I need your people here so they don't take him to jail."

"Where are you?"

"I'm at the back of the store about to go outside. I think she went that way."

"Okay, we'll let you know if the tracker moves."

"It won't. Even if she gets back to the car, Mason flattened the tires."

"Okay. We're on the way. Be careful."

Shee hung up.

She opened the door, and the alarm squealed. The humidity hit her like a wave of steam as she stepped out, gun at the ready.

She didn't see Joy, but there were plenty of places to hide. The truck stop parking lot sprawled ahead of her—massive eighteen-wheelers and smaller trucks creating a maze of tires and metal on the property. The sun had gone down, and the intermittent roars of engines and hiss of air brakes cut through the dark.

She looked to her left and right and didn't see Joy headed in either direction—paths that would lead her back out front to her car. She might have already rounded the corner or might be out hiding amongst the trucks.

Tall overhead lights burst to life, and Shee thought she saw legs running on the opposite side of one of the trucks.

Got you.

Shee sprinted toward the front of the first truck, hoping to cut Joy off. She pressed herself against the headlights and peered around the corner.

No one.

She jogged out and squatted to look under the next vehicle.

Nothing.

"You want to come up for a visit?" she heard a man's voice say. It came from the next truck in line.

"Hey, sweetheart, come back. I won't bite," he said as Shee hustled around the front of his vehicle.

He glanced at her as she appeared and did a doubletake. "What about you—*whoa.*"

The large man hanging out the passenger side window of his truck noticed the gun in her hand and withdrew in a hurry.

"Where'd she go?" asked Shee.

"Easy, I don't want no trouble," he said.

"I'm a cop," she said. It seemed the easiest way to get him to comply, but she would need to see someone about her constant law enforcement lies. It was getting too easy.

"You're looking for the other one?" he asked.

"The dark-haired woman you were just talking to."

He hesitated but saw no reason to protect the woman

who'd spurned his advances.

"That way," he said, pointing under the next parked truck. "I thought she was a lot lizard."

Shee's lip curled. *Delightful.*

"Stay in your truck. She's armed," said Shee.

His window rolled up, and he disappeared inside.

Shee bent to walk beneath the next truck. Crouching beneath the trailer, she spotted Joy at the rear, peeking around the tires, looking to see if someone was chasing her. Shee worked her way toward the back, staying low. She guessed Joy was working her way out front again, giving the store a wide berth. She imagined that, out front, Joy hoped to hop into a car idling at one of the gas pumps—if not her own. She didn't know the tires on the Mercedes were flat yet.

Joy's feet moved.

She was making a run for it.

She sprinted toward the front of another truck parked farther east in the lot.

Shee popped out from under the trailer to pursue.

"Freeze, Joy," she called, her gun raised.

Joy didn't hesitate. She spun and fired.

Shee hadn't seen that coming. She wasn't sure why—the woman was desperate and had a gun, after all.

Maybe this was why Mason seemed so concerned she'd do something stupid.

Hm.

Ah, well—no time to worry about it now. She'd add it to the growing list of things she should probably talk to a therapist about.

Shee didn't know where Joy's bullet went, but it didn't hit her—she suspected it wasn't even close. It had been a wild shot.

She held her gun steady on Joy, her stance wide to make it clear she'd taken the time to *really* aim.

"I won't miss, Joy," said Shee. "Put down the gun."

Standing beside the passenger door of the other trailer, Joy kept her weapon aloft and pointed at Shee. There was a good thirty feet between them. Shee felt her odds were good—Joy probably wouldn't hit her with even a well-planned second shot, but she'd feel a lot better if the woman put the gun *down*. There was always the outside chance Joy was a marksman. Who knew? She owned a gun, clearly. Wasn't scared to fire one. Wasn't squeamish about killing people—she'd *stabbed* Liam to death—a lot messier than shooting someone across a parking lot.

"Put the gun *down*," Shee repeated.

Joy remained still.

Dammit.

Now she'd have to choose whether to shoot first or continue to the standoff—

Before Shee could decide, the passenger door of the truck cabin swung open between them, blocking her view of Joy's face.

"Get out!" screamed Joy.

Shee saw her arms move. She guessed Joy had swung her weapon at whoever opened the cabin door. Was she going to try and hijack the truck? That seemed unlikely. She didn't imagine Joy knew how to drive a tractor unit.

No, she was taking a hostage.

"What?" she heard another woman say.

The door partially closed again. The woman in the truck had shielded herself for another second, but she'd probably hop out in a moment, and Joy would have her hostage.

Screw it.

Shee squatted and aimed low. The movement seemed to have caught Joy's attention, but the second she needed to refocus on Shee so low to the ground was the only second Shee needed.

She fired.

Joy yelped and collapsed as if someone had swept her leg. Her gun fired into the air. The woman in the cabin shut the door tight.

Shee sprinted to the fallen woman and tossed her own gun

aside to jump on her. She needed both hands to secure Joy's weapon before she recovered from the shock of being shot in the leg.

She assumed she'd caught her in the leg.

Shin? Knee? Thigh?

She'd *aimed* for *leg*—she wasn't sure what she hit.

It had worked. That's all that mattered.

Joy's teeth gritted in the orange glow of the overhead pole light. Her body tensed, bracing for impact as Shee pounced. She tried to swing her gun back up but ran out of time. Shee grabbed it before the muzzle could point her way. She pinned Joy's wrist to the ground.

Joy was a smaller woman, and Shee hadn't expected much of a fight, but the murderous bitch clung to the gun like it was the last *Titanic* life jacket. She thrashed as they wrestled for control of the weapon.

"Why do you have vice grips for hands?" grunted Shee as she tried to twist the gun away.

Joy rolled towards her, trapping the gun between their bodies as they bucked. Shee realized that, at any moment, the weapon could go off and kill either of them.

Oh, that's not good.

Don't be a hero, Mason had said.

Yep. Seemed like sage advice now.

She'd wildly underestimated little Joy's will to escape.

The overhead lights glinted off the rainwater pooling in the cracked asphalt around them, burning blankspots in Shee's vision as they writhed on the ground. The uneven surface dug into her flesh.

Shee kneed Joy in the thigh, but it had no effect. She tried again, this time kicking lower. Joy howled.

Shin. Yep, shot her in the shin.

The pain loosed Joy's grip on the gun.

Shee jerked the weapon free, momentarily triumphant. Then it continued moving, slipping through her wet hands and skittering across the asphalt.

She watched it dance away.

Shit.

Joy struck her under her chin with something—an elbow? Shee's teeth snapped together.

Ow.

Joy tried to scramble to her feet, but Shee twisted and dove for her legs.

"Not so fast—"

She'd had enough.

Joy fell to the hard ground, knees first—Shee wrapped around her ankles like an anchor.

She pulled herself up the woman's body, agitating that bad shin as much as possible as she moved. Joy screamed in pain. Shee grabbed her arm, flipped her face down, and jerked her hand toward her head until Joy begged her to stop.

"Do not effing move," Shee hissed in her ear.

Joy remained still but for her steady panting. In the upper position, Shee did the same. She needed to catch her breath and think for a second. She wasn't sure how she would get to her feet with the tigress in tow—not without starting the whole tango over again. The woman fought like she'd been snorting PCP all afternoon.

She heard sirens. Close. Someone had alerted the local police.

Shee inched forward like a caterpillar creeping across Joy's back, pushing her full weight on her, always keeping that arm twisted.

"I swear I'll break your shoulder if you move," she warned.

"You bitches are *crazy*," said a voice behind her.

Shee glanced over her shoulder and saw a man and a woman standing near the cabin, staring down at them.

"I'm a cop," said Shee. Sprawled on top of Joy, she assumed the guy wouldn't ask her to produce a badge. "Go get help."

The girl broke off and ran in the *wrong* direction, hustling deeper into the parking lot. Not a fan of cops. Luckily for Shee, the man nodded and lumbered toward the store.

A few minutes later, cops rounded the back of the truck, guns raised.

"Don't move," they barked.

"The one on top is a cop," said the trucker who'd led them back.

Shee sighed.

She had some explaining to do.

CHAPTER THIRTY-SIX

CHAPTER THIRTY-SIX

Rowan watched the television above the bar at Bahama Betty's, sipping her wine. She didn't usually watch television—she didn't even own one. After watching her mother grow wider and dumber for decades, her butt parked in front of the TV, she swore she'd never own one. She never wanted the temptation of sitting in front of one.

That being said, she *did* want to keep an eye on the news. Joy had been on the local news quite a bit in the last few days—*she* had as well. Rowan had been fielding calls for days from television shows and publications hoping to buy her story.

Come one, come all—I'm selling.

She couldn't believe the amount of attention *Portia* got. Joy could probably sell her story for even more. Rowan was a small-time player in comparison. She'd make a nice little chunk, but her sudden notoriety wouldn't be the score to set her up for life.

"Too bad I'm not a killer," she mumbled into her rosé.

Joy had a lot of nerve calling *her* a whore when she was doing the same thing. She just *killed* them afterward. That was the only difference. Well, that, and she made a lot more money.

Rowan felt a wave of jealousy.

In theory, Joy had been on the right track—except for the whole *going to jail for life* bit. She hunted money, dated it, and got rich. She didn't get gifts—she got *everything*.

Respect.

Rowan nodded to herself.

That was the answer. She had to stop counting on men to shower her with gifts. She needed to not only *land* one but pull him far enough into the boat that she ended up in his will—

No. *No.* Stop it.

She had to stop these fantasies. She'd almost ended up *dead.* No more get-rich-quick schemes, no more men—

"Buy you a refill?" said a voice to her left.

An older man stood beside her. Her gaze swept over him out of sheer habit—fancy shirt, an expensive watch, R.O.C. dangling from his neck—An air of *money*.

Rowan took the last sip of her wine.

Dammit.

She smiled.

It's just a free drink.

She could still get free drinks, couldn't she? What was the harm in that?

"I'd love one, thank you," she said.

He smiled with expensive teeth. He wasn't *terrible*-looking for his advanced age. A little pale, maybe? Something was up with the bags under his eyes, the sallow tone of his flesh—*cancer*? He didn't seem well—

Hold the phone.

"White wine?" he asked.

"Rosé. It's better for my figure."

He chuckled. "Oh, you have nothing to worry about there," he said, chuckling. "Look at you. You must go to the gym every day."

She shrugged. "You too," she said.

Terrible lie.

"Maybe we could go together sometime," she said.

"Oh no, not me," he said with a wheezy laugh. "I have a heart condition."

"Oh," said Rowan. "Do you? Oh *no*."

She held out a hand.

"I'm Rowan. Nice to meet you."

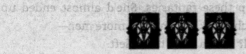

CHAPTER THIRTY-SEVEN

There was a short period of *confusion* after the police showed up at Cluckie's. The local police detained Joy, but also Mason and Shee. Snookie arrived to explain everything before they threw them in jail. They had a backup plan anyway—Ollie offered to represent them if Snookie couldn't fix things.

Wiseass.

Back at the Loggerhead, Angelina threw a little party to celebrate the end of another successful job. Joy was in custody, and Snookie felt confident they had plenty of evidence to prove she was Portia. They could keep her on Shee's attempted murder alone until they sorted the Portia details.

The FBI swept in and claimed Joy's capture as *their* success, as expected.

Officer Artie showed up at Angelina's party. He approached Mason on the back porch when Angelina went inside to freshen her drink.

"So you two look good," said Mason, sipping his beer.

Artie nodded. "Thanks for the heads up that she'd be looking for me. I had just enough time to get ready."

"You had the props ready?"

He chuckled. "Yep, I had the book you told me to get. I even read some of it. It was pretty good. I can see why she chose Benjamin Franklin."

Mason nodded. "So, it went well?"

Artie took a sip of his wine. "Yep. We're going to dinner tomorrow—and I'm here, right? She's looking at me *different.* I can tell. This could be it."

"Well, you take good care of her," said Mason with a smirk. "Don't make me regret being a double agent."

Artie snickered. "I won't. I can't thank you enough. I just needed my chance."

They clinked beers together.

Angelina reappeared, and Artie moved to her like he was magnetized.

Mason shook his head.

He'll have to slow his roll if this is going to work.

Mason noticed Shee approaching.

Speaking of slow rolls…

"What are you two up to?" she asked. "You looked like you were conspiring."

Mason shook his head. "Nah. Just thanking him for his help, even if we didn't need the license plate in the end."

Shee watched Artie chatting with Angelina.

"He's still trying."

Mason nodded. "I told him he'll need to play the long game."

She chuckled and playfully elbowed him in the side. "Like us. The long, *long* game."

Mason grinned and rubbed at the thick scar on his arm.

"*Yep.*"

THE END

Keep reading for sneak-peek first chapters of other books by Amy Vansant.

The Girl Who Found Joy

Thank you—<u>Please review on Amazon</u>!

ABOUT THE AUTHOR

USA Today and *Wall Street Journal* bestselling author Amy Vansant has written over 30 books, including the fun, thrilling Shee McQueen series, the rollicking, twisty Pineapple Port Mysteries, and the action-packed Kilty urban fantasies. Throw in a couple of romances and a YA fantasy for her nieces...

Amy specializes in fun, exciting reads with plenty of laughs and action. She lives in Jupiter, Florida, with her muse/husband and a goony Bordoodle named Archer.

You can follow Amy on <u>AMAZON</u> or <u>BOOKBUB.</u>

BOOKS BY AMY VANSANT

Pineapple Port Mysteries
Funny, clean & full of unforgettable characters
Shee McQueen Mystery-Thrillers
Action-packed, fun, romantic mystery-thrillers
Kilty Urban Fantasy/Romantic Suspense
Action-packed romantic suspense/urban fantasy
Slightly Romantic Comedies
Classic romantic romps
The Magicatory
Middle-grade fantasy

Made in United States
Troutdale, OR
02/08/2023

Made in United States
Troutdale, OR
05/29/2025

31755202R10155